"What's this? Jennifer Tyson speechless?" Devin asked, his insolent gaze raking over her.

What did he want? Jenny asked silently. Why, after all this time, was he here? From the look on his face and the tone of his voice, it wasn't to exchange pleasantries, but that was fine with her. All she wanted was for him to leave—as soon as possible.

"What do you want, Devin?" she asked, finally finding her voice.

"Now, Jenny, is that any way to greet me after—what's it been?—six years? After all, it's not like we're strangers. Or have you forgotten?"

His words jarred her memory. Apparitions nudged at her, daring her to remember, taunting her. Apparitions she'd successfully kept at bay for a long time—until now. With practiced determination, she pushed them away.

No, damn him, she hadn't forgotten....

Dear Reader,

The year may be winding to a close, but here at Intimate Moments the excitement hasn't waned. We've got some of your favorite authors—several of them award-winners—for you this month, as well as another of the talented newcomers we've been bringing your way in recent months.

Marie Ferrarella offers *Callaghan's Way,* featuring American Hero Kirk Callaghan. Back in town after a long absence, he runs smack into childhood friend Rachel Reed—and her irresistible young son. In *A Soldier's Heart,* Kathleen Korbel proves once again why she's known as one of the genre's most powerful writers. There's just no way to read one of her books without identifying completely with her perfectly drawn characters.

Round out the month with *Scarlet Whispers,* by Diana Whitney, a tale of small-town secrets and steamy passions; *Fugitive Father,* by Carla Cassidy, a top-notch secret-baby story; and Pat Warren's *Only the Lonely,* featuring Giff Jacobs's quest for revenge and the woman who crosses his path at just the wrong—or is it the right?—time. Finally, there's that new author I promised you. Her name is Elizabeth Sinclair, and in *Jenny's Castle* she makes a debut I think you'll really enjoy.

And don't forget to come back next month, when we'll be bringing you more of the terrific love stories you've come to expect from Silhouette Intimate Moments.

Enjoy!

Leslie Wainger
Senior Editor and Editorial Coordinator

Please address questions and book requests to:
Silhouette Reader Service
U.S.: 3010 Walden Ave., P.O. Box 1325, Buffalo, NY 14269
Canadian: P.O. Box 609, Fort Erie, Ont. L2A 5X3

JENNY'S CASTLE

Elizabeth Sinclair

Published by Silhouette Books
America's Publisher of Contemporary Romance

If you purchased this book without a cover you should be aware that this book is stolen property. It was reported as "unsold and destroyed" to the publisher, and neither the author nor the publisher has received any payment for this "stripped book."

ISBN 0-373-07606-1

JENNY'S CASTLE

Copyright © 1994 by Marguerite Smith

All rights reserved. Except for use in any review, the reproduction or utilization of this work in whole or in part in any form by any electronic, mechanical or other means, now known or hereafter invented, including xerography, photocopying and recording, or in any information storage or retrieval system, is forbidden without the written permission of the editorial office, Silhouette Books, 300 East 42nd Street, New York, NY 10017 U.S.A.

All characters in this book have no existence outside the imagination of the author and have no relation whatsoever to anyone bearing the same name or names. They are not even distantly inspired by any individual known or unknown to the author, and all incidents are pure invention.

This edition published by arrangement with Harlequin Enterprises B. V.

® and TM are trademarks of Harlequin Enterprises B. V., used under license. Trademarks indicated with ® are registered in the United States Patent and Trademark Office, the Canadian Trade Marks Office and in other countries.

Printed in U.S.A.

ELIZABETH SINCLAIR

admits she loved composition assignments back in grade school. While other kids glared at the teacher, she was always excited at the prospect of creating a new world. However, it wasn't until her own children were all in school—and the house remained clean for more than a few minutes at a time—that she found the time to *really* write.

And though it took some years before she realized her dream of being published, Elizabeth says the wait was worth every minute. She credits her husband, Bob, with giving her the kind of love, patience and understanding that have added a special touch to her stories.

To my friends Anita, Brooks, Debbie
and Brenda, who sweated as much as I did
but never lost faith in me.
My love and unqualified thanks, ladies.

To Linda, Toni and Bobby for all those
hated hours you spent in the romance sections
of bookstores when you were kids.
I hope this makes up for it.

Mostly, to the man who fixes my computer,
helps me plot, shares *my* castle and
has my undying love,
my husband, Bob.

Chapter 1

"Coldhearted bitch."

"You talkin' to me?"

Devin Montgomery swung away from the hotel window to face the middle-aged P.I. wearing a rumpled gray suit and sprawling his overweight body across the sofa as if he owned it. "No. Thinking out loud."

Walking to the coffee table, he picked up the financial report the private investigator had brought with him. He scanned it with a critical eye and asked, "Just how serious is her money bind?"

The P.I. lit his third cigarette in less than an hour and inhaled deeply, studying the man who'd hired him over a year ago—carte blanche. In his twenty-five years of snooping into the private lives of New Orleans's citizens, Joe Tate had never seen anyone display such cold, calculated hatred. Almost from day one he'd suspected Montgomery had a yen to taste Jennifer Tyson's blood, and wasn't about to settle for anything less.

"Serious," he finally said, when Devin flashed him a glare of barely restrained impatience. "In the last three weeks, she's made the rounds of every bank and loan office in town."

"And?"

"And nothing, zilch, the big goose egg. Her little business is going down the toilet, and no one's willing to pay for a life raft." He took a long drag on the cigarette and stamped it out in the glass ashtray on the table at his elbow.

With one last glance at the papers he held, Devin dropped them to the coffee table. "What kind of business?" He'd read the report over later, when he could concentrate. Right now, he wanted fast answers.

"A little shop called The House of Miniatures in the Pontalba Building on Jackson Square. Been in business about four years."

"Who owns the building?"

"The mortgage is in the hands of an estate. The old geezer died about three years ago. Family's been tryin' to unload it ever since. They live in Europe, and havin' property here is too much of a hassle for them."

"For sale, huh?"

The P.I. noted the flicker of excitement in Devin's expression.

"What does she sell?"

"Dollhouses, doll furniture, stuff like that. At one time the place kept its head above water, but when the economy went sour..." Tate indicated the direction the business had taken by inverting his thumb.

"Dollhouses," Devin mused. Taking a seat in the chair facing Tate, he drummed his fingers thoughtfully on the arm. "She have a supplier?"

Tate shook his head. "Carves the stuff herself. Seems her grandfather taught her. Buys very little. Wood, sandpaper, decorations for the houses, that kind of thing. Has a couple working for her..." He paused and patted the breast of his suit jacket. After making the rounds of all his pockets several times, he extracted a small, dog-eared notebook from his hip pocket. Grinning apologetically at Devin, he wet his finger with his tongue and shuffled through the pages.

Shifting in the chair, Devin fought to keep his cool. If this guy hadn't proved his effectiveness by locating Jenny when no one else could, he'd have doubted his ability to find his way home. Resigned to overlooking the P.I.'s shortcomings, he reminded himself that he still had questions about Jenny—and Tate, unfortunately, held all the answers.

"Ah, here it is," the unkempt man announced. "They're an elderly couple. Retired. Name's Mason—Belle and Harry Mason. The old man builds the dollhouses, wires them with electricity and does some of the finishing. The old lady does general work, cleans the houses, crochets bed coverings, curtains, tablecloths for the houses. Been with her about two years."

"What kind of relationship do they have with her?"

Tate flipped the notebook closed, stuffed it in his jacket pocket and raised two entwined fingers. "Close. Like one big happy family."

Too agitated to remain motionless, and needing to escape the smell of the cigarette Tate lit, Devin rose, shoved his hands in his pockets and walked back to the window. "Is she married?"

"Nope."

Exhaling a breath he hadn't been aware of holding, Devin glanced over his shoulder at Tate. "Boyfriends?"

Tate shook his head. "None. If she's not in her shop, she's upstairs in her apartment—alone. In the three weeks I been watchin' her, there hasn't been a man near her, except customers and the old geezer who works for her."

Fighting a smug grin of satisfaction, Devin absently followed the progress of the excursion steamboat *Natchez* far below as it fought the currents of the Mississippi to dock at the Toulouse Street Wharf. How unpredictable and treacherous those waters were, he thought distractedly. Like a woman's heart.

Unbidden, a picture of Jenny rose up to taunt him, looking as she had the last time he saw her—fresh, young, vibrant, and only eighteen, or so she'd led him to believe until her father told him otherwise. Had her unripened, lovely body matured into the lush, sensuous one it had promised to become? Was she still as strikingly beautiful as his memory painted her? The stirring in his groin roused him from his fantasies.

"How can you be sure they're just customers and not boyfriends?" he asked, more to fill the silence and redirect his mind than because he doubted Tate's ability to recognize the difference.

"Trust me," the P.I. replied, throwing an arm over the back of the sofa. He crossed an ankle over his knee and smiled knowingly.

"Any family?"

"Negative. I've never seen a young broad live like she does. That shop seems to be her whole life." He nearly added he thought it was a waste that a looker like her didn't spread the wealth around, but the expression on Devin's face rendered him mute.

Montgomery stared down at the river, some twenty stories below. From beneath his dark, arched eyebrows, his mossy green eyes glowed menacingly with a strange gratification. White teeth gleamed from behind a humorless smile; his fists worked spasmodically at his sides.

Tate looked away and squirmed in his seat, thanking providence that he wasn't this Jennifer Tyson. Something told him that whatever Montgomery had in mind for her, it would be very unpleasant.

"Popie! Popie!"

The door burst open, and a bundle of pink lace and flying black curls stumbled through it, making a beeline for Devin.

"Don't run, Scamp. You'll fall," Devin scolded gently as he turned and hoisted the little girl into his arms, exposing the metal brace on her leg.

Joe Tate stared in astonishment as an expression of loving tenderness warmed Devin's face, melting away the frozen hatred. It was like seeing a snowbank hit by a blast from a blowtorch.

"Popie, Mrs. Filbert bought me a be…be…" She glanced with questioning eyes toward the stiff-backed Scottish nurse who'd followed her in.

"*Beignet,*" the woman said, coaching her.

"Yeah," the child grinned, turning back to Devin. "They're French doughnuts, but they're square, not like regular doughnuts. We ate them outside, and the wind blew sugar all over my face."

"Sugar?" Devin cried in mock horror. "What on earth do you need that for? I think you're sweet enough already. Let me have a taste." He buried his face in the child's neck and nuzzled her with his nose.

"Popie, you tickle," the girl cried, laughing and tilting her head to hide her neck.

Devin raised his face and frowned playfully at her. "Just as I thought. You've wasted my money. You're definitely sweet enough already."

"Mr. Montgomery," Mrs. Filbert interjected, "it's time for Amy's nap."

Seeing the objections ready to roll from Amy, Devin placed his finger over her lips. "I'm busy now, Scamp. You go along with Mrs. Filbert like a good girl. You and I will have a long chat about your adventures at supper."

Amy threw her arms around his neck as he hugged her close and placed her carefully on her feet. "Okay, Popie. See you later!" she called, taking the nurse's hand and limping from the room.

"Your kid?" Tate asked.

"Yes," Devin replied, following Amy's departure with loving eyes.

"Pretty little tyke." The investigator paused, frowning thoughtfully. "Looks a little like—" Devin's thunderous look stopped him from completing the statement.

Tate's observation upset Devin. If he saw the resemblance, would Jenny? Time would tell. He'd rather that didn't happen for a while, but if it did, he would handle it.

He returned to his contemplation of the river, weighing the information the P.I.'s keen observations had produced. If Devin had planned it, he couldn't have done a better job. Without money, and with no real friends, no romantic ties and a strong attachment to a dying business and two dependent senior citizens, she would be at his mercy.

"I'll have my secretary mail you a check," he said, dismissing Tate. "I want a full copy of your report by tomorrow noon."

The middle-aged man stood and stared at Devin's back. "You'll have it, Mr. Montgomery. Always a pleasure doin' business with you. Want me to continue to keep an eye on your lady—?"

Devin rounded on him. "She's *not* my lady," he snarled. "I'll advise you when your services are no longer required."

Silently, Tate nodded and left the hotel room, breathing a sigh of relief when he was free of the fog of hatred that seemed to surround Devin Montgomery. He almost felt sorry for the Tyson dame. Quickly checking his thoughts, he attributed his temporary lapse to the softening effects of old age. Montgomery's fat check would put him on the right road, he thought, smiling and whistling as he strolled down the hall.

The door had barely closed when Devin picked up the financial report on Jennifer Tyson. He studied it with the same degree of intensity a scientist devotes to the inspection of a bug under a microscope.

Coming to a decision, he laid the sheaf of papers aside carefully and picked up the phone. After punching in a series of numbers, he waited, tapping the edge of the table with his finger.

"Jim? Devin Montgomery. Are you going to be in your office for a while today? Good. I want to talk to you about buying one of the buildings in the French Quarter. Yeah. On Jackson Square."

He hung up and sat back with a satisfied smile. Things were going better than he'd hoped. Once he bought the building that housed Jenny's little shop, he'd send his attorney around to advise her she was about to be put out on the street if she didn't pay up her back rent.

Then, in true knightly fashion, he would offer her an out that she would find impossible to turn down, putting her right where he wanted her—in his house, and under his thumb. And she would never know the extent of his hold over her until the time came for her to leave.

He would enjoy seeing her living on the fringes of the family she'd always said she wanted, never quite being a part of it, never quite able to taste and savor the closeness he delighted in with his daughter.

He considered the prospect of once again sharing a bed with Jenny. Although sleeping with her had never been a hardship, he didn't want to get caught in that trap again. He had yet to meet a woman who could equal her in that department. Even at the tender age of seventeen, she had been a fiery, active companion. Now that she'd matured and had more experience, he thought she should be beyond belief, but then he reminded himself that discretion was the better part of common sense.

The grin widened when he considered the two senior citizens she employed. What a bonus. If she balked, he would make sure Adams pointed out what a devastating effect it would have on them. Surely she hadn't grown hard-hearted enough to stand by and watch them starve trying to make ends meet.

Don't get too confident, his conscience warned. *She didn't have any qualms about sticking your daughter in a children's home and walking away.*

Bounding from the chair, he stalked to the bar in the corner of the luxurious suite and poured a liberal amount of Scotch into a glass. The liquor burned its way down his throat, helping to quiet the rage that grew in him every time he thought about Amy being raised as he had—another forgotten, unloved statistic in a cold building full of more statistics, or shuffled from one foster home to another like a troublesome pet, never knowing the love and security of her own family. Jennifer Tyson had a very large debt to pay, and if things went well, she'd be making her first installment before the end of the week.

Jenny's hopes for a busy day in the shop faded with the weather. Outside her window, late-spring rain fell in torrents. Tourists were not apt to be walking the streets of the French Quarter today. This downpour would push them toward the museums or closet them in their hotel rooms, out of the elements. Those few who were brave enough to venture out would make little difference to her business.

Thankful that the Baroness Pontalba had seen fit to flout Creole custom and put inside staircases in the building, she descended to her shop with lagging footsteps. She checked her watch and unlocked the front door. Out of force of habit, she then proceeded to the workroom, where she started the coffee she kept brewing all day as the *lagniappe* she offered her customers. The "something extra" cost her very little and promoted goodwill. And lately she could use all the goodwill she could lay her hands on.

As she dipped the last scoopful of the mixture of chicory and coffee into the brewing basket, the bell over the shop door tinkled, signaling the arrival of one of those brave souls she'd been thinking about. Since Belle wouldn't arrive for a while yet, and Harry was off to the doctor's for a checkup, she was in the shop alone.

"Be right there," she called over her shoulder, and deftly slid the basket in place over the coffeepot. Pushing the brew button, she paused long enough to hear the first gurgle, the signal the pot had begun its cycle. Satisfied the coffee would soon be ready, she picked up a towel to dry her wet hands and stepped through the curtain.

"I'm sorry to have kept you waiting," she said cheerfully, wiping the water from her hands and tossing the towel on a nearby display case. Turning to her first customer of the day, she froze when her gaze collided with a pair of painfully familiar pale green eyes.

"Hello, Jenny."

Even if she hadn't been facing him, she would have recognized that voice. The sound of it slid over her skin like warm, rich velvet, reminding her of its power to turn her knees to water. It hadn't lost one ounce of its potency, she thought, reaching for the edge of the display case for support.

She mouthed his name, but no sound left her lips. Shock rendered her incapable of more. She felt as though she'd hurtled through a time warp into the past. Wordlessly she stared at the man she had once loved so deeply, the man who had turned his back on her when she needed him most. Slowly, without relinquishing her hold, she worked her way around the display case, putting it between them. Still she stared, unable to believe he was here—six years too late.

Standing just inside the door, the shop's light dancing off his black hair, turning the strands to shimmering silk, Devin overpowered the tiny shop. A casual blue polo shirt clung tenaciously to the muscles of his broad chest, exposing a dark tuft of hair at the V in the neck. Sinewy biceps swelled against the material as he stuffed his hands in the pockets of his tight jeans, pulling them snug across his slim hips. He advanced into the shop, his well-toned thighs rippling beneath the washed-out denim.

Stopping on the opposite side of the counter, he pinned her with an appraising gaze from those strange silvery green eyes, close enough for her to see the thin band of amber outlining each iris. If she'd found him disturbing from across the room, at this distance he nearly annihilated her entirely.

His thirty-four years hadn't changed him. Except for the laugh lines creasing the skin on either side of his generous mouth, hinting at the wrinkles they would one day become, he looked much the same. After assessing his dark coloring, square jaw, high cheekbones and dark brows, one would never think of him as a successful folklore novelist. He'd always reminded her of an Apache warrior—except for those penetrating, icy eyes. She knew only too well that locked behind their glacial facade lurked the secrets that made up this complex man.

"What's this? Jennifer Tyson speechless?" Devin asked, his insolent gaze raking over her in turn.

What did he want? Why, after all this time, was he here? From the look on his face and the tone of his voice, it wasn't to exchange pleasantries, but that was fine with her. All she wanted was for him to state his business and leave as soon as possible.

"What do you want, Devin?" she asked, finding her voice.

"Now, Jenny, is that any way to greet me after... What's it been? Six years? After all, it's not like we're strangers. Or have you forgotten?"

His words jarred her memory. No, damn him, she hadn't forgotten. Apparitions nudged her, daring her to remember, taunting her, niggling at her. Apparitions she'd successfully kept at bay for a long time. With practiced determination, she pushed them away.

"Devin, spare me the for-old-times'-sake speeches. Why are you here?" Unable to remain still under his intense scrutiny, she flicked her hair behind her back and wet her nervous lips.

For a while, Devin couldn't answer. His gaze followed the sweep of her tongue across her full lips. Her beauty had all the impact of a fist slammed into his gut. His mind raced, filled with other times she'd used that very gesture to gain his attention.

Hot on the heels of the physical reminder came the resurgence of the pain she'd caused him and Amy. His stomach tightened into a knot.

Oh, no, he warned himself. *It's not that easy anymore, Jenny. It'll take more than a swoosh of that mane of black silk and a coy gesture to derail my plans.*

"My child," he finally stated flatly, eyeing her for a reaction.

Jenny's heart rose into her throat. Her fingers whitened as they maintained their death grip on the display case. Anything else! her mind screamed. She would talk to him about anything else, but not the child. Ever since the night Gramps had told her the baby had been born dead, she hadn't spoken of it to anyone. Time hadn't made verbalizing it any easier.

Slowly, Devin's voice penetrated the haze of panic surrounding her. "She has her heart set on you furnishing a dollhouse for her." He strolled around as he talked, inspecting the dollhouses on display.

Jenny gaped at his back. She *has* her heart set... She *has*... *has*... *has*... It slowly dawned on her that he was talking about another child, a living child. Breathing a sigh of relief, she tried to ignore the tug on her heart at the idea of him fathering a child with another woman. What difference did it make to her?

Wanting to be rid of him, but governed by a gloomy financial picture that didn't include turning business away—not even his—she let go of the counter and moved to a nearby shelf. "If you'll tell me the style," she offered, pivoting toward him, pleased that her quaking emotions didn't transmit themselves in her voice, "I'll help you pick the furniture from what I have in stock."

"Not for this dollhouse," he said, swinging to face her. "This is special, unique. It's a duplicate of our home, fashioned over a hundred and fifty years ago for the original owner's daughter. The furnishings have to be replicas of the ones in the house now." He advanced on her slowly.

Jenny compared his stride to that of a black panther she'd seen in the Audubon Zoo, sleek, graceful, predatory. Dragging her eyes from his, she picked up a small rocker. "You'll find that I've got some styles here to fit the era you're speaking of. However, custom-making all the furniture for a dollhouse is a very lengthy and expensive project just for a child's toy."

"This won't be the first time I've been accused of over-indulgence where Amy's concerned."

"Amy?"

"My daughter. The dollhouse is a gift for her sixth birthday next month."

Sixth? It didn't take a genius to add two and two and get the picture. The bastard! It hadn't taken him long to fill his empty bed. Her temples began to pound, drowning out his words. Her fingernails dug into the wood on the counter.

After six years of wondering, asking herself why he'd never answered her letters, why he'd turned his back on his own child, the answers were clear. Why hadn't the possibility of another woman occurred to her long ago?

Because you were so in awe of him, so much in love, so blinded by him, you couldn't have seen it in a mirror if it had been written across your forehead, the voice of reason whispered.

The shop's walls seemed to close in. Her hands tightened their death grip on the edge of the counter. Her mind cautioned her over and over, *Don't pass out. Hold on. Not now. Not in front of him. Don't let him know how much it matters.*

Her knees buckled. A strong arm caught her around the waist and lowered her to the stool she kept behind the cash register. She almost moaned out loud as feeling began to return to her numbed body. She felt eviscerated.

The pain had been bad enough when she thought he'd just turned his back on his responsibilities, but to find there had been another woman— It went beyond bearing.

"Breathe. Take a deep breath," a voice said encouragingly.

She obeyed. The room swam back into focus just as she heard the soft tinkle of the bell over the door.

"Lord almighty," Belle exclaimed, going nearly as white as the woman Devin supported with an arm around her shoulders. "What's happened? Jenny, Jenny honey, are you all right?"

Weakly Jenny smiled at her employee and friend and nodded. "I'm fine," she said in a thready voice, grateful when Belle scooped her from beneath Devin's arm and nestled her against her ample bosom.

"What on earth happened?" Belle demanded of Devin.

"We were discussing some furniture for my daughter's dollhouse, and she suddenly went white and collapsed." Devin studied Jenny's face closely, waiting to see if she would refute his words, recalling exactly at what point her knees had crumpled.

"Well, it's no wonder," Belle scolded gently. "All this worrying you've been doing over money lately. It's a surprise to me you haven't folded under the pressure before this."

Jenny tried to summon the strength to silence Belle, but she was too late. Avoiding Devin's assessing eyes, she leaned into the secure haven of Belle's embrace.

"I think I'll go upstairs and lie down for a while."

Devin's gaze fixed on them as Belle assisted Jenny through the curtain. Awaiting Belle's return, he walked around the shop, his attention drawn by a castle near the door. On its highest spire hung a small white sign—Not for Sale. Odd, he thought. Even to his untrained eye, the workmanship showed the skill of a master craftsman. Why wouldn't she want to sell something she could make a bundle on?

Each stone had been hand-cut and put in place. The rooms were filled with period furniture. A small throne room boasted two gilded chairs upon which sat two dark-haired monarchs. Carefully he slipped the king from his perch. Looking down at the tiny figure, it occurred to him that the hair and eye coloring of the minute king matched his own. A bitter smile curved his lips as he slipped the figurine back into place.

"That's her pride and joy," Belle said, coming up behind him with a bag of pralines clutched in one hand. She held it out to Devin. "Care for some? They're my only weakness, aside from Harry, my husband." She grinned as Devin dug into the bag.

"Jenny built this?" Devin asked, gesturing toward the castle and taking a bite of the sweet candy.

"Yup. Said she started it about five years ago, before she even had a glimmer of an idea to open a shop." Belle studied Devin. "You two know each other?"

"Oh, yes. Jenny and I go back quite a few years," he said, being deliberately obscure about the time period. "At one time, we were very...close." If he played his cards right, Belle could be of use in his scheme to get Jenny to do the dollhouse—the first step in his plan. "I couldn't help but overhear your comments about Jenny's money problems."

Belle shook her head sadly and popped another piece of candy into her mouth. "It's this damned economy," she said. "When Harry and I first started working here, she wasn't hauling in a fortune, but she made a tidy living for herself. Now she's lucky if she can pay the rent." She stopped abruptly. Lord, she hardly knew this man, and she was blabbing Jenny's private business to him.

"I want Jenny to do custom-made furniture for my daughter's dollhouse—copies of the originals. I got the feeling she was going to turn me down. It would be a substantial sale for her." He watched with growing satisfaction as Belle's eyes lit with hope. "If she had to come to my home to do it, would you and your husband be able to take care of things here until she got back?"

"Sure. Harry and I know as much about this place as she does. But why would she have to go to your house?"

He'd never dreamed this would be so easy. "I have in my possession a diary, very old, very valuable, that tells all the specifics of the furniture that was in the house one hundred and fifty years ago. I'd hate to have anything happen to it, so I'm reluctant to have it out of my possession."

Belle snorted. "You wouldn't have to worry. Jenny'd take good care of it while it was here."

"That's just one of the problems," Devin explained. "Some of the custom-made pieces aren't mentioned in the diary, but I have them in the house. She'd have to come there to measure them."

"I still don't see why she couldn't do the work here," Belle said doubtfully.

Having expected every argument and prepared for it in advance, Devin explained quickly, "My home is quite a distance from here—north of Baton Rouge. It would be much more convenient for her to work there than to travel back and forth every time she needed a measurement or a fact about a piece." He placed a hand on Belle's chubby fingers. "Besides, if things have been so tense for her lately, I'd be pleased to offer her the opportunity for a nice rest in the country. Amy would love having her there, and so would I. It's the least I can do." Not far from the truth, he thought, praising himself silently.

"Just what are you willing to pay for this project?" Belle asked, feeling the strain of the past few weeks begin to ebb.

Devin named a price.

Belle choked on her candy. "My God!" she squeaked. Reaching out, she clutched Devin's hand. "You can bet I'll talk to her about this," she said.

Feeling elated, Devin squeezed Belle's hand and left the shop.

Jenny watched in relief from an upstairs window as Devin crossed Jackson Square. She had no idea what he had up his sleeve, but she had a strong suspicion the dollhouse furniture made up just a small part of some larger picture, and she wanted nothing to do with it—or him.

Chapter 2

"I'm sorry, Miss Tyson. I have my orders. The gentleman who bought the building insists all leases be brought current. Anyone who does not comply will be evicted. You've missed the last three months, and he won't tolerate arrears. You must be paid up-to-date by week's end, or he'll begin eviction proceedings." The sour-faced little man snapped his briefcase shut with a decisive click. "Of course, whatever stock you have on hand will automatically revert to him to cover your arrears, should you default on the three rent payments."

"But you can't—" Jenny sputtered.

He held up a blue-veined hand. "I'm afraid it's all quite legal. His orders were quite specific. He insists your back rent be paid in full by the end of the week. Read your lease agreement, Miss Tyson. Paragraph four, line two. You'll find it there." He slid his briefcase from the counter. "I must be going. Have a nice day," he drawled as he exited the shop.

"I wonder if anyone's ever bothered to point out to the little twerp that he should revise his exit line," Belle grumbled in one of her typical stage whispers.

Jenny cursed the luck of having the building change hands right now. The old owners would have waited until she was better able to catch up. This new guy sounded like Simon Legree. *And I'm his Eliza,* she thought. She could almost feel the hot breath of the hounds of failure on her neck. But she had no one to blame but herself—certainly not that obnoxious little lawyer.

Jenny sighed. "Don't hold it against him. He's only doing his job."

"And enjoying every minute of it, too," Belle added, glaring in the direction the new landlord's attorney had tripped across the square.

Plopping down on the stool behind the counter, Jenny propped her elbows on the edge and rested her chin in her hands. "Well, it's not as if I wasn't expecting it. The DuBois family's agent has been more than generous, allowing me those three extensions. I can't expect everyone to be that understanding. And it's not like we didn't know the building was up for sale." She swallowed her own explanation. "I just wish it hadn't sold right now," she added under her breath.

Belle's warm arm slid around her boss's shoulders, enveloping her in a familiar cloud of lavender perfume. "Jenny..." she began.

"No, Belle. Please don't bring that up again," she said, sitting up straight, knowing what was to come. In the past few days, she and Belle had sparred daily over her flat refusal to accept Devin's offer. Jenny wished she could tell her why. "I won't consider Devin's proposal. There has to be another way."

Even as she said the words, she knew how futile things looked. She'd exhausted her options long before Devin made his appearance. Her gaze drifted around the shop, avoiding the castle and the reminders it embodied. Could she give all this up?

It held so much of her. It *was* her, from the bright blue paint and puffy white clouds on the walls to the grass green rug. It represented her world. She had expended a great deal of time and energy here, setting it up to look like a tiny town nestled inside the four walls, safe from outside influence. But she should have known the grime from outside would eventually seep through the cracks and tarnish her Shangri-la.

Automatically her gaze slid to her castle, the castle she'd constructed to keep her mind off her losses, the castle she'd kept in plain sight to remind her every day of the betrayal of the man she loved, the castle she'd then used to further remind her never to let another man get that close. The little sign on the highest tower glared at her—Not for Sale. Well, neither was she, no matter what price Devin dangled under her nose.

But could she give up everything she'd worked so hard to attain? With growing uneasiness, she knew that taking this job would mean making concessions that went far beyond the shop, far beyond moving into his house.

"What am I going to do, Belle?"

"The way I see it, you don't have a lot of choices. Either you give up, or you fight." Belle took a small folding camp stool from beneath the counter, along with a shoe box marked Cleaning Closet, and waddled over to one of the Victorian houses. Unfolding the stool, she settled her overflowing bulk on it and placed the box at her feet. "Somehow, I never saw you as a quitter."

Belle's words were still ringing in Jenny's ears an hour later as the shop door closed behind her with a *whoosh* of cool air, and she stepped into the humidity of Jackson Square. One other time, she'd quit, and the consequences had reverberated with agonizing pain. Oddly enough, that time had involved Devin Montgomery, too.

Searching for a distraction, she tried to immerse herself in the hustle and bustle of Jackson Square. Along the wrought-iron fence enclosing the square, artists had installed themselves at their easels, walled in by samples of their work in bright oils, watercolors and charcoals, each of the pictures exhibiting the diversity of the artists who'd painted them. In front of St. Louis Cathedral, a crowd gathered to watch the antics of a street magician as he performed feat after feat in response to their enthusiastic laughter and applause. Vendors hawked rice cakes and pralines from the trays hung around their necks, the aromas of their wares filling the air with the sweet odors of sugar and molasses. The haunting strains of "Greensleeves" hypnotized the tourists as it tripped from the guitar strings of a young man propped against the wall of the Cabildo, exchanging his talents for the coins deposited in the cup at his feet.

Making her way to a bench at the side of the park closest to the river, Jenny could hear the soft clatter of the hooves of the horses pulling gaudy carriages full of sightseers over the worn cobblestones of the French Market. Ordinarily, she would have sat back, cleared her mind and enjoyed the pageantry, but today was far from ordinary, and the colorful magic of the Vieux Carré grew dim in the shadows cast by the reappearance of her past.

A large red ball landed with a hollow *thunk* at Jenny's feet. Startled, she looked up to see a little girl chasing after it. Without acknowledging Jenny's presence, the child scooped up the ball in her chubby arms and ran back to the man waiting to hoist her above his head and twirl her in the air. Her delighted laughter blended with the other noises of the square as she and her father disappeared behind the pigeon-bedecked statue of Andrew Jackson. The loving demonstration added to Jenny's distraught state.

She slipped her arms from the sleeves of her beige gauze jacket, her attention moving to the giant live oak in the corner of the fenced-in square and the couple nearly concealed by the great tree's girth. Locked in each other's arms, they were oblivious of the world around them. The picture they made threatened the release of a torrent of unwelcome memories—memories of the first time she'd met Devin.

Back then, Jenny had firmly believed in happily-ever-afters and the unknown force that had guided her steps through the early-spring rain and onto the doorstep of Devin's cabin retreat.

Once that one small recollection emerged into the sunlight, the rest tumbled after it like water over a precipice. Leaning back on the bench, she abandoned the fight and closed her eyes, giving unvoiced consent to her subconscious to let the parade begin. Strolling tourists gave scant notice as her memories transported her from the humid air of the Mississippi to the sweet, pine-scented mountains of Tennessee, back to a time when life had held the magic of first love and only other people had suffered grief and pain.

The sparse raindrops came as a welcome coolant to Jenny's hot skin after her long trek over the mountain trails. Intermittent shafts of weak sunlight peeked through sparse openings in the boughs overhead, dappling the newly washed earth with a muted radiance. A small stream gurgled close by, filled to capacity with the runoff from the hills. She inhaled deeply of the pungent odors of wet earth and moldering leaves and the ever-present pine resin—the fragrance of home.

Engrossed in the transformation of the forest, she failed to see the approach of a new storm. When the thunder boomed and lightning slashed a path of electrified fire through the sky, she shivered in the sudden cold. The heavens opened and water sluiced over her, plastering her denim shorts and white cotton halter top to her skin. Wind wailed through the pines, bending the trees in submission, moving them aside to expose the spectacular display of lightning as it skipped across the blackened heavens. An angry rumble of thunder reverberated through the ground beneath her feet. Another lightning bolt pierced the gathering dark of the late afternoon as the sky churned angrily and the rain intensified.

She remembered a seldom-used cabin farther up the trail, and hurried toward it, hesitating only momentarily when she saw the single finger of smoke rising from the chimney and the amber glow of a light in the front window. Gooseflesh blossomed on her wet skin as chill after chill coursed through her. If she didn't get out of the rain soon, she'd have pneumonia. Still, she paused, unsure. The top of a pine tree snapped under the pressure of the relentless wind, crashing to the ground somewhere close and deciding for her.

Knowing that in the hills hospitality came with the land, and no one questioned what lay behind closed doors, where the inhabitants waited to extend the hand of welcome to strangers, she raced up the front-porch steps and pounded on the door. There was no response. Without a second thought as to what she might be getting into, her mind caught up in visions of dry clothing, a blazing fire and a friendly welcome, she knocked again. She had just about given up any hope of finding refuge when the door flew open to reveal not the welcoming face she'd anticipated but a decidedly unhappy occupant.

"Good God," the man growled, and grabbed her wrist, hauling her into the cabin. "What in the name of hell are you doing out in a storm like this, and half-dressed?" he demanded, his gaze raking her scanty attire.

The cabin's warmth had barely started to coax the chill from her body when she began wondering what she'd gotten herself into. Impetuousness had long been her worst failing, but this time she'd outdone herself. She froze, staring fixedly into his pale eyes.

"You can stop looking at me as though I'm going to cook you and eat you for supper," he said, grinning in response to the absolute horror he saw register on her stricken face.

"I'd gone for a walk and didn't see the storm coming. It frightened me," she managed to choke out, backing cautiously away from him.

"That's understandable," he said gently, his face softening as he cast a glance out the window. "This is one of the worst I've seen."

Shivers rippled over her, bringing a fresh crop of goose bumps to her exposed flesh. "I should leave."

"Not until you dry off." He took her arm and led her across the room to stand in front of the blazing fire. "Stay there, and I'll see if I can find something for you to put on." He disappeared through a door to the right of the fireplace.

As the warmth of the blaze began to seep into her cold limbs, she surveyed his domain, unconsciously looking for a telephone.

A desk positioned near a bare window on the far side of the room showed its age in the deep scars of use gouged into the soft pine. Amid the clutter on its top, she could make out the keyboard of a typewriter. Piled on either side of it were stacks of paper, reference books, a dog-eared atlas, pens and pencils protruding from an old jelly jar, and a new dictionary with the pages propped open by a plate holding a half-eaten sandwich. To the right of the typewriter, a gooseneck lamp illuminated the paper coiled around the platen of the machine and a collection of several dirty coffee cups.

Unless it lay buried beneath the rubble, there was no telephone in the cabin. A new shiver, unrelated to the cold, ran over her limbs.

"You write?" Jenny asked, striving to sound nonchalant, when he came back into the room carrying a faded pair of jeans, a gray sweatshirt and a pair of white athletic socks.

"I try," he said dryly, handing the clothes to her and taking her arm again to steer her into a bathroom. "Change in there. I'll make coffee."

Locking the door securely, she quickly peeled off her wet clothes, toweled herself and pulled on the dry clothing. Everything was miles too big for her, and she had to roll the legs of the pants up several times before she dared take a step.

Cinching in the waist with a belt she found hanging behind the door, she emerged into the room again to find him bent over, retrieving the wads of paper dotting the floor around the desk. He seemed to sense her presence immediately. Depositing the paper in a wastebasket, he turned to her. As he slowly looked her over from head to foot, his face shifted into a wide grin. The grin built into a chuckle, escalating into robust laughter.

Jenny looked down at herself, and had to agree she presented a rather comical picture. The rolled-up jeans resembled big blue doughnuts around each calf, and the sleeves of the sweatshirt hung at least five inches beyond her hands. The socks fit rather well, if she didn't take into account the three inches protruding beyond her toes. Her hair, which usually fell in fluffy waves, clung to her shoulders in limp, dripping clumps.

"I'm sorry," he croaked. "You look worse than when I dragged you in here, if that's possible."

Even though his comment held a lot of truth, it stung. "Thanks." Jenny flashed him a saccharine smile, her youthful dignity in shreds. "Few women I know could enter a beauty contest after being caught in one of our downpours." She threw him a disdainful look and bent to towel her hair dry in the heat from the fireplace.

Damn man, Jenny thought as she rubbed at her wet hair. Who did he think he was, laughing at her? Through the drying strands of her hair, she stole a look in his direction. Her anger faded, replaced by a warmth not provided solely by the fire. His expression had sobered, and his gaze was traveling from her hair over her extended buttocks and down to the oversize socks. A sharply inhaled breath expanded his wide chest when her sweatshirt slid down her bent frame, exposing her bare back.

She found herself returning his frank appraisal. Even upside down, he was a breathtaking specimen of manhood in his late twenties—tall, lithe, with muscles bulging beneath the material of his white T-shirt. His strong hands gripped the sides of the desk on which he'd rested his hips, pulling the material of his jeans tight across muscular thighs.

She quickly applied the brakes to her thoughts. Sans underwear, and at the mercy of this stranger, she couldn't afford to show any interest in him. Straightening, she snapped her head back, throwing her damp hair behind her and yanking the sweatshirt over her hips.

"How old are you?"

Averting her eyes, Jenny folded the towel with fumbling hands and laid it on a chair beside her. "Eighteen," she finally said, biting her tongue on the lie. Well, it wasn't all that much of a lie. Technically, she was in her eighteenth year, even if she wouldn't attain it for another ten months.

A faint glimmer of sunlight sifted through the window over his shoulder. The rain had stopped as suddenly as it had begun. She had no reason to remain.

"The weather's cleared," she said, her voice quavering with uncertainty. "I should be going. I can return your clothes later today, or first thing tomorrow."

"No, you don't." He snared her arm as she sidled past him. "I made coffee, young lady, and you're going to have some before I let you leave here. I don't want to be accused of allowing you to catch your death."

She pulled away, frightened by his commanding voice. Looking into his eyes, she saw humor lurking just beneath their moss-colored surface; she relaxed and smiled.

"Besides," he went on, "I've lost all the inspiration I had today and am suffering from a spasmodic disease called writer's block. It's not fatal—at least not to me—but a little conversation might unclog my thinking mechanism." He held out one of his large hands in friendship. "Devin Montgomery, aspiring novelist," he said.

Feeling much more at ease, Jenny took his hand. "Jennifer Tyson, aspiring...woman," she added for lack of anything else to say, his warm touch sending her heart into overdrive.

"I think not." His eyes gleamed devilishly as they traveled the full length of her body, taking in the ill-fitting clothes effectively concealing any trace of her shapely figure. His expression, however, told her the memory of her gloved in wet shorts and a halter top remained vividly clear in his mind. "You've been a lot more successful at reaching your goal than I have at attaining mine."

Jenny colored, disengaged her hand, and moved to the small table holding a battered enamel coffeepot, two chipped mugs and a mismatched sugar and creamer.

To her amazement, once the embarrassment died, she found she liked his compliments. She'd never been faced with having to accept flattery from a man before. The only remarks she'd ever encountered about her looks consisted of the wolf whistles that followed her down Main Street. The few dates she'd ever gone on had quickly turned into wrestling matches to preserve her dignity. Most guys considered aesthetics a bonus, something to stimulate their infantile hormones, not something to be complimented. Devin's remarks were sincere, and not in the least offensive.

A friendship took root on that stormy day. At first Jenny devised excuses to spend time with him, but as the weeks flew by, she fell in love and forgot the excuses, heading for the cabin as soon as her father had dragged his hung-over body to the mill.

Devin was never irritated by her impromptu visits. On the contrary, he seemed to look forward to her company as much as she did his. Sometimes they walked off his writer's block in the woods. On other occasions, they sat by the fire and talked of their dreams and fantasies. She told him about the family she'd have one day, and the little house they'd all live in.

"I used to have dreams like that," he said, looking suddenly forlorn and turning toward the crackling fire with a faraway look in his eyes. "But fate and Social Services had other plans."

"Social Services?"

He picked up some splinters of wood from the logs they'd carried in earlier and tossed them into the fire, watching hypnotically as they were consumed. "They're great at preaching the need for kids to have families, homes and love. But when it comes down to the wire..."

Jenny waited for him to continue, feeling the loneliness emanating from him. He'd never spoken about his life before he came to Tennessee. Curiosity prompted her next question. "Devin, where's your family?"

He glanced at her, then back to the fire. "I don't have any—at least none I know of. I spent my childhood being hustled from foster home to foster home. When I was sixteen, I took off on my own. Two years later, I enlisted in the United States Navy.

"When I got out, I had a high school diploma, the urge to write, and no idea how to go about it. So I got a job in an insurance company and went to college at night. Last year, I quit my job and spent my savings on a secondhand typewriter and a used car, and here I am."

He turned and smiled at her, but the loneliness crowded the happiness from his eyes.

"Do you still dream about a home and family?" she asked hopefully.

Laughing with a hard, brittle sound, he stretched out before the fire and rested his head on his bent arm. "No. Aside from my writing, there's no place in my plans for any kind of commitment. I want to write about America's back roads, and its people. To do that, I have to travel around the country. I can't do that with a family hanging on my pant leg. I'm happy just as I am, footloose and fancy-free."

"Sometimes things happen that aren't part of our plans. What if something did happen, and you found yourself with a wife and child? Wouldn't it be their choice whether they traveled with you or not?" she offered, her secret dreams of a life with Devin fading rapidly with his words.

"It won't be a decision I'll have to make. I'm being very careful not to make the mistake of acquiring a family." He grinned at her.

Jenny's heart sank, but she drew hope from the thought that she could change his mind. And so they continued. With no phone, no TV set, not even a radio, they were undisturbed by the outside world, snug in their idyllic existence.

Soon, Devin allowed her to read his manuscript and asked for her opinion. Once she discovered that his novel depicted the hill people of Tennessee, she began jotting down bits and pieces of folklore she remembered hearing the older residents of the town repeat. She took pleasure in working side by side with him, cementing the growing bond between them that much tighter.

But it wasn't tight enough for Jenny. The fact that Devin seemed to look upon her as nothing more than a friend distressed her. Worse yet, despite his words to the contrary, she feared he would never see her as a desirable woman, and would leave Tennessee without her.

Barely two months after she first walked into the cabin, she decided to take matters into her own hands, certain she could make him change his mind. Playing the seductress did not come easy to her. She wouldn't have been able to summon the nerve to consider it at all if she hadn't caught Devin sneaking sidelong glances at her or caressing her skin with his thumb as they walked hand in hand through the woods. She already knew she loved him more than anything on earth. But did he feel the same way?

The day she planned to take the big step, she spent extra time dressing and doing her hair, brushing it until it shone blue-black, leaving it loose around her shoulders the way Devin liked it. Wearing lipstick, tight jeans and an equally snug sweater, she set out to seduce Devin Montgomery.

Nervously she entered the cabin. The unoccupied interior glared at her. Had he left without telling her? A cheery fire flickered in the fireplace, calming her fears.

Walking outside and looking around, she heard the sound of splashing water coming from the direction of the creek. She took a deep breath and moved toward it. Pushing through the scrub pine and trailing vines, she came upon a sight that robbed her of her breath, leaving her shaken and inexplicably warm.

Devin emerged from the gurgling creek, naked, tanned and breathtaking, his muscles rippling and glistening with water droplets. Never having seen a naked man before, she was mesmerized by his masculine beauty. She froze in her tracks, watching breathlessly as he rubbed a towel languidly over his skin. In her mind, *her* hands replaced the towel traveling over his flesh, caressing his shoulders. *Her* hands played in the black curls on his broad chest. *Her* fingers combed through the damp hair at his groin, touching his manhood.

The wanton thoughts took her by such surprise, she started to turn, but then she paused. The opportunity she'd been waiting for, dreaming of, had presented itself. Why was she walking away?

Slowly she stripped off her sweater and jeans. With trembling fingers, she peeled her flimsy underwear from her body. Taking a deep breath, she separated the branches and stepped into the circle of sunlight with the unabashed confidence of a woman who knows her allure.

He saw her at once. His hands stilled. His gaze traveled over her, hot and blatantly hungry. "Jenny." The look in his eyes registered in her mind as a cherished memory. To her dismay, he restrained himself. His expression went blank. "No, Jenny. Please. Put on your clothes. We can't let this happen." His plea emerged as a hoarse whisper, divulging how strongly the sight of her seductively youthful body affected him, giving her the impetus to fulfill a dream.

She ignored his protests and, with the grace and agility of a mountain cat, walked slowly toward him, concentrating on the way his appraisal made her feel alive and tingling. His gaze caressed her flesh, gently stroked her breasts, swelling them and hardening her nipples. His attention dropped to her stomach and on down to the dark V at the apex of her thighs. She shivered convulsively.

Stopping just a few inches from him, she inhaled his scent—it was masculine, woodsy, fresh. Her breathing ceased. Her blood slowed. Her entire being came to a grinding halt—waiting for the first touch of his hands on her skin.

Devin's hungry eyes locked with hers as he traced the rosy tip of her breast with one finger, slowly, erotically circling the areola, smiling when her breath exploded from her lungs in a moan of pure pleasure. He seemed poised, as if he were waiting for her to vanish. When she didn't, he cupped her breast gently with his large hand.

"Jenny." His breathing grew more rapid. "You have the most incredible skin. So soft. So smooth," he whispered, staring at her white flesh, his free arm snaking out to pull her to him, enveloping her in his warm embrace. He groaned.

The sudden contact of his flesh against hers, the feel of his hands caressing her from shoulder to hip, melded together in a lightning sensation. Scorched nerve endings sizzled from her head to the tip of her toes, settling in a blaze between her thighs.

"Do you know what's happening?" Devin asked, a muscle in his jaw flexing. His breathing was erratic, and his lips were resting against her hair. "You're so young. Are you sure you're ready for this, Jenny?"

She managed a slight nod of her head as she tilted it back and looked in his eyes. A groan broke the silence of the woods. Burying her hands in the thick hair at the back of his neck, she allowed him to support her as he lowered her to the bed of pine needles beneath their feet. The amber halos in his eyes widened, devouring the silvery green. His head lowered. His lips engulfed hers in a kiss so gentle it was like a dream. As the kiss intensified, she knew it was no dream, but the realization of one.

Devin's hands left her shoulders and moved in a velvet-soft caress over her collarbone and into the valley formed by her breasts. His lips pursued the same path.

When she felt his mouth close over a distended nipple, she cried out his name and thrust herself against his lips. Digging her fingernails into the rock-hard muscles of his shoulders, she could feel the control he kept in rigid check in the taut flesh beneath her fingers.

Punctuated by the rasp of his labored breathing, Devin pleaded with her. "Please, Jenny. I don't want to hurt you. All these days with you so close, all the hours wanting to touch you..." His mouth covered her eager lips.

The sensations produced by his body covering hers intensified her need for him. Arching her back, she showed him without words how much she wanted him, and reveled in the fact that his need equaled hers.

"God, we shouldn't do this." His voice emerged from his throat strained and raspy.

"Devin," she whispered, deliberately allowing her breath to caress his ear. "Don't deny us this. I want it to happen. You want it to happen."

Her whispered pleas worked their magic on his constraint. He adjusted his long legs between hers and slowly lowered his hips toward her, cupping her buttocks in his hands, cushioning the initial entry. Covering her lips with his, he swallowed any noise she might have made.

Jenny soon forgot the pain as their bodies learned the rhythm of their lovemaking, adjusting and flowing into a smooth movement of flesh on flesh. All their senses were attuned, their hands discovering new forms of delight. Locked in a war of sensual pleasures, their frenzied bodies tangled on their pine-needle bed, straining for release. A simultaneous explosion rocked them. Their voices cried out in unison, shattering the morning silence with their mutual climax.

That day set the tempo for the weeks that followed. As each day passed, their lovemaking became sweeter, more intense. They were unable to get their fill of each other. Other things did change, however. After the first time they made love, Devin made certain to use protection. Neither of them dreaming their one unguarded encounter would put into motion a series of events that would nearly destroy them.

Several weeks later, Jenny woke to her third morning of nausea. After consulting the calendar, she joyfully ruled out the flu and allowed herself to admit she was carrying Devin's child.

At first she couldn't wait to share the news with him, but as the day wore on she recalled Devin's declaration that he wanted no ties to a family. For that matter, he'd never said he loved her in so many words. Doubts began to form. Knowing he wasn't the type to shirk his responsibilities, and concluding that he would marry her out of duty if need be, she balked at telling him. She didn't want his commitment because he felt obligated to give their baby his name. She wanted it to be because he loved her. Hugging her secret close, she headed for the cabin.

That night, the sun had nearly set when they stretched out in front of the blazing hearth.

"What happens when you've finished your book?" she asked, trying to be casual, combing his hair with her fingers while his head rested in her lap.

"I'll send it off and hope someone likes it enough to publish it," he said, eyes closed, enjoying her caress.

Her fingers abandoned their task. She reached for the coffee cup on the floor beside her. "I mean, what will you do? Will you stay on here, or will you go back to New York?"

"Go back, I guess."

Nearly choking on the hot coffee, she set the cup aside. A lump formed in her throat. "What...about us?" she asked softly.

"We'll write," he said, turning to look up into her blue eyes. "In the fall, I'll come back for a visit."

"Write? Visit?" She repeated the words as if they were a death sentence.

Devin pushed himself up, aligning their lips. "Hey! Why so grim? I'll be back. I promise. I love you, Jenny."

The words she'd waited an eternity to hear only brought more pain to her heart. Devin had no idea what love was. "But not enough for anything permanent," she said, pushing him away and rising to her feet. "I'm supposed to sit here in the mountains and wait until you get around to visiting me. Is that what you have planned, Devin?"

"No."

"What, then?" she demanded, fighting the tears straining at her throat.

"I don't know. Jenny, I told you how I felt about a family. It's just not the right time for a permanent arrangement. We have time." He looked up at her, his face in shadows. "Give me a chance to get my career off the ground. Then we can make all the permanent plans you want."

"*Permanent* isn't a dirty word, Devin," she told him, hating the way he made it sound like a loathsome disease. She bit her tongue to keep from blurting out that time had run out—time now consisted of a few short months before their child would arrive. "It's synonymous with commitment, marriage." There, she'd said it, some small part of her still praying she'd misunderstood his lack of enthusiasm, praying he would change his mind, praying he would say he loved her enough to marry her. He had to want more from their relationship than a few stolen hours in a mountain cabin. He had to, but the words never came.

Devin clambered to his feet. "Marriage? But we can't get... I mean... I never... My career..."

Jenny cringed as all her dreams tumbled around her feet. "Damn *your* career!" She moved away from him. "What about us? What about *our* future?" She watched in horror as he avoided looking at her and offered no answers to her anguished questions. Her mind finally awakened to a fact she'd put off considering. "You never meant for us to marry, did you, Devin?" she finally managed in an agonized whisper. "I was never any more to you than a distraction."

"No. That's not true. I just never thought—" He grabbed for her arm as she walked past him. "Jenny, try to understand..."

She deafened herself to his pleas, past understanding how he could say he loved her and yet not want them to have a life together. Picking up her sweater from the sofa, she faced him.

"Please, Jenny. Can't we talk about this?"

"What's the use in talking? Will it change anything?" Shaking her head, she walked to the door. Without looking back, she opened it and walked out of Devin's life.

That night was the most hellish she had ever lived through. By morning, she'd made up her mind about what she had to do. Her beloved mountains no longer provided solace for her—without Devin they held only painful memories.

"I want to go away from here," she'd told her father over breakfast.

Raising bloodshot eyes to stare at her for a second, he reached for the bottle at his elbow and filled his cup with moonshine. "I ain't payin' your fare," he mumbled against the rim of the cup before he tilted it to drink.

Using the small reserve of cash she'd accumulated from occasional baby-sitting jobs, Jenny purchased a bus ticket to Asheville, North Carolina. By late that morning, she took her last look through the window of a Greyhound at the father who'd never wanted to be saddled with a kid—just like Devin. Tears raced down her cheeks as she said a silent goodbye to Devin and their love and turned away. Her grandfather had wanted her with him for years. He was about to get his wish.

It took only three lonely, agonizing weeks for Jenny to admit the mistake she'd made in running from Devin. She began writing letters to him daily, begging him to forgive her foolishness, telling him she wanted their relationship to continue in any form he decided on, and informing him of the small life they'd created. When they went unanswered, she refused to give up, and boarded a bus for Tennessee.

The stillness that greeted her at the cabin deafened her, but the barren wasteland inside, declaring the cabin unoccupied, screamed out at her, shredding her soul. There hadn't been any misunderstanding on her part. Devin didn't want her or their baby. She'd been an amusement, a plaything, to fill the boredom when he wasn't writing. She and their child were an encumbrance, a responsibility he didn't care to take on. How could she have misjudged him so completely?

Sobs tore from her for the naive young girl who'd believed his declarations of love, who'd believed a man from the city might be content tied to a nobody from the sticks.

Like any child in need of reassurance, she went to the house she'd called home for seventeen years. In her heart, she knew there would be no understanding there, but, driven by her sorrow, she tried anyway. It was empty, just like her soul. Empty and lonely. A neighbor confirmed what her grandfather had already told her. Her father had died of alcohol poisoning a week earlier.

Jenny collapsed on the porch and gave in to the tears burning her throat. She cried for her father and his useless existence, for herself and her shattered dreams, but most of all, she cried for the life growing inside her and the fact that it would never know its father.

Hours passed before she dragged herself back to the bus station.

Determined to go back to North Carolina and have her baby, she tried to look forward to starting a new life.

Jenny's mind snatched her from her memories and deposited her back in the reality of Jackson Square, as if to protect her from further pain. She blinked at the bright sunlight and looked around her in embarrassment, wondering if anyone realized she'd just relived the most heartbreaking, and yet the most erotic, moments of her life.

Activities went on around her as if nothing had happened. The child chased the ball and threw it back to her laughing father. The couple had abandoned their hideaway beneath the oak tree, probably for more private surroundings. Empty spaces marked the spots left by the artists who'd gathered up their canvases and paints and gone home. The magician had vanished, taking the laughter with him. The crowds thinned as the tourists surrendered to their empty stomachs, making their way to the many restaurants housed in the square mile of the French Quarter. The musician's song had come to an end.

Their lives moved on as usual. Only Jenny's remained motionless, poised on the brink of the future, teetering on the edge of the past, as she waited for Devin to reappear. God, how much of her life had already been consumed waiting for Devin to appear?

She needed activity. Leaving the Square, she strolled toward the Moonwalk, fighting valiantly to keep the rest of her memories closeted in her subconscious. In that short span of time, back in Jackson Square, she'd relived a part of her youth, a summer interlude with a man she'd come to love. The happy memories. Another set remained tucked safely away. Lacking the strength to face them, she left the tragic past for another time. Right now, she felt bruised and beaten.

Though six o'clock had come and gone, when she returned to the shop, Belle was waiting patiently.

"I sent Harry along home," the older woman said, taking in the drawn face of her young boss.

"You should have gone with him, Belle."

"I didn't want to leave until I knew you were okay."

"I'm fine." Jenny patted the chubby hand Belle had placed on her arm, forcing a wan smile.

"Well, you don't look fine. Not sleeping. Not eating. Jumping at the slightest noise. It's like you're waiting for a monster to jump out from behind every door and eat you up."

Sardonic or not, Belle's analogy brought the first real smile in days to Jenny's lips. The woman had no idea how close she'd come to stumbling on the truth.

"It has something to do with that visit from Devin, doesn't it?" Belle's forehead creased in a frown. "Did he give you a bad time? Harry said we should have been here with you. I knew I should have come in early that day."

"How could you have known? It wasn't as if he gave me any forewarning. You have nothing to reproach yourself for. And if it makes you feel any better, Belle," Jenny said, placing her arm around the woman's shoulders, "he was a perfect gentleman." She bit her tongue, recalling his sizzling glances and how they'd burned into her like a branding iron. Too much had happened for her peace of mind.

"Then what is it, dear? What's got you so upset?"

"Belle," she said, trying to appease her friend's motherly instincts, "he's a part of my past I don't like to think about. He's given birth to memories I'd rather not have to face. When he goes, so will they."

"And when is he going?"

"I don't know." *Soon,* she prayed. *Soon.*

"Just what are these memories you can't face? Were you in love with him?"

Jenny swallowed. Belle had to be the reincarnation of one of the interrogators of the Spanish Inquisition. "Yes, Belle, I was in love with him."

Belle mulled Jenny's words over. "It appears to me, the problem may be you still are. It might be why an old flame showing up out of nowhere can rattle your cage so bad, and why you insist on turning your back on the first real money you've been offered in a month of Sundays."

Belle left the shop shortly after dropping her bomb on Jenny. The young woman sat alone in the darkened interior for a long time, wondering if Belle's conclusion had any validity. Did she still love Devin? Was she kidding herself when she claimed she felt nothing for him? Could there be more? She shuddered just considering the possibility.

Pushing aside the whole ridiculous idea, she locked up the shop and climbed the stairs to her apartment. But the notion followed. She couldn't still love Devin. Only a masochist would go on loving a man who'd turned his back on her and their child. Belle had to be wrong. She just had to be. Panic gripped Jenny as her relentless conscience prodded her. *But what if she isn't? Dear God, what if she isn't?*

Chapter 3

"Popie, can we go home now?"

Devin glanced up from the papers his attorney had delivered for his signature that morning, the papers that would put Jenny's fate in the palm of his hand.

"I have more business to do before we can go home, Amy. I thought you were having a good time here. Mrs. Filbert took you on a boat ride, and to the zoo. You even rode the trolley car yesterday."

Amy doubled her good leg beneath her on the couch and allowed the other to dangle over the edge. The corners of her mouth turned down, and her little hands fidgeted in her lap. "When will you be done with your business?"

"One more day," he said. That should be more than enough time for Jenny to realize his offer was her only way out. "Why don't you go into your room and color for a while? Mrs. Filbert said she was going to take you shopping this afternoon, and tonight we'll have dinner at your favorite restaurant, just you and me."

Amy brightened. "You mean the one with the fountain?"

"That's the one." Devin grinned and opened his arms to catch her as she bounded off the couch and deposited herself next to his chair. "You'll need to pick out something extraspecial to wear tonight. The Court of Two Sisters doesn't let ragamuffins in."

Squealing, Amy hugged his neck and kissed his cheek. She slipped quickly from his embrace and limped to the door. Turning, she faced him with a broad smile. "You're the best daddy ever. I'm glad you came and got me from the home. Sally Anne said you were just adopting me, but I told her, no, you weren't, that I was really your little girl and you were my real daddy."

He returned her smile and swallowed hard. "That's right, Scamp. You're my real little girl."

His gaze remained on the closed door long after she disappeared through it, recalling another time when Amy had bowed her head and made nervous pleats in her dress. Funny how a few words could bring back memories . . .

"This man is your real daddy, Amy," Mother Superior said gently to the quaking little girl at her side.

"My name's Becca," she murmured.

"Oh, but you're gonna have a brand-new name to begin your brand-new life. Your daddy's come to take you home to live with him for always."

Large, fear-filled eyes raised to look at Devin. He sucked in his breath. If he had any remaining doubts about this child's parentage, they were whisked away with that one forlorn look. She was the very picture of her mother. "Amy, we can keep your old name if you want."

The little shoulders lifted in a shrug. "How's my grampy gonna find me if I go away?"

The nun glanced at Devin and shook her head. She sat and lifted Amy to her lap. "Amy, we talked about your grampy. Don't you remember we said he went to live with the angels?"

Amy nodded, her eyes trained on her hands, which were twisting and turning the sash of her dress. "Can I take Dora and my bears to his house?" She pointed at Devin, keeping her eyes glued on her other hand.

Devin felt his heart tighten in his chest, cutting off his air and clogging his throat. He sent the nun a questioning look.

"Dora is Amy's doll friend," she explained, brushing stray wisps of black hair from the child's forehead. "The bears are a collection of carvings a gentleman who used to come see her all the time made for her."

Devin recalled the doctor's explanation that Jenny's grandfather visited Amy on a regular basis.

"Well, then, we certainly can't leave anything that important behind," Devin exclaimed, smiling at the bent head.

The nun slipped Amy from her lap and walked her to the door. "Why don't you run along and help Sister Mary pack your things while your daddy and I finish up a few details here?"

Casting a quick glance at Devin, Amy scooted through the door.

"I'm sorry, Mr. Montgomery. I thought we'd prepared her, but it's so difficult for a little mind to grasp these things. I'm sure she'll be better as she gets more used to you."

He nodded at the nun and cleared his throat. Emotions too powerful to deny, emotions aimed at the woman who'd left his daughter to be raised by strangers, rendered him speechless.

"As I told you on the phone, Mr. Montgomery, the results of the blood test you had done match Rebec—Amy's—perfectly. There's no doubt she's your daughter. That, along with Dr. Hines's signature on the notarized affidavit stating you're her blood parent, was all we needed to be able to release her into your custody." She paused, choosing her words with great care. "I do hope you'll be patient with her. In all her four years, she's never known a real home. I'm told you're a writer."

Devin nodded, slowly regaining control of his rage.

"Does that mean you'll be traveling a lot?"

Understanding where this was leading, Devin leaned forward in his chair. "Amy will have a home where she can grow and flourish, Sister. You have my promise. I used to move around a lot, but now that's all changed. I'll make sure my traveling is minimal and that whenever possible Amy is with me."

The nun nodded and pushed the stack of forms toward Devin. "Then I guess all we need do is sign these and make it legal."

Amy returned a few moments later. Another nun carried the girl's meager belongings in one small suitcase. Tucked beneath her arm and clutched close to her chest was a shoe box, which Devin decided must house the precious carved bears.

As their car passed down the long drive, away from the only home and family Amy had ever known, Devin noticed the glistening of silent tears rolling over his little girl's cheeks. How could Jenny have done such a heartless thing? How could she have turned her back on her own flesh and blood? How many times as a child had he asked himself the same question about his own mother?

It was at that moment that Devin swore that if it was within his power, Jenny would pay for what she'd done both to him, and to Amy, with her selfishness.

* * *

With indecision still dogging her footsteps, Jenny slipped into the empty shop the next afternoon and closed the door quietly behind her. The sound of raised voices coming from the workroom drowned out the tinkling of the bell announcing her return.

Although she tried not to eavesdrop, the thin walls and the flimsy curtains separating her from the Masons made it impossible not to overhear their conversation.

"Harry, if we tighten our belts, there's no reason we can't survive on our pension checks," Belle was saying without much conviction.

"We're barely making ends meet now, my dear," came Harry's strained voice. "If we don't have our paychecks from here, we'll have to do more than cinch up our belts."

Belle snorted. "You just make sure Jenny doesn't hear you talkin' like that, old man. She's got enough on her plate without worrying about us, too."

Harry made a shushing sound. "If we don't put a stop to this talk now, she's liable to come back and hear it anyway."

"The bell will let us know if she comes in. But you're right," Belle agreed. "No sense in taking chances. We'll talk about this at home."

Surreptitiously Jenny moved back to the door and opened it wide enough to close it firmly, reaching up and jiggling the bell as she did so.

"I'm back," she called, noting she was met with momentary silence before Belle hustled through the curtain, a cheery smile painted on her lips.

"Well, you look a bit more chipper. Am I to take it you've come to a decision?"

Harry peeked out from behind his wife, the shop's lights reflecting off his bald head.

For a moment, Jenny looked into their dear faces. Images of Belle swiping her sponge wand full of window cleaner across the mullioned panes of a Victorian dollhouse accosted her. Following quickly in their wake came a picture of Harry's head bent over the task of threading minute crystal beads on hair-thin wire to create a swag for a tiny chandelier.

Their love for this place went as deep as hers. What would become of them if the shop closed?

"I don't know," she whispered. "I just don't know."

The following morning, Jenny made the coffee, a half-formed decision chasing around in her mind. She knew what she *should* do. She should accept Devin's order for the dollhouse furniture and ensure the continued existence of her shop. In doing so, she would secure the Masons' supplementary income.

However, she couldn't shake her misgivings about working in such close proximity to Devin. It wasn't that she still loved him—Belle was dead wrong about that. She'd gotten over that long ago. What tortured her was the idea of being reminded daily of the child she'd never hold, never love, never see grow to adulthood.

She glanced at the date on her watch. If she didn't pay her lease by tomorrow, she'd be out on the street, and Belle and Harry with her. The choices had boiled down to two—losing the shop or losing her hard-won peace of mind.

Little did anyone realize what a battering her pride would undergo if she took help from Devin. Even knowing she'd be exchanging her professional services for his money wouldn't assuage her dignity. She'd wanted never again to rely on him for one shred of her happiness, and here she was with not only her well-being hanging on his benevolence, but the Masons', as well. Had it just been her, she'd have taken her lumps and told him to go to blazes, but she didn't have the right to play with Belle's and Harry's future.

The shop bell tinkled softly. Jenny glanced up to greet her customer. Unprepared for the sight of Devin, hands on his hips, the same stubbornness lighting his eyes, she took a deep breath and a step backward from his masculine magnetism. There had been a time when she would have moved heaven and earth for this man, she thought. She still would, she amended, if she could dump it in the middle of his arrogant face.

Taking the necessary steps to position himself exactly on the opposite side of the display case from Jenny, Devin planted both hands on the glass and looked her in the eye. "Well, Jenny, what have you decided?"

Staring into the face of a man obviously savoring the taste of victory, she surrendered. "You win, Devin," she said, dipping her head to hide the angry tears the agreement brought to her eyes.

Reaching across the intervening space, he ran his fingertip along her clenched jaw, tilting her face up to look at him. "I usually do."

"This time," she added with grim softness. Fighting the prickling of awareness along her skin where his finger rested, she stared at him unflinchingly.

He dropped his hand to the countertop, and his face hardened, but then collapsed into a broad smile. "I remember another time when I lost a battle to you, Jenny. If the results are the same, I'll look forward to the defeat."

There was no need for him to elaborate on the incident of which he spoke. After all, she'd lived through it in her memory the previous day.

"I've made a list of the things I'll need to work with at your house. You'll have to supply them. The Masons will be using the tools I have here while I'm gone." Congratulating herself on her businesslike tone, she handed him a sheet of paper. "I always require a fifty-percent deposit before I begin." She named a figure.

Devin stuffed the list in his pocket and pulled his checkbook from the inside pocket of his suede jacket. "Pen," he said, holding out his upturned palm like a doctor performing surgery.

Jenny handed him hers, struggling with the reflexive urge to recoil when his fingers captured hers for a brief second.

Trying not to let on that her touch had sent a lightning bolt careening up his arm, Devin slid the pen from her cold grasp. Filling out the check with a bold flourish, he passed it across the glass top to her, along with another piece of paper. "Sign the receipt for the deposit," he instructed.

"How trusting," she commented dryly, and signed her name, experiencing a twinge at the thought of how much their relationship had deteriorated.

"Trust is a commodity I've learned to be selective in handing out," he drawled, his eyes turning frosty.

The sting of his words and his expression rankled. "Haven't we all?" she shot back pointedly.

"Tell me something," he said, extracting an ivory-colored business card from the rack next to the cash register and running his finger across her name. "Why didn't you ever marry?"

Mesmerized, she watched him move his thumb in a slow caress over the small castle embossed in the corner of the card. A shiver ran down her spine, as if her nerve endings were somehow connected to the raised picture. Angry at her reaction, she shoved the signed receipt at him.

"Facts about my personal life aren't part of the deal."

Curiosity sparked by more than a perverse desire for an answer, he pushed. "Why, Jenny?"

"I repeat. Your deposit did not buy you the right to pry into my personal life."

"Didn't it?" he asked quietly. Raising his compelling gaze to her, he pinned her like a mounted butterfly. "I'll find out, Jenny. So why not save us both a lot of wasted energy. Why?"

Her fingernails dug painfully into her palms. If he'd expected her to crumple at his feet and say it was because she'd never gotten over him, he was in for a big surprise. She couldn't imagine why he was so interested, but if he wanted an answer so bad, by God, she would supply one.

"I decided marriage wasn't for me after all. Who needs a husband and kids hanging around your neck like an albatross?"

Devin flipped the card onto the counter with his thumb, his expression turned to stone. In a flash, he'd rounded the case, grabbing her shoulders in his steely grip. "I could..."

"Could what, Devin? Hurt me?" Slowly she shook her head, never breaking eye contact. "Not anymore. You lost that power a long time ago."

Abruptly he turned her loose. *You're wrong,* he thought. More than once, since the first day he walked into the shop, he'd seen the pain his words inflicted. He hadn't lost one bit of that power, and she knew it. What she didn't know was that he intended to brandish it like a sword.

Lack of sleep and emotional fatigue had finally caught up to her. Pulling back, she leaned on the display case for support, drained of all her strength. "Devin, why are you doing this?" she asked wearily. "And don't tell me it's because of the dollhouse furniture."

He came very close to bellowing his answer at her. "We have things to settle," he answered evenly.

"What things?"

He scanned her face for the merest hint that she knew what he was talking about. Her bland expression indicated she hadn't a notion. If facts hadn't proved otherwise, he could have sworn she knew nothing about what had happened to Amy. But that was impossible. He had proof: her family Bible, with the entry for Amy's birth; a birth certificate bearing both their names; her grandfather's deathbed request to his family doctor, asking the physician to contact Devin so that Amy would have family to care for her; and her own admission that there was no place in her life for children.

Damn it! Why couldn't she have just told him, instead of taking off? If she had come back to Tennessee, told him she was pregnant with his child, they would have been married. Amy would have been with them instead of spending her first years in an orphanage, and all three of them would have been spared this pain.

"Popie?"

Devin blinked, releasing Jenny's gaze. She took a step away from him as if he had threatened her. Both adults turned in unison to the child standing just inside the door.

"Amy, where's Mrs. Filbert?" Devin asked, examining the empty doorway behind the girl for a sign of her nurse.

"She said she had to run an errand, so she brought me here."

In stunned silence, Jenny watched as the small child came to her father's side. Her heart constricted when she noticed the slight limp and the metal brace running from below her knee to clamp on the sole of her shoe. Jenny's questioning gaze flew to Devin.

He had been studying Jenny's reaction to Amy, and he gave a brief shake of his head in reply to her silent inquiry.

Magnetically her attention returned to the child. She was a miniature version of her father; the same silky blue-black hair hung in soft ringlets to her waist, framing her cherubic face; the same mossy gray eyes looked back at Jenny from the little face as Amy smiled up at her. Jenny's heart twisted, the pain cutting deeper than any she could ever have imagined.

"Hi."

"Hello, Amy," Jenny replied, forcing herself to smile down at the child.

"Popie, she knows my name." Tucking her small hand in her father's, Amy beamed at Jenny. "My popie gave me that name. It's French for beloved, but the French people spell it with two *e*s instead of a *y*."

Jenny was astounded. The child was very smart for five. "It's a lovely name."

"I really have two names," Amy stated emphatically.

"You mean you have a middle name, too?" From the corner of her eye, Jenny detected Devin's agitated movement.

"No. I used to have another name, but—" Amy began.

"Amy, why don't you look at the dollhouses while Jenny and I talk?" Devin said, hustling the child away from Jenny.

Obediently Amy scampered off, the metal brace beating on the wood floor. She headed straight for Jenny's castle.

"Devin, her leg..."

Taking Jenny's arm, he steered her away from Amy. "She was born with a twisted foot, a result of how she was carried during pregnancy. Had they treated it in infancy, she'd have worn a cast for a few weeks and been fine. Because her bones are harder now, she'll have to wear the brace until it straightens out." He paused, his attention leaving his daughter and returning to Jenny. "She's flawed, but she's mine, and I love her. She's made me very proud to be her father."

Jenny sighed, watching Amy's animated expression as she investigated the castle. "No, Devin. She's not flawed. She's precious, and your pride is well placed. I envy you."

Devin started at her words. Studying her face for some sign that she was patronizing him, he found none. He flinched as a crack opened in the wall of hatred he'd built around himself.

"How long?" Jenny's gaze never left the little girl.

He continued to look at her with a dumbfounded stare, trying to find a reason for remarks that contradicted her statement about needing neither children nor a husband cluttering her life.

"The brace. How long will she have to wear it?"

Roused from his stupor, he had to think for a second before he could make sense of her question. "Perhaps another few months. The doctor isn't certain at this point. It all depends on how quickly her bones reform."

"How awful for her," Jenny said, bathing him in a gaze filled with empathy for both of them.

His stern face was transformed when he watched his daughter, expressing more love than Jenny would have thought one man capable of. Rather than being warmed by the sight, she was enraged.

Caustic accusations clogged her throat. She fought the urge to hurl them in his face. *What about our child? Why couldn't you have cared this much for our baby?* Only Amy's presence helped her win the battle to control herself.

"Not really," he was saying. "It doesn't seem to bother her. She's quite amazing. Nothing slows her down. She runs and plays just like any other five-year-old tornado." He paused and returned his attention to Jenny. "Amy loves life. She reminds me of another girl who devoured it with both hands." He studied her for a sign she recognized herself in Amy, but none came. Grimly he asked himself how a mother could fail to recognize her own child? What about that invisible thread, touted by all the baby specialists, supposedly binding a mother and her offspring?

"Popie, can we buy this?" Amy asked, turning sparkling eyes to her father and pointing at Jenny's castle.

"No, Scamp." He indicated the sign on the castle's tower. "That sign says the castle isn't for sale."

"Oh."

The disappointment in the child's face tugged at Jenny's heartstrings. For the very first time, she found herself reconsidering her decision not to sell it.

"She's lovely, Devin." Jenny watched in amusement as Amy carefully inspected the castle's interior.

"Just like her mother," Devin mused softly.

The words carved their way into the tattered remains of Jenny's heart. She didn't want to hear about the woman she'd unknowingly shared him with.

"Popie, Popie, there's a real prince and princess in here!" Amy pointed excitedly to the throne room. "Come see, Popie! Quick! Come see!"

Smiling indulgently, Devin left Jenny's side and walked to where his daughter was wiggling with glee over her discovery.

Holding her breath, Jenny watched Devin bend to peer into the castle, hoping he wouldn't see the resemblance between them and the miniature monarchs.

Sliding his large hand into the room, he withdrew the tiny figurines, cradling them in his open palm. He studied them for a time before shifting his equivocal gaze to Jenny.

Jenny hurried to his side and took the black-haired dolls from him. Carefully she replaced them on their respective thrones. "Actually, Amy, they're a king and queen."

"Is there a princess?" Amy asked, unaware of the crackling tension between the adults.

"No." Jenny's throat closed around the word. "No. There's no princess."

"My popie says you're going to make furniture for my dollhouse." One of the Victorian houses captured Amy's attention, but she cast a last wistful look at the castle before moving away.

"Yes. Yes, I am," Jenny said absently.

He'd been that sure, she thought, sure enough to risk disappointing his daughter. But then, there had been no risk, and somehow he had known it and used the knowledge against her. Why?

Devin and Amy left the shop a few minutes later. Jenny picked up the check and dropped it into the cash-register drawer. The drawer was nearly closed when the amount on the check made her do a double take. His deposit would cover all her overdue bills, and then some. Puzzled, she slowly pushed the drawer closed, her gaze going to the retreating figures of the tall man and the little girl as they walked hand in hand across Jackson Square.

All at once Jenny knew what the fly must have felt like when the spider issued its silky invitation.

Chapter 4

Devin chose a spot where he could watch Amy play with her dolls on the lawn while he enjoyed his morning coffee on the veranda and waited for Jenny's impending arrival. His heart swelled as he looked at his daughter. He shuddered when he considered how close he'd come to never knowing her at all. That, more than anything, made it impossible for him to forgive Jenny. He'd been so sure he knew her, but had he? Did he now? Would he ever?

As he watched Amy, she flung back her head, throwing her long black curls over her shoulder, stirring memories of the first time he had seen Jenny. They tugged at him, memories of a drenched girl who had sought refuge from a raging storm—and brought one of her own.

Jenny had been the loveliest thing he'd ever seen, even in her drenched state. It had taken a few short minutes for his heart to agree. The struggle he'd waged against his baser instincts during those weeks was like none he'd ever engaged in, before or since. No matter how often he reminded himself of her youth, his blood had never failed to come to a rolling boil around her. When she finally took matters into her own hands and walked out of the trees that day by the creek, gloriously naked, temptingly willing, his defeat had been a foregone conclusion.

The cobwebs began to fall away from the memory of the staggering conclusion to their idealistic days in the mountains, the memory he'd fought against endlessly in the past year, the memory that rekindled all the pain of her treachery. Now, as a deliberate reminder, he welcomed the agony of it....

The sun played across the uneven glass in the window, splaying a rainbow across Devin's hand, much as Jenny had spread her colors across his life.

With the harsh words of their argument from the night before still ringing in his ears, he'd awakened that morning to realize just how senseless his misgivings about getting married had been. If he hadn't been so stunned by her abrupt introduction of the subject, he'd have been able to do more than just sputter in an attempt to explain.

A struggling writer with no more than a few dollars in his bank account to call his own had no right to be thinking about marriage, to be subjecting Jenny to a life of nomadic hand-to-mouth living. Wryly he acknowledged being embarrassed to admit his poverty to her. But, hell, other couples had made it on less. Why not them? He craved nothing more than to have Jenny as his wife, and if she could accept him as he was, then he would marry her in a minute. She would be the family he'd never had. To hell with his projected plans for a career. He could have both. She was right. They could travel together. He was more than willing to have her at his side daily. One thing he wasn't willing to do was take the chance of losing her completely.

Devin looked upon the advent of Jenny in his life as nothing short of a miracle. From the moment she'd entered it, the days had passed in a parade of love and laughter. His work had progressed at an astounding rate with her encouragement, and it was better than he'd dreamed possible, inspired by Jenny's love, nurtured by Jenny's belief in him, and imbued with her gentleness.

Growing up an orphan, he had never experienced being needed by anyone—until Jenny came along. She, in turn, made up the center of his existence, the axis his world turned on.

Anxiously he watched the trail from the village for signs of her. To keep himself busy, he packed a picnic to take to their favorite spot by the creek, where he would tell her how wrong he'd been and ask her to marry him.

Time passed on dragging feet. By late afternoon, she still hadn't come. As darkness descended, his worry turned to sickening fear. Had he lost her with his stupidity?

Disregarding the possible consequences of his turning up on her doorstep, he left the cabin, climbed in his secondhand car and headed toward the village. The moon had risen above the pine trees when he stepped to the door of her house and knocked.

"Whattaya want?" Lester Tyson demanded, spewing forth the odor of liquor into the night air as he faced the man on his porch.

"Is Jenny here?" Devin looked around the slouching figure of her father, his heart twisting with dread. Was she all right?

"The slut's gone. Run away." Tyson swayed unsteadily, his rheumy eyes slitted in an effort to focus on Devin. "Who the hell are you? You that no-good she's been runnin' off to see every day?" He snickered at Devin's look of surprise. "Thought I didn't know, didn't cha? Hell, it didn't take much brains to figure it out. She ain't no better than her ma when she was seventeen."

"Seventeen?"

Lester Tyson squinted. "Well, I'll be damned. Lied to ya, did she? Told ya she was old enough to be foolin' 'round with a grown man? Well, I'll be damned."

His alcoholic laughter rang in Devin's ears. Devin recovered slowly from the shock of his world suddenly careening out of orbit. "Where did she go?" He leaned to the side to see around Tyson, still unable to believe what he was hearing.

"Don't know. I took her to Knoxville this mornin', and she climbed on a bus goin'... someplace." He made a passing swipe with his hand, throwing his rocking body off balance. Stumbling and righting himself, he took another long draw from the bottle clutched in his hand. Wiping his mouth on his sleeve, he glared at Devin. "You're the one, ain'tcha?"

"I love Jenny, if that's what you're asking. I want to marry her." Devin tethered the fury eating at him, urging him to smear this poor excuse for a human being all over the floor of the porch. Tyson was lying. He had to be.

Tyson took another gulp of whiskey. "Marryin' ain't nothin' but a pack of trouble. You live with a woman who ain't good for nothin' 'cept whinin' and havin' brats. Know what that gives ya? Double nothin'." He sneered, poking Devin's chest with a dirty fingernail for emphasis. Then he laughed and jammed the bottle to his lips, draining its contents.

Watching helplessly as Lester Tyson got progressively drunker, Devin felt a sense of hopeless despair overtaking him. "Where is she?" He ground out the words between teeth clenched to keep rein on his temper.

"Gone, I tell ya. She jesh—" He swung his arm and lurched forward, off the porch. The bottle flew through the air and smashed against a rock, its shards scattering over the ground like dirty raindrops. Lying facedown in the road, Tyson moaned and went still. He'd passed out.

Vaulting the porch railing, Devin ran into the house. He scoured each room in a frenetic bid to prove Jenny's father wrong. When he came to her bedroom, with its empty closet and dresser, the truth slammed into his heart. *She was gone.*

He left the house, stepping over the unconscious form in the road as if Tyson's body were trash set out to be picked up. With shoulders bowed under the burden of his pain, he walked to his car, each step echoing harshly through his soul. Why? Why hadn't she known he'd change his mind? Why hadn't she trusted in his love? The same questions pounded at his brain, over and over.

He waited for word from Jenny, sure she would come to him. When nothing but silence was forthcoming, he paid repeated visits to Tyson, hoping to find him sober enough to answer the question burning through his brain—where was Jenny? But it seemed that no matter how early or how late he knocked on the door, Tyson had already absorbed the better portion of a bottle of Tennessee moonshine.

The hours lengthened into endless days. Devin sank deeper and deeper into depression. After ten grueling days, he drove to Tyson's house, bent on beating the answers from him if necessary.

When he arrived, there was no one home. He decided then that he would do what he should have done long before. Determinedly he headed toward the bus depot in Knoxville. Jenny was not the type of girl anyone would forget easily. The slim possibility existed that the ticket agent would remember her.

The dingy building's interior smelled of disinfectant and stale air. At the end of the row of wooden benches across one wall lay the scattered pages of a newspaper. A trash can, overflowing onto the cracked linoleum floor, stood sentinel against a yellowed wall beside the ticket windows.

Devin headed straight for the balding man behind the glass partition, barely noting the deterioration around him. "Excuse me?"

The man never glanced up from his paperwork. "Yeah? Where to?"

"I don't want a ticket," Devin explained patiently. "I'm looking for someone."

The ticket agent lifted his head, cocked a bushy brown eyebrow, looked around the waiting room and then back to his paperwork. "Ain't nobody here but me," he said, in a tone clearly meant to discourage further questions. "Next bus don't come for two hours."

"I'm looking for a girl. She left on a bus from here about ten days ago." Devin paused, waiting for some sign the rude man had heard him. None was forthcoming. He plunged on. "I don't know what bus she took, but she's a striking girl. Very pretty. Long dark hair, blue eyes, about so high," he finished, holding his hand midway up his chest.

The agent might have been deaf, for all the attention he paid Devin's impassioned plea for help. Enraged and frustrated, Devin slipped his hand through the opening at the bottom of the glass partition and grabbed the man's wrist.

"Dammit! All I want is an answer! Did you see her? Where did she buy a ticket to?"

Twisting his hand, the ticket seller freed his wrist and glared at Devin. "Mister, I don't have to tell you anything. But I can tell you this, your attitude ain't gonna get you any answers. What it's gonna get you is an overnight stay in the local jail if you try another move like that."

Devin ran his hand through his hair. "I'm sorry, but it's very important that I locate her. Please, did you see her?"

Evidently Devin's change of tactics and his restrained, polite tone touched a chord of sympathy in the man. "Listen, fella, I sell the tickets to people who want to buy them. It's not my job to ask questions about who they are and where they're goin'." He reached behind him and picked up a clipboard holding a sheaf of papers. He shoved it through the hole for Devin to look at. "See this? These are the buses scheduled to run outa here this week. You got any idea how many people it takes to fill this many buses?" He tossed the clipboard aside. "I probably won't remember one face that comes through here, much less where they're goin'."

Defeat bowed Devin's shoulders. "Thanks," he mumbled, and walked toward the door.

Face it, Montgomery. She's gone. You drove her away with your talk of careers and no family ties. You've got no one to blame but yourself for losing the woman you love.

How often did she tell you she wanted to see something of the world beyond the mountains? You should have known then that when you wouldn't finance her fantasies, she would write you off, he mused with rancor, sipping his cold coffee.

"Fancy" had hardly been an apt description of him back then, or in the months following his return to New York City. His agent had been thrilled with the book he'd written in Tennessee, but it had taken months before Devin would agree to its publication. Somehow, by keeping the manuscript, he'd retained a part of Jenny. Ironically, when it was published, it had become Devin's first bestseller, the launching pad for his career as a successful author. Eventually he'd been forced to gather the fragments of his life and move on.

For two years, he tried to forget her, with other women, parties, his unexpected success as an authority on the people of rural America—and, for a few months, booze. But her image continued to tease at the fringes of his mind, laughing at him, taunting him, turning his love to hate....

"Is she here yet, Popie?"

He blinked away the memories and watched his daughter limping toward him. Clutched in her hand was Dora, her rag doll. "No, sweet thing. If she were here, I would have told you." He pulled her and her friend onto his lap, and kissed her forehead. "Do you think Dora is going to like Jenny?"

"Oh, yes. I've told her all about Jenny, and she thinks she'll be wonderful." Amy patted his hand to reassure him. "Is Jenny's room ready?"

"I had Harriet make up the bed this morning, and she put the bouquet you picked in a vase of water, right on the dressing table."

Amy smiled with pleasure. "I wish you'd given her the bedroom next to me," she said wistfully.

"I think it's better if she uses that one for a workroom. She can't sleep in there, too, can she?"

"I guess not." Amy hid her face behind her hand and whispered. "She'd get sawdust on her nightie."

Devin laughed and wryly considered the room he had allotted Jenny. He wasn't at all sure she wouldn't prefer sawdust on her nightie to sleeping next door to him.

"Popie, Harriet said the room where Jenny's gonna sleep used to be the mommy's room. Does that mean Jenny's gonna be my mommy?"

Devin nearly choked on a mouthful of coffee. Carefully he set his cup back in the saucer and pulled Amy closer. *One more thing you'll pay for, Jenny,* he thought.

"No, Scamp."

"Where's my real mommy, Popie?" Amy asked, resting her head on his shoulder.

Answering his daughter's simple question should have been easy. He should have been able to tell her that her mommy didn't want her, that she had dumped her mere hours after she was born. But, although it should have been easy to destroy any hope of a relationship between Amy and Jenny, the words wouldn't come. "She went away a long time ago."

"Why?"

Frantically Devin searched for the right words, but none came to mind. "I think she just didn't want to be anybody's mommy."

"Didn't she love us?" Amy asked.

Devin looked away from his daughter's face, the face that was so like that of her mother. "I thought she did once, Scamp, but I guess I was wrong."

"But..."

"Mr. Montgomery, I believe the young lady you're expecting just drove up," Harriet, his housekeeper, announced from the doorway.

"She's here! She's here!" Amy squealed, clambering from her father's lap and hurrying past Harriet to the front hall as fast as her encumbered leg would permit, her black curls flying.

Devin followed quickly, vehemently denying to himself his own eagerness to see their houseguest.

Jenny sat behind the wheel of her car, staring at the house. It was the most enormous thing she'd ever seen. Graceful, white and frosted with lacy banisters—a castle. Not like the one she'd built, but nevertheless a castle. Devin had indeed prospered.

Her appreciative gaze traveled over the half-circle veranda that formed the base for the eight massive Corinthian columns lending their support to the gallery running the full width of the upper story. Tall windows evenly crossed the upper and lower levels, the symmetry of the lower broken midway by a double door with a brass knocker.

Stately old oaks embraced the roofline like protective lovers, their roots deep in the soil of a lush green lawn that stretched on forever, dotted with azaleas and roses dripping blooms on the verdant carpet. Their perfume combined to add to the burden of the humid air from the Mississippi, flowing slowly south beyond the levee.

Returning her attention to the front door, she started as it burst open and Amy came loping toward her. Jenny got out of the car just as Amy stopped, a few feet away.

"Hi," Amy said, sudden shyness pulling her eyes to the tops of her shoes.

"Hi, Amy."

"I'm so glad you're finally here, Jenny," she spouted, bashfulness forgotten.

Jenny took Amy's hand and squeezed her fingers affectionately. "So am I. You have a beautiful home, Amy."

"Thank you," the child said, smiling shyly up at Jenny, then turning toward the house. "Popie, she's here!" she cried to the man standing stiffly at the edge of the veranda.

"So I see," he answered, his gaze riveted on Jenny's brown skirt and pale yellow cotton blouse. She looked like an ice-cream cone—and, he added silently, good enough to eat. His heart rate increased by several beats. "Why don't you come inside, Jenny? You're probably tired and thirsty after your long drive," he suggested, an edge to his voice.

How was she going to stand this? she wondered as she allowed Amy to lead her up the wide stairs to Devin. Apprehension nagged at her shaky peace of mind. She wished an escape route would magically appear, but there was little hope of it happening. For some reason, Devin wanted her in his home, and he wasn't going to settle for anything less.

"Let me show you the house," Devin suggested much later, when Mrs. Filbert had hustled Amy off for her daily leg exercises and a nap. "I thought seeing some of the pieces you'll be reproducing in miniature might be helpful."

"I'd like that." Jenny placed her teacup on the table beside her and rose to follow him into the huge entrance hall.

The hall extended from front to back, with spacious rooms jutting off on either side. They walked directly across and into the magnificent ballroom taking up the majority of the north wing. Stark white walls and high ceilings made the room seem even larger than it was. At the far end, an oversize bay window projected into the back lawn, its undressed panes stretching from floor to ceiling, offering a panoramic view of the meticulously landscaped lawn and rose garden.

"That's where the musicians sat when the Clays, the original owners, entertained, so that they didn't interfere with the dancers," Devin explained as she stepped into the huge protrusion in the room's otherwise symmetrical proportions.

Purposefully he came to stand behind her, close enough to see the hair escaping her loose ponytail vacillate with his every breath.

"You need a rose arbor."

"I had plans to have one built over there," he explained, pointing over her head to the bright blooms in the garden closest to the fieldstone walk.

"What stopped you?"

"I lost interest when I began to think about its upkeep. The humidity off the river would have meant painting the arbor yearly. It was just one more expense, one more responsibility I didn't need, added to the endless list attached to this place."

His casual explanation gave rise to a tide of bitter resentment in Jenny. She moved away. He really hadn't changed at all. Take on a project—or a woman—and just walk away before someone asks you to be responsible for what you've created.

Calming herself, she let her gaze wander to the ceiling. It wouldn't make her time here any easier to constantly resurrect old resentments.

"Up there—" Devin pointed at the border of the high ceiling that had captured her interest "—is some of the most beautiful plasterwork in Louisiana." He chuckled. "Or so I'm told."

The sound of his natural laughter, and its disturbing effect on her taut nerves, caused Jenny to consciously rivet her attention on the medallion above her head.

Around the top of the high walls, plaster leaves, vines and flowers, interwoven in intricate detail, matched the design in the medallion crowning the ceiling and circling a painting of Adam and Eve in the Garden of Eden. Devin perused her as raptly as she did the entwined lovers. He's doing this deliberately, she thought, removing herself from his line of vision.

Absorbing herself with rapt attention to two imposing Doric columns standing on either side halfway down the room, she endeavored to ignore his glinting eyes. Instead she concentrated on the path of the flowers wrapped serpentinely around each column. Then she jumped when he spoke from right beside her.

"Clay built this room for his daughter Amy's debut into society. The guest list, according to Mrs. Clay, was hand-picked by him. From her diary accounts, Clay protected his daughter with a vengeance, and didn't like the idea of her becoming too involved with the riffraff of New Orleans. As a result, they spent a great deal of time here at Claymore, away from the city and its questionable inhabitants."

"Do you plan on keeping such a tight rein on your daughter?" It was really none of her concern, but she found the idea of anyone suppressing Amy's free spirit abhorrent. It struck an all-too-familiar chord from her own childhood.

Devin moved closer, drawn against his will like a piece of steel to a magnet. "I'd never impose my desires on Amy. Being her father doesn't give me the right to decide her happiness. Once she's old enough to make her own decisions, she's on her own to live both with them and up to them. Anytime she needs advice, I'll be there, but the rest is up to her."

His warm breath, tickling her cheek, sent shivers racing down Jenny's spine, while his words, ironically, brought her peace. Amy would never have to suffer as she had, and for some reason she couldn't begin to understand, that was very important to her. Speculating on how different her own life might have been if her father had been a different kind of man, she quickly amended her thoughts. Hadn't she learned the hard way that the past was the past, unchangeable and better left alone?

"I hope this isn't the end of the tour," she said, a bit too brightly, moving to inspect a small inlaid mahogany table near the door. It was a safe distance from Devin's oppressive presence and the painful reminders of her youth.

"It's only just begun," he murmured smoothly, allowing her the small retreat, the resumption of the tour the farthest thing from his mind.

The inspection of the first floor lasted for nearly an hour, taking them through an enormous dining room with a seating capacity of fifty-four, a morning room, used by the lady of the house; a music room, equipped with an antique spinet, and a book-lined library holding everything from the classics to today's bestsellers.

As they mounted the wide, winding staircase to the second floor, Devin rested his hand on the small of her back to guide her. She could feel his palm burning through the material of her blouse into her skin. Her pace quickened.

Run, Jenny, run, Devin told her silently. *Sooner or later, you'll realize you've run out of corners in which to hide. But I'll find you, no matter where you go. And when I do, you'll wish you'd never been born. I'll tell you exactly who that little girl is, and send you packing....*

He could only imagine the satisfaction he would derive from watching her defeat, watching the pain eat away at her heart, leaving an empty numbness in its wake. What he longed for most of all was to see the look on her face when she found out he'd rescued Amy from where she'd so callously dumped her, never intending to tell him he had a daughter.

Oh, yes, Jenny, revenge will be so sweet.

Like a fox stalking a rabbit, he followed his prey up the stairs as she slipped deeper and deeper into the blind alley of her own emotions.

"I've given you Mrs. Clay's room," he said, steering her into the last of the second floor's beautifully appointed rooms some time later. By far the loveliest of all the rooms she'd seen, it was large enough to hold The House of Miniatures.

"Devin, it's absolutely gorgeous. I've never slept in anything this elegant." She outlined with her fingertips the carved pineapple crowning the turned mahogany posts of the canopied bed. "It's my favorite color," she whispered, turning her attention to the pale blue spread, the canopy cover and the drapes puddling on the floor at each of the two large open windows. The fragrance of jasmine sweetened a soft breeze as it wafted through the filmy undercurtains.

Devin chuckled sardonically. "I'm afraid I'll have to let Catherine Clay take the credit for the choice of decor, and its shades. Your preference in colors was just one more thing you neglected to tell me before you moved on to bigger and better things."

"We never knew a lot of things about each other," she replied, ignoring his well-aimed gibe. The memory of the activities that had taken the place of conversation back then, the things she'd naively interpreted as love, crowded into her mind.

She really looked at him for the first time since she'd arrived. His hard expression snatched the breath from her lungs, sending prickles of wariness down her spine.

He moved closer to her. His smoky gaze locked with hers. "Before you leave here, I plan on knowing every facet of Jennifer Tyson."

Thrown off balance by what sounded like a threat, her question emerged as a feathery whisper. "Why, Devin?"

"Is there really a need to explain?"

He was suddenly too close. She couldn't breathe. Her body wouldn't move. *Push him away. Don't let him do this.* She watched as the amber halos in his eyes widened, eating up the darkening ghostly green.

"Jenny," he whispered, and pulled her to him. He caught her whimper of protest with his mouth.

Even though she could tell by the tone of his voice that his actions were in defiance of some inner emotional upheaval, she could feel the weakening in her limbs. She fought the draw of him, pressing her hands against his chest to break the stranglehold he had on her waist and the back of her head. But it was no use. Her body wouldn't obey her brain's commands. Surrendering to her inner urgings, she slid her arms around his broad shoulders, holding him close.

Time slipped away, carrying her with it to a Tennessee pine forest. The pungent aroma of the tall trees invaded her senses. All the fight drained from her. Fighting him was so difficult. Allowing the tide of passion to sweep her away was so easy. Just before the final surrender, her good sense rebelled.

"No," she gasped, her lips stiffening beneath his ravaging mouth.

But he didn't stop. His arms tightened like the jaws of a vise, pinning her to him. His mouth devoured her, deepening the kiss until she had no will left with which to fight. Her greed for the feel and taste of him eroded the foundation of her resolution to keep a distance between them. Her lips opened, admitting him, meeting his invading tongue with her own.

She was like a woman who had gone without water for years and suddenly found herself confronted with a clear mountain stream. There seemed no end to her need to partake of what he offered.

"Popie?"

The adults sprang apart. Amy's voice sluiced over them like ice water.

"Yes, Amy?" Devin said, the quiver in his tone revealing the residue of emotion left by their scorching kiss.

"Popie, were you kissing Jenny?" she asked with a child's innocence.

"No, Scamp. Jenny had dust in her eye. I was just getting it out for her."

Jenny quickly nodded in agreement, not trusting her voice. Her nerves still tingled. Her lips throbbed, and she had to hold on to the bedpost to keep her knees from buckling.

A few hours had passed since she'd entered Devin's home, and in that short time she'd managed to let him know that his touch could still send her off like a Fourth of July rocket. To her abject shame, he'd scaled the barriers around her emotions like a champion mountain climber. Amy's undetected arrival and keen observation only made the shame more acute.

But somehow the realization of how easily and quickly the lie had slipped from his lips penetrated the emotional fog surrounding her.

"How come she had her arms around your neck?" Amy looked from one to the other.

"Amy, aren't you supposed to be resting?" he asked, adroitly sidestepping Amy's probing question and using the time to tamp down the emotions that holding Jenny again had given rise to. He had to keep a tighter rein on his libido and concentrate on the only reason Jenny was here.

"I was too excited to rest. Mrs. Filbert said I could show Jenny her workroom. Can I, Popie?"

"Jenny might need some time to...pull herself together." Devin challenged Jenny to deny what he could see smoldering in her blue eyes.

Unable to hold his gaze, Jenny turned away and forced a smile for Amy. "I'd love to see my workroom," she answered, in a voice that was surprisingly steady, considering that her insides felt like whipped cream.

"I'll leave you ladies to it. I have some writing to do." Casting a furtive glare at Jenny, he disappeared through a door at the side of the room.

Leaning against the closed door, he sifted through what he'd just learned. No matter how vehemently Jennifer Tyson might deny it, she still responded with all the fire and enthusiasm of the old Jenny. A new twist to his plan that he hadn't considered before began to evolve in his head. What better way to pay her back for the pain she'd caused him than to make her fall in love with him, then dump her? His grin broadened. It certainly wouldn't be any hardship on his part. The best aspect of their little mountain tryst had been their lovemaking. Jenny was a woman made for it, warm, responsive, eager, inventive—what that crude P.I., Tate, would refer to as a "natural." Why not enjoy himself while he waited for the time for the final blow?

He pushed himself away from the door, avoiding his reflection in his dresser mirror and the niggling little voice that kept asking how he planned to erase the feel of her, the taste of her, when she was no longer there.

Curious about the exit route Devin had taken from her bedroom, Jenny asked, "Where does that door go, Amy?"

Amy slipped her small hand in Jenny's and led her from the room. "It's Popie's bedroom. He has his computer in there so he can write without nobody bothering him. He gets real cranky when he's bothered while he writes."

The child continued to talk, but Jenny heard little of what she said. A gunshot in the night would have been less of a shock. Devin would be sleeping a step away from her.

Reminded that in the old houses the master and mistress shared the master suite, with a common, connecting door, her heart began to pound. As soon as he'd told her she'd been assigned the bedroom of the former mistress of Claymore, she should have known, should have protested. But she'd been so befuddled by the lush enormity of her surroundings, she'd totally missed it.

Calming her clamoring senses, she made a mental note to check for the key and put to use the lock commonly found on the lady's side. After what had just happened, distance—and lots of it—spelled emotional and physical safety, and a locked door ensured it.

Quickly she directed her thoughts to safer terrain. That Devin still wrote came as no surprise. A satisfied readership had proclaimed his success for years. As she walked beside Amy, she recalled the many times she'd forced herself to pass a bookstore because it displayed his latest best-seller. She'd never been able to bring herself to buy one. It had taken her a long time to get over the ache she'd experienced with her first glimpse of his likeness on a book jacket. Reading his words would have been torture.

"This is it," Amy announced, throwing open the door to a large, sunny room at the back of the house.

Jenny gasped. How had he managed all this in such a short time? Her gaze traveled over the worktables stationed at the edge of the room, equipped with every possible convenience for a wood-carver. Evidently, when Devin issued a command, it was obeyed to the letter. She hoped he didn't expect her to fulfill his every whim so easily. If so, he was in for a very rude awakening.

On the bench in the room's center hung C clamps, tweezers, pliers, small hammers and other hand tools in various shapes and sizes. A gooseneck fluorescent light with a magnifying glass attached swung on an adjustable arm over the bench. X-acto knives arranged according to size protruded from a slot along the side of the bench. Several kinds of glue and an electric glue gun stood in readiness. She examined the state-of-the-art jigsaw, no bigger than a portable sewing machine, occupying the center of the table. For years she'd planned on buying one of them, but extra funds had always found other places before she had a chance.

"Jenny." Amy tugged at her sleeve. "Come see my doll-house."

Reluctantly Jenny dragged her attention from the jigsaw and looked to where Amy stood proudly next to her toy house. Slowly Jenny walked around it.

An exact duplicate of Claymore, it rested on a land-scaped platform, surrounded by sentinel oaks dripping Spanish moss from their tiny branches, which caressed the eaves of the house. The front and the back of the house opened by means of two doors to display lilliputian rooms leading to gardens of minute roses, azaleas and flowering jasmine.

"Amy, this is lovely."

"My popie says there isn't a doubt in his mind, it's the most prettiest house in Lou . . . Lou . . ."

"Louisiana," Jenny finished automatically. "And he's right. It is the most prettiest." She understood why Amy had insisted on authenticity for the furnishings, although she still wasn't convinced it was all Amy's idea, as Devin had led her to believe. Of course, he'd deny it if she confronted him with her suspicions, but she sensed Devin's hand in his daugh-ter's insistence on realism.

Amy came to her side to point out some of the special features. "See this," she said, picking up the knob of the tiny newel post.

"Do you know what that was for?" Jenny asked, bend-ing to see inside the lower floor.

"No."

"After building the house, the people took the mortgage paper from the bank and put it in there. When the house was paid for, they took the paper out and burned it at a grand party."

Jenny drew a stool close to the house, sat, and placed Amy on her lap. After the child went to great pains to smooth the wrinkles from her dress, Jenny told her other stories of the old Southern homes.

When she'd exhausted her supply, Amy happily took over, pointing out secret compartments, windows and doors, opening and closing each one to demonstrate their uniqueness. The aurora borealis chandelier, hanging in the dining room over the spot where the table would eventually be placed, was a touch of elegance few dollhouses could boast.

Several hours had passed when they finally closed the doors to the house and walked around the workshop, picking up tools while Jenny described their use.

"Do you like everything?"

"Yes," she said, hugging Amy's body close. Grudgingly, she admitted that Devin had created a marvelous workshop for her. "I love everything. This is the best workshop ever."

"Popie says if there's anything missing, you have to tell him," Amy instructed in her best adult voice.

Looking around her, still awed by the efficiency of the room, Jenny could see nothing missing from the list she'd supplied, and could see several things he'd added on his own. He'd even remembered the tack cloths for cleaning the dust from the wood before staining it. Instead of smoothing over the unease she was feeling, it served merely to intensify it. Was this yet another debt he would hold her accountable for?

"I think your popie has remembered everything, even the wood." She surveyed a shelf on the other side of the room stacked with balsa in long, thin sheets, as well as blocks of white pine, basswood, poplar and oak.

"Jenny—" Amy tugged on her hand "—will you teach me to carve wood?"

Laughter broke from Jenny. "Scamp, you're too young to handle all those sharp tools," she said, unconsciously adopting Devin's nickname for his daughter.

"When I get bigger, will you?" The little girl's eyes were trained on Jenny, the irises large, and dark with excitement—just like Devin's.

Jenny looked away. "We'll see."

"How old were you when you learned?"

"A lot older than you are," Jenny managed to say. She could feel the memories pleading to escape, memories of the lonely nights with her grandfather, watching him magically transform a shapeless piece of wood into a testimonial to his artistic talent. But, most of all, memories of a time when she had had a small treasure of her own forming inside her.

Amy's relentless questioning continued. "Who taught you to carve?"

"My grandfather."

The little girl's eyes brightened. "My grampy made clown bears for me. Wanna see?" Giving Jenny no time to consider, Amy latched on to her hand and pulled her down the hall to the room next door. Excitedly she crossed the deep-piled rose carpeting to a glass-fronted cabinet set against one wall.

"Here they are. Popie had the cabinet made for them so they wouldn't get broke."

Astounded, Jenny stared at the small wooden bears. The exquisite workmanship nagged with a familiarity she couldn't put her finger on. Perhaps she'd seen this craftsman's work at one of the many miniature shows she'd attended, she thought.

"They're lovely, Amy. May I see one?"

"Oh, no. Popie says they're never to leave the cabinet. He says they aren't toys, and they'll get broke if I let anyone play with them. He says they're irre...irre..."

"Irreplaceable," came a deep voice from behind them. "I'm certainly glad to hear you've remembered something I've said."

Amy giggled and ran to him, squealing as he hoisted her in his arms.

"You two seem to be hitting it off," he commented, tickling Amy, pleased with the way his presence seemed to throw Jenny off balance. He pushed his advantage by moving closer, hoping to distract her from the carvings.

"Amy was just telling me about her collection," Jenny blurted, tearing her welling eyes away from the picture of Amy cuddled close in her father's arms.

"They're a gift from a friend who took a liking to Amy." Devin set Amy on her feet, holding on to her arm till he was sure she wouldn't lose her balance.

Amy hurried back to Jenny's side. A frown of concern furrowed her dark little eyebrows. "You got dust in your eye, Jenny?" she asked innocently. "My popie can get it out. He'll make it stop hurting."

Jenny's gaze locked with Devin's. "I doubt it, Amy. I don't think anyone can ever make it stop hurting." Without a word, she rushed past them, intent on putting distance between herself and the family that could have been hers—should have been hers.

Devin frowned after Jenny, perplexed by her words and her sudden departure. What an odd thing for her to say, when it was he and Amy who had suffered the pain and agony of her selfish abandonment.

"Popie?" Amy tugged at her father's trouser leg. "Is Jenny okay?"

"I think so, Amy," he replied distractedly, continuing to stare at the empty doorway.

"Maybe we should go see." Amy started for the door.

Roused from his contemplative stupor, Devin snagged her hand. "No. Jenny's had a long day. I think we should let her have some time to unpack and get some sleep. She'll feel better in the morning." Seeing Amy's continued concern, he added, "How about a walk in the garden with your old popie?" The child agreed, but as they walked together from the room, Devin fought to erase the image of Jenny's tear-streaked face from his mind.

Devin didn't allow himself to think about what Jenny had said until the following morning, despite the fact that for the rest of the day an uneasy feeling nagged at him. The face staring back at him from his bathroom mirror gave him the answer. Compassion. He'd felt compassion for her. It was a dangerous commodity for him to be handing out to a woman he was bent on hurting.

Sap. The accusing eyes shot back at him. *Didn't you learn your lesson the first time? You know what she's like, all soft and clinging, worming her way into your life and then tearing it to shreds. Playing on your sympathies, getting your heart involved, and then letting you bleed to death from the wounds she inflicts. How many times do you need a reminder? Just look at your daughter, if you doubt the woman's callousness.*

As much as he wanted to heed his conscience's warnings, he couldn't erase the memory of the look on her face. What had she been referring to, this woman who was so adept at hurting others?

Thoughtfully he squeezed a dab of toothpaste on his brush and sawed it over his teeth. Was she using her wiles to wheedle her way back into his good graces? Considering what she'd done until now, that wasn't such a far-flung assumption.

Now that she'd seen he was no longer the impoverished struggling writer she'd left behind in Tennessee, she would probably calculate all this very carefully. Once she was safely ensconced in his house and saw how wealthy he was, she had decided that she had a sucker on the hook. With the use of a few well-delivered tears, she'd thought to rope him into marriage. After all, she had a floundering business to protect, and what better way than with a husband who had a fat bank balance? Since she'd seduced him once, looking for a ticket out of the Tennessee hills, he had no trouble believing she would try again.

Well, this time he'd beat her at her own game. He'd fallen for that once. This time he knew her for what she was, a heartless opportunist who let nothing stand between her and what she wanted, not even a small child's happiness.

If it came to that, he would welcome her into his bed, but that was where the similarity to their past "relationship" ended. This time he would be the one to walk away unscathed. But first she needed a lesson in humility, a reminder of her place at Claymore. And he was more than ready to provide it.

Jenny took one last glance at her mirrored image. Devin was being difficult enough; the last thing she needed, or wanted, were any of his snide hints. Her appearance would be impeccable, her conversation businesslike and her debut at Devin's table as brief as possible, giving him little or no opportunity to goad her further.

She smoothed the front of her lemon yellow sweater and turned sideways to check the line of her darker yellow slacks. Patting a few recalcitrant wisps of hair back into the fall over her shoulders, she gave herself the high sign and left her room.

The dining room was empty, except for the lord and master reigning from his place at the head of the breakfast table.

"Where's Amy?" she asked, ignoring his missing greeting.

"She had an early doctor's appointment."

Dreading the thought of spending the duration of a meal alone with him, she strolled to the table. There was no setting for her. She looked at him and found him studying her.

"You'll be eating in the kitchen."

Stunned, Jenny stared at him, speechless.

"What did you expect? That you'd be clasped to the 'bosom of our family'?" He saw her flinch, but ignored it. "You are here as my employee—nothing more, nothing less. As such, you will eat in the kitchen with my other employees." He rose and rounded the table to stand beside her. Jenny clutched her cold fingers together and faced him. "Don't make the mistake of thinking that little seduction scene you engineered yesterday meant anything."

She gaped at him, unable to believe his accusation. "Me? *I* engineered it? Why, you pompous, overbearing—*You* were the one who started stalking me the minute Amy left the room. I was doing my utmost to avoid that kind of confrontation."

"Avoid? My dear Jenny, I seem to remember you clinging to me like a wanton. I hardly call that avoiding me. Nor was that feeble *no* you uttered before putting a death lock on my neck."

Taking a step back, Jenny waited while her seething temper cooled to a rolling boil. Again her brain warned her that there was more to this job than making a birthday present for Amy. He was going out of his way to be as obnoxious and hurtful as possible. Why? She studied his closed expression. "Why am I really here, Devin?"

"When you ran away from me, Jenny, you left a lot of unfinished business behind. Before you leave Claymore, I expect we'll be even."

"Who are you?" she blurted. "I don't know this stranger you've become."

"You will," he promised with a tight grin. "You will. Now I suggest you get your breakfast and get to work."

She watched as he turned his back, strolled casually back to his chair and picked up the morning paper, dismissing her completely.

As she walked to the kitchen at the back of the house, she tried to decide whether she was more angry or hurt. That little scene he'd just played for her told her one thing. He was making it clear where she stood. She should consider herself neither friend nor family. She was a stranger, an employee, and he was making certain she never forgot it.

Oddly enough, while it hurt, the thing that bothered her more was his covert suggestions. They had definitely been flavored with the hint of threat.

Chapter 5

The following morning, engrossed in her preliminary plans for the creation of Amy's dollhouse furniture and still puzzling over Devin's attitude of the previous day, Jenny started when the door to the workroom swung slowly open. A dark head peeked around it.

"Can I come in?"

The sight of Devin's daughter brought a cheery smile to Jenny's lips. "Of course." There was something about the child that made her want to hug her every time she appeared.

Amy returned Jenny's grin and limped hesitantly toward her. "Popie said not to bother you today. He said you needed time to settle in and get accus . . . accus . . ."

"Accustomed," Jenny supplied.

"Yeah, accustomed to your workshop." Amy studied Jenny, then looked around the room and asked sheepishly, "Are you accustomed yet?"

Laughter bubbled from Jenny as she caught Amy's hand and drew her close to her side for a hug. "Yes, I'm accustomed." Amy's delighted smile washed over Jenny like warm syrup.

"Good." Amy smiled.

In addition to being enchanting, engaging, bright and warm, Amy had a naturally loving nature. At each encounter, Jenny could see more and more of Devin in her. Along with the physical likeness, Amy had also inherited his ability to charm anyone she came in contact with.

"What's that?" Amy pointed to the list Jenny had been going over.

"It's a list of all the furniture I have to make for your dollhouse."

"Wow! There sure is a lot. Why are there stars next to some of them?" Amy studied the sheet of paper as if it were a treasure map.

"Those are the pieces Mrs. Clay had made specially for the house. Some of them are funny sizes, like Mr. Clay's bed, so I have to work with different measurements than I usually do."

"*B...E...D...* That spells bed," Amy announced proudly, moving her chubby finger down the list. "And that's my name. *A...M...Y...* Amy," she added, pointing to the notations for the room in the dollhouse that was to be a replica of Amy Clay's.

"That's right," Jenny said encouragingly.

Amy paused in thought. "Jenny. Do you like my room?"

"Very much," Jenny replied, half listening, concentrating on checking the list for omissions.

"So do I. It's much nicer than my other room was."

"Other room?"

"The one I shared with Sally Anne at the children's home, where my popie found me." Amy fiddled distractedly with the gold bracelet circling Jenny's wrist.

Her words snared Jenny's attention. "Children's home? You were in a children's home?"

"Uh-huh."

"But why?" Jenny asked, not expecting Amy to answer.

"I don't know, but my popie says sometimes kids go there by mistake, and that's how I got there. And 'cause he was my real honest-to-goodness daddy, he came and got me." Grabbing Jenny's chin, Amy turned the woman's face to her. "Do you think I got there by mistake?"

Hugging Amy close, Jenny smiled. "I'm sure of it. I don't think anyone would have put you there on purpose," she said soothingly, disturbed by the thought that anyone could love Amy so little as to confine her in a home for unwanted children. What kind of woman had mothered her, to allow such a thing? Was she so unfeeling?

Another thought occurred to her. Was Amy's mother dead? No one ever seemed to mention her, and Jenny was hardly in a position to encourage Devin to seek her out to share family secrets. And if she *was* dead, why hadn't Devin taken the child instead of putting her in a home? Jenny was shocked that he would have allowed such a thing, considering his own lonely childhood. Unless...unless he hadn't been any more ready for a family then than he'd been when they last saw each other.

With the resilience of a child, Amy bounced on to a new topic of conversation, leaving Jenny puzzled and upset by this new vein of thought.

"Why did Mr. Clay need a bed made special for him?"

Shaking herself mentally, she fumbled through her mind for an answer. "'Cause he was so tall, if he slept in a regular bed, his feet would have hung out."

Amy clamped her hand over her mouth to cover the giggle fighting to escape.

The change in the little girl's face mesmerized Jenny. Her eyes sparkled like sunlight on pewter. Her ebony ponytails danced about, dislodging one of her bright yellow ribbons.

Tying the ribbon back in place, Jenny could feel the amusement shaking Amy's body and found herself laughing with her.

"I thought I'd find you here."

They turned in unison toward the stern voice.

"I thought I told you not to come in here. Jenny's working. You shouldn't be disturbing her." Devin scowled at his daughter.

Amy squirmed down from Jenny's lap and stood at her new friend's side, looking contrite. "Jenny said it was okay for me to be here, Popie."

"*I'm* your father, and *I* said you were not to come here. Harriet is waiting to give you breakfast, young lady. Now, go on downstairs, and tell her Jenny and I will be along in a moment."

"Can I come back after I eat?"

"May I," Devin corrected automatically.

"May I?"

"It's all right, Devin," Jenny put in, hoping to ward off any more angry words.

Devin glanced at Jenny, his flinty gaze clearly telling her he didn't appreciate her intervention. But he held back the words in Amy's presence. "It's up to Jenny."

Avoiding Devin's scowl of disapproval, Jenny nodded to Amy. "Of course."

Reluctance showing in every step, Amy obeyed Devin. Flashing a parting smile at Jenny, she gave her father a wide berth and scurried out the door. Both adults watched her exit with exaggerated interest.

Turning back to Jenny, Devin studied her in silence, assessing her brief white shorts and aqua blouse. "Good morning, Jenny." He deliberately imbued his words with a provocative tone. "You spoil her. Don't let it happen too often."

His husky greeting spiraled through Jenny, whipping out the soft reprimand for her permissiveness with Amy. The words didn't belong in a room full of wood shavings and sandpaper and the smell of turpentine. They should have been whispered against naked skin, tangled in damp sheets smelling of the essence of shared love. Good heavens, what was happening to her? Was she going stark raving mad?

"Good morning, Devin." She forced the words past lips stiff and dry with nerves. Had Devin heard her conversation with Amy? Did he think she'd pumped the girl for details of their private lives? Was that the reason for his sharpness with the child? She moistened her lips nervously. "I can't seem to not spoil her," she added belatedly. "I'm afraid I'm a willing victim of her charm." She flung her mass of hair over her shoulder.

Along with any trace of coherent reasoning, his anger evaporated. He fought to stifle a moan. She was like a piece of forbidden fruit. He stood by helplessly as his gaze burned a path from her wet mouth to the expanse of naked skin below the knotted tails of her blouse.

Keep your emotions out of this, Montgomery. She's bad news—you know that. As far as you're concerned, if it comes to that, she's nothing more than another woman to warm your bed for a few nights.

Breaking eye contact with concentrated effort, he picked up a piece of pine from the workbench and ran his thumb rapidly back and forth over a small brown knot in its surface, playing for time to calm the throbbing beat of the blood racing through his veins. The aroma of the wood came to life under the friction of his caress, flooding his nostrils with the odor of pine. As if it had grown fangs, he dropped the wood, hoping to force the memories of crushed pine needles beneath naked bodies from his mind.

Jenny's nose caught the aroma at the same time and with the same resulting nudge to her memory. Her gaze flew to his face. Their eyes locked. A weakness invaded her body. She was suddenly reeling from the power of his presence, conscious of the sound of his breathing, unable to drag her eyes away from his mouth.

Devin caught his breath. That look of pure need brought to mind another time, another place.

Why couldn't he take what her look seemed to offer? He knew from past encounters that she would welcome his advances. And he'd made up his mind to do just that. But each time something stopped him, some warning voice telling him that if he took Jenny to his bed he'd never let her go. That wasn't his aim in bringing her here. Resolutely he started toward her, intent on putting an end to his quandary and proving that nagging voice wrong, once and for all silencing its incessant taunting.

Recoiling from his heated study of her, Jenny skirted his path, slipping away from him to fumble with some knives.

Not to be denied, Devin followed, nonchalantly running his fingers through a pile of sawdust, leaving deep furrows in their wake and stirring to life the essence of fresh-cut pine as he inched toward her.

"I should be able to start carving today," she commented nervously, picking up the piece of wood Devin had discarded, as well as her knife. Pressing the blade into the soft block, she prayed he'd leave her to work in peace. As she continued to gouge random slivers of wood from the block, she could feel Devin's eyes following her movements.

The silence swelled between them, laden with the pungent fragrance of pine sap. Jenny took a deep breath and concentrated on her work, trying to block out his presence.

"You've never said that before," he murmured, coming close enough to watch the sun pick out the blue lights in her hair.

"Said what?" Half listening to his words and acutely aware of his nearness, Jenny resumed carving as an alternative to screaming at him to leave her alone.

"Good morning, Devin," he quoted.

"That's silly. I'm sure I have. Don't you remember all the mornings when I came to the cabin? Surely I must have said it then." She could have bitten off her tongue. His haphazard conversation had destroyed her mental balance.

"Oh, yes, Sam, I remember. I remember vividly. Do you?"

Jenny couldn't answer. The unbidden emotions given birth to by that name on his lips and the tantalizing images it evoked rose around her like a prison wall. No one called her by the shortened version of her middle name, Samantha—only Devin—and only when he was hungry for her. She sank down on the stool, her legs suddenly too weak to hold her.

"Do you remember the early-morning swims we took in the stream, clothed in nothing but sunshine? Or are you remembering chasing the chill from our bodies on the bearskin rug, in front of a blazing fire?" he whispered, cornering her with words.

He ran the tip of his finger down her neck and beneath the collar of her shirt, smiling when she shuddered.

"Are you cold, Sam? Can I help you chase away the chills?" He dipped his finger into the valley between her breasts, tracing a path up to her throat, where the skin vibrated with her heartbeat. "Or is the problem heat?"

"Devin," she finally managed to squeak out, slipping from the stool and stationing herself far from his inflaming touch. "Devin, you have to stop this. This has to be a business arrangement. Old, useless memories don't fall under that heading."

"They may be old, Jenny, but they aren't useless. Anything that brings Sam to life can't be useless," he purred. Reading her retreat as a challenge, he pushed his advantage, relentless in his need to get her to admit to what she was feeling—what *they* were feeling.

"Sam is dead, Devin, dead. Everything she stood for died with her. It'll make it easier on both of us if you understand that and accept it." Jenny backed away, both mentally and physically, in a desperate bid to ease the coil of emotions snarled in her stomach.

"Oh, no, Jenny." Devin stalked her, plastering her against the workbench, her denial goading him to prove her wrong, helplessly aware that what had started as a step in his plan to trap her had suddenly become an emotional web, with him at its center. "She's very much alive. I've had glimpses of her. I know she's hiding somewhere inside the cold woman who calls herself Jennifer Tyson. She's alive, and I'm going to find her." He reached for her. She slipped to one side, evading his grasp. "Always running, Jenny. Always trying to outdistance me."

"Devin, we have a business arrangement. We..." Her mind was tripping in a thousand directions, searching for the words to stop him. "Why?" she whispered imploringly.

He halted suddenly and ran a frustrated hand through his hair. "Because you're driving me crazy," he snapped, his voice strained with the power of his emotions. Unmindful of what his thoughtless words revealed, he went on relentlessly. "Every time I see you, I want to—"

"Popie, Harriet says breakfast will be cold if you don't stop lolly...lolly..."

"Lollygagging," both adults finished for her, their gazes locked in silent combat.

"Yeah." Her dark brows furrowed. "Popie, what's loll-gaggling?"

"Lollygagging," he corrected gently. "It means fooling around."

"Were you and Jenny fooling around?" Her large green eyes surveyed them for any hint of this terrible thing they might have done.

Devin could see Jenny battling hard to regain her composure. His lips curved in a sardonic smile. "Not quite, Scamp, not quite."

His tone, and the unflinching determination in his eyes, told Jenny this encounter was far from over. Without a word, she slipped past him and took Amy's hand, sure she heard him chuckle as they stepped into the hall. The damn man was enjoying watching her squirm.

Breakfast in the kitchen had its advantages, Jenny thought as she finished the last of her hot corn bread, omelet and coffee. Had she still been welcome at Devin's table, it would have meant enduring the embarrassment of their encounter in the workroom with his every glance, his every veiled word, his subtle sarcasm. Her nerves were frayed enough without that.

As soon as she'd swallowed her last bite, Jenny excused herself and returned to the sanctity of her workroom. Locking the door against unwanted visitors—even Amy—she prepared to carve her first piece of furniture.

Determinedly she barred her mind against Devin as thoroughly as she'd barred the door. Concentrating on the piece of basswood, she dived into her work. She fingered the wood, tracing the grain, searching for the spirit of the wood. Her grandfather had told her that every piece of wood had its own spirit, and that for a carving to be a good one, it had to be found before the first cut. She took up her knife and began.

Many hours later, she put the roughly formed piece aside, stretched her stiff back and stood on cramped legs. Her watch read midnight. The crudely formed petite morning-room settee and chairs on the workbench gave mute testimony to her uninterrupted labors. Only when Harriet brought her a tray with soup and a sandwich for dinner had she realized she'd missed lunch. Stopping long enough to gobble down Harriet's offering, she'd submerged herself in her labors again, using them to block out Devin and this new form of torture he'd devised.

Now, her eyelids drooping, she moved her body by rote. She'd gone brain-dead. Deciding that, if nothing else, she'd sleep well, she locked the door behind her and headed down the hall to her room on the opposite side of the house.

Closing her bedroom door and promising herself a nice long soak the next morning, she stripped away her clothes and slipped into a pink nightgown, sighing in appreciation as she slid beneath the covers. The bed felt wonderful to her aching limbs. Her eyes fluttered closed.

Something roused her sometime later. She listened. It was faint, but it sounded like horses' hooves on the cobblestones of the French Quarter—*click, click, click.* Slowly, as she strained to hear, it dawned on her she was listening to the sound of Devin's computer on the opposite side of the wall behind her headboard.

The idea of him next door, with only a wall separating them, brought her wide awake, her senses magnetized by the sound from the next room. Her gaze swung to the connecting door. Damn him! She wouldn't put it past him to have arranged it this way on purpose, just to taunt her. The horror of it was, it had worked.

It took little imagination on her part to conjure up a picture of Devin at work. She'd seen him so many times in the mountains, the sight had become as familiar to her as the rising sun. She'd often sat quietly in the cabin and watched him write, muscles dancing across his wide shoulders while his strong hands pounded away at the stubborn keys of his old portable typewriter, an errant lock of hair hanging across his forehead, his beautiful eyes trained on the paper as he worked.

Hours later, without warning, the clattering keys would stop. He'd turn to her and flex the stiff muscles in his back as he rose and came to flop down beside her on the floor by the hearth. Unbidden, she would slip into his embrace, and all thought of anything but their shared passions would vaporize in the heat of their joining.

Jenny shook herself. These insistent memories were making her life hell. Throwing back the bed covers, she slid from the bed, knocked against the bedside table and padded to the window to stare at the quiet, moonlit landscape below. Her gaze darted about the expanse of lawn and driveway, as if she were searching for peace of mind, searching for a way to rid herself of this unreasonable awareness of a man she no longer loved, could never love again.

The night abounded in beauty. A full lemon yellow moon hung in the heavens like a child's ball. Stars twinkled merrily against a backdrop of deep black velvet, their brightness undimmed by the intrusion of city lights. Shadowy Spanish moss swayed in an eerie dance to the soft music of the warm breeze caressing her skin with a lover's fingers. Night creatures scampered across the silver paths of moonlight into the protective shadows of the stately oaks. A symphony of sounds rose from the night: the hooting of an owl, the chirp of cicadas, the croaking of a frog, all orchestrated to beckon to the soul of a lover. The serenity soothed her raw nerves, calming and healing her like a tonic. She sighed and inhaled the perfume of night-blooming jasmine.

"Can't sleep?"

Too late recalling that she'd neglected to lock the connecting door, she spun toward the voice and found herself caught up in the arms of the man standing at her back—the man she wanted desperately to put from her life. Moonlight illuminated Devin's smile. Mindlessly she zeroed in on his tight jeans, his broad, naked chest and his rumpled hair.

"You startled me."

"I'm sorry, but you were so absorbed in the scene outside the window, I guess you didn't hear me. I didn't mean to frighten you. I heard your restless movements. Sleeping in a strange house can be trying for the first few nights."

Liar. You know why you're here. The memories the two of you evoked this morning battered you all day, and you came to her because only she can heal the bruises.

The intoxicating lethargy produced by the warm Southern night oozed over her anew with Devin's touch and his quiet voice. When his hands dropped back to his sides, she turned gratefully to the window again. In the dark, she could almost believe that the chasm of pain and betrayal yawning between them didn't exist.

"It's just so beautiful and peaceful here."

"Nothing like New Orleans?" he whispered, not wanting to disturb the mood, surprised by the sudden rush of the first genuine peace he'd known in years. Fear of bringing it to an abrupt end kept him from asking himself why.

She chuckled. "There's no place on earth like New Orleans. More goes on there in one minute than anywhere else in the world in an hour. The whole city is a hyperactive child with adult morals. I've always loved it."

"Do I hear a but?" Devin's breath brushed her ear. His arms stole tentatively around her waist. When she offered no resistance, he drew her back against his body. This was insane, and he knew it, but he had to touch her.

"Yes. Faced with the quiet beauty of the country, the city seems too raucous, too... too alive."

The sound of her giggle reminded him of Amy.

"I guess I'll always be a country girl at heart. There are times when the throbbing excitement of New Orleans infects me, but most of the time I long for the tranquillity of forests and endless meadows. It makes me slow down and appreciate what surrounds me."

Devin didn't reply. His arms tightened on the enigma he'd captured in the moonlight.

Drugged by Devin and the night, Jenny settled back into his embrace. This was wrong. She was probably playing right into his hands, but she couldn't pull away—it felt so *right.*

"Jenny."

Her name whispered through her hair. Was that longing, sorrow, she heard? Helplessly she melted against him. He swung her around in his arms with no preparation, no words, covered her eager lips with his own.

Need rose in her, filling the empty spaces of her heart with painful longing. For years she'd tried to forget Devin Montgomery, but now she was forced to admit that no other man could come close to making her want and burn as he did. No other man could make her abandon common sense and forsake promises she'd made to herself—just Devin.

She clung to his broad shoulders, molding herself to his torso and returning his kiss with all the hunger accumulated during years of famine. Beads of moisture lubricated his skin, aiding her hands as they slid over his flesh, unconsciously seeking the elusive spirit living inside the man. She pressed closer as he cupped her aching breasts.

Devin's surprise at her response turned to greedy acceptance at the intrusion of her tongue seeking his. He melted under the heat of her tongue seeking his. He melted under the heat of her uninhibited touch, holding her closer. The naked passion of Sam made itself known in the sharp sting of her nails digging into his shoulders. Damn, she felt good.

Cautioning reason broke through the sensuality engulfing Devin. The helplessness seeping into him served as a sharp reminder of what had happened the last time he was under her control, and doused his heat as effectively as a torrent of icy rain. She was sucking him under again, and he was letting it happen, encouraging his own destruction. It wasn't supposed to be this way.

Not until his lips pulled away and he took a step backward did she feel him withdraw. Cold swept over her where his body had touched her. Her throat muscles contracted, preventing speech. Just like six years before, she'd fallen into his arms like a ripe peach, and just like before, he was rejecting her. From somewhere deep inside, a protective screen of indifference rose to shield her.

"This shouldn't have happened," he ground out, wishing his body had the power to reason like his mind.

"We all make mistakes," she rasped, countering his rejection with acid coolness and moving to the safety of one of the hearthside chairs. Slowly, she sank into it, grateful for the support for her rubberized body. Her mind would register nothing but that he hadn't wanted her, that he'd been the one to pull away first. She faced the shame of knowing she would have allowed him anything...*anything*. And he knew it. Using the time to collect her erratic emotions, she ran her nail across the scrollwork on the arm of the chair.

Devin's groin knotted with unfulfilled need. He'd never wanted any woman the way he wanted Jenny at this moment. Just the sight of her sent his hormones racing out of control. He tore his gaze from her, knowing how close he'd come to opening himself up to the horror of repeating his old mistakes, knowing what she could do to him with that knowledge. His bitterness at his own stupidity almost choked him.

"Sex always did make us forget, didn't it, Jenny?" He tossed the words out with blind disregard for the feelings of the woman huddled in the chair, wanting only to heal his own bleeding wounds.

Her gaze flew to him. "Was there ever an *us?*" A humorless laugh sprang from her lips. "But you're right on one count. The root of all our problems is buried in that one little word—*sex*. What happened tonight was unfortunate, but let's not put more meaning on it than it deserves."

Her casual dismissal of what had just happened between them brought back all the rage of six years ago, the heartache, the frustrating helplessness, propelling him to her side. He squatted and took her shoulders in a firm grip, forcing her to face him.

"Listen to me, Jennifer Tyson. What happened just now was neither unfortunate nor insignificant. And we'd be fooling ourselves outrageously if we tried believing there's nothing between us." He gave her a shake. "There's more than you can even imagine."

"Get your hands off me!" she cried, unsuccessfully trying to tear free of his grip. "I'm tired of your veiled innuendos. If you've got something to say, say it. How much more am I supposed to stand?"

Quickly Devin searched for the words to cover what he'd nearly blurted out in anger. "You make it sound like some medieval torture, Jenny," he said, as smoothly as his tangled emotions would allow. "There's still this heat between us. It started in Tennessee. Over the years, it's lain dormant, but don't try to kid either of us into believing it died. It's very much alive. We just proved that. Why not enjoy it for what it is? Lust can be quite satisfying, you know. None of the emotional entanglements that go with love."

Fatigue washed over her. She was bone-tired of this emotional seesaw they climbed aboard every time they were alone. And it terrified her that Devin was always the first to jump off—never her. She was tired of his insults, his subtle insinuations, his demands. It was time to call a halt. Exhaustion loosened both her tongue and her temper.

"And just what is *it,* Devin? A quick trip to your bed? No thanks. Face it. There's nothing to enjoy. This arrangement was doomed from the start. We can't keep this up. I think it would be better if I went back to the city to work."

"No!" He released her and stood. For a moment, his gaze bored into her, daring her to follow through on her words.

"There's no reason for me to be here. If you're worried about the Clay diary, keep it here. I'll take down the information I need."

"I wouldn't do that, if I were you," he said, with cold deliberation. "You might find the consequences of such a rash move . . . financially unfavorable." Taking a seat in the chair facing her, he threw a casual leg over its arm, his relaxed posture at odds with his tense expression and tight lips.

"What are you saying?"

"You may recall the not-so-small matter of a deposit I gave you toward completion of this project you've agreed to do. I assume you ran right out after I left and paid all your bills."

She nodded dumbly, wondering how he knew so much about her affairs. Icy fear slid down her spine as she began to question where this was heading. Her insides filled with an expanding sense of dread; a panic-induced nausea rose in her throat.

"If you leave Claymore before the furniture is completed, I'll have to ask for the money back."

"What?" She sat up straight and stared in openmouthed awe at him. She hadn't thought Devin capable of such cruelty. "I can't pay you back."

"I know." His smile fell somewhere between conciliatory and Machiavellian. "In which case, I'll be forced to take your shop and its contents as payment." The smile left his lips as he delivered the final thrust. "An easy matter, since I'm your landlord now, and you haven't been all that prompt making your rent payments. According to my attorney, you've been late more than you've been on time over the last year."

"You? You bought the building?"

He nodded slowly. "And I have a strong aversion to tardy payments owed to me."

Swamped by the confusion of trying to understand what had driven Devin to his recent behavior, Jenny countered his casual threat with inner panic. Wildly she offered her only defense. "They were always made, even if they were late," she shot back. "Any judge would take that into consideration."

"Jenny, Jenny," he said shaking his head sadly. "Your last three payments were only made because of my money, and the threat of eviction. Not a good record to present for defense in a court of law." He sighed. "I'd hate to have to take a business it took you so long to build."

"I can build another one."

"Perhaps, but without any money, it'll be a long struggle. And what will happen to Belle and Harry in the meantime? Nice people. It'd be a shame for them to lose their income, just because you didn't have the guts to stick something out." The patronizing smile returned. "Of course, there are alternatives to working off your debt," he added neutrally.

Jenny sprang to her feet. Her hands curled into tight fists of outraged anger. "You bastard!" she whispered, understanding perfectly what he was suggesting and itching to use her balled-up hands on him. But knowing he would still emerge the winner stopped her. And why not? He held the trump hand.

If it had been only her, she would have gone to any lengths to see Devin's almighty ego deflated, but as he'd pointed out, she wasn't the only one who'd suffer. Belle and Harry deserved more than that from her after sticking by her through the leanness of the past year. It didn't take long for her to understand he'd played his ace.

Casting a baleful glare at him, she knew any arguments she made would be ineffectual. She accepted defeat. "Very well. I'll finish the job for you, but the minute it's done, I'm leaving." Flouncing to the door connecting the rooms, she flung it open. "Get out."

His eyes bore into her flesh like cold steel splinters as he unwound himself from the chair and strode to the open door. Stopping in front of her, he ran a fingertip down her face. "Too bad." Taking a step into his room, he stopped and turned back to her. "Don't try running out on me this time, Jenny. You won't like the consequences."

Jenny used all her strength to push the door closed behind him with a resounding crash. Reaching to twist the key in the lock and prevent any more nocturnal visits, she stared at the empty keyhole. He'd thought of everything.

"Who the hell does he think he is, Don Juan? Does he think he can go around demanding a 'flesh payment' for services rendered? Not to mention the fact he seems to have forgotten who ran out on who." With frantic anger, she paced the confining expanse of the carpet surrounding her bed. It wasn't until she realized how close she'd come to delivering the payment of flesh without his even asking that she crumpled on the bed.

Had she just won a victory? If so, what was it? Sentenced to spending time in a situation that closely resembled a Chinese water torture could hardly be considered victorious.

Devin's attitude toward her fluctuated like the pendulum of a clock. One minute he was almost the man she'd known, the next he was a total, unfeeling stranger. However, his actions boarded on the irrational with respect to keeping her at Claymore. Why? And why hadn't she fought harder to leave?

Adroitly she sidestepped the answers to both questions. Could all this be his way of paying her back for not waiting around all those years ago for him to carry on a sporadic affair?

Weariness overtook her. She felt like one of her carvings. Little by little, the master craftsman whittled away at her resolve, exposing more and more of her tender core. And each time he cut into her exterior with his emotional knife, the pain came closer and closer to her heart. How long would it be before he could see that he was eroding her indifference and pulling forth emotions that she'd thought long dead?

Resigned to the inevitable, she climbed back into the rumpled bed. While the idea of Devin stepping back into her life as anything more than a client frightened her, ironically, it also warmed her. She fell asleep, assuring herself she could maintain the business relationship. Her heart, however, told her she was traveling down a one-way street with no detours, and the final destination was her emotional destruction.

Devin paced the library, considering the several days that had passed since the scene in Jenny's bedroom. Strain marked his face. His writing had taken a downhill turn from mediocrity to sheer drivel. Organized, constructive thought lasted for only a few minutes before Jenny's face superimposed itself on his computer screen. The woman was driving him mad.

After all he'd accomplished thus far, he waited for the elation of a battle won, victory nearly in his grasp, but it never came. In its place was a self-loathing that was beginning to grow stronger every time he sent home a thrust and it hit its mark. In its place was a heaviness that weighted down his soul. In its place were doubts, fears that perhaps he'd misjudged Jenny after all.

The strident jangle of the phone brought Devin alert. Grateful for the intervention, he grabbed the receiver.

"Hello."

"Devin, great news! I know how you feel about personal appearances, but we got a chance that's too good to pass up. A booking for an interview on the 'Today' show in two weeks. They called at the last minute, but who's proud? Your publisher thinks I'm God."

"Cancel it," Devin barked into the phone without a moment's hesitation.

"What?" came back the astonished reply from his friend and agent, Dave Schaefer.

"I said, cancel it."

"Are you crazy? Do you realize any author would give a year's royalties for this chance?"

Devin frowned and leaned against the corner of the desk. "Dave, you know and I know my books will survive without a TV interview. They have in the past. I can't leave here now," he added, thinking of the consequences that might arise from leaving Jenny and Amy alone. He couldn't take the chance that his whole plan would blow sky-high. Besides, he knew Jenny was finishing, and in two weeks she'd probably be done. In which case, the time to close his trap was drawing near. He still had to win her over and into his bed.

He judiciously avoided thinking about the feeling that had nudged at him incessantly for the past few days—that Jenny was becoming very vital to both his and Amy's lives.

"Dammit, Devin, the network went to a lot of trouble to arrange this. The publishers are going to be very unhappy if you don't fulfill this obligation. Your sales were down on your last book. A bit of national exposure won't hurt before we release this new one on the crafts of the Louisiana Cajuns."

Devin chuckled at Dave's idea of *down,* recalling the six figures on his last royalty check. "Should I apply for welfare?"

"This is no joking matter!" Dave roared back. "The publishers say they want to see you on the tube in two weeks. Period. This is not your choice to make. Be there," Dave added before cutting the connection.

"Damn!" This couldn't have come at a worse time. Slamming down the receiver with undue force, he took a seat behind his desk and stared at the polished mahogany, as if he'd find the excuses he needed to get out of the interview somewhere in the rich patina of the wood. Unable to concentrate even on that, he rose from behind the desk and strode to the open veranda doors. The sound of raised voices drew his attention.

Just beyond the doors, Jenny and Amy sprawled on their backs on a blanket. Using the door frame to conceal his presence, he savored the picture.

Stretched out full-length, Jenny had one shapely leg bent at the knee, and the other lay flat. Her bare toes wiggled and flexed, drawing attention to the graceful arch of her slim foot. The length of her tanned legs seemed to go on forever before disappearing beneath the cuff of snug chocolate brown shorts.

Devin sucked in his breath and shifted, in search of a way to ease his growing discomfort. Jenny arched her back to adjust her position. The two brown owls on her white T-shirt stretched across her breasts, their large, knowing eyes boring into Devin's accusingly.

His gaze trailed over her face as she lifted a hand to sweep her hair off her shoulder, exposing her long, swanlike neck. The vivid memory of how she'd smelled and felt against his lips as he traced a string of kisses over that pulsing vein before the cabin's flickering fire accosted him. With it came the picture of firelight dancing over her naked flesh, the feel of her against him, the aching need to feel her around him....

With an effort, he halted his thoughts. Struggling to catch his breath, he concentrated on what Amy and Jenny were saying.

"Look at that one, Jenny," Amy said excitedly, her voice rising. She pointed toward the sky from her resting place in the crook of Jenny's arm. "It's a horse."

Devin leaned forward and glanced up at the puffy clouds decorating the bright blue sky.

"And there's an Indian chasing it," Jenny's clear tones added. "Oops, the cloud changed. Now the Indian looks like a lady." Her girlish giggles joined Amy's.

"Maybe she's the farmer's wife, and the horse got away from her," Amy chirped.

Jenny laughed anew at Amy's explanation for the sudden change in the cloud formation.

"Oh, Amy, look over there. It's a castle."

"Just like the one you made," Amy said reverently, staring at the spot in the sky where a large cloud extended vapor turrets above a battlement of cottony white.

"When I was a little girl, I used to dream of living in a castle," Jenny told Amy wistfully. "The castle was big and tall and shiny white. Just like that one. I was the princess, and my mother and father were kind and understanding rulers."

"Wasn't there a prince?" Amy asked excitedly, drawn into the story of make-believe, forgetting the game of identifying objects in the clouds.

"Oh, yes. There's always a prince. He was a very handsome prince, too. He rode a white horse, and his armor was so bright, it nearly blinded people when the sunlight shone off it."

Devin stirred uncomfortably, recalling the drunken father, sparse meals and squalid living conditions Jenny had endured as a child. A far cry from her dream.

"Where's your mommy and daddy?" Amy inquired innocently, raising up on her elbows to look down at the face of the woman beside her.

"They're both dead, Scamp." Jenny brushed a kiss against Amy's temple. "I have a grandfather, but I haven't seen him in a very long time."

Silence fell over them, each of them absorbed in her own thoughts. With their heads close together, Devin was reminded that Amy showed all the signs of growing into a beauty like her mother. Her lithe child's body would develop all the same curves, her dainty features would transform into the lovely, expressive face of her mother, framed by the same billowing black hair. Swearing at his musings, Devin started to turn back to the library, conscious for the first time that Jenny had no idea her grandfather was dead. Then Amy's excited voice stopped him.

"You could live with us, Jenny. We could be your family. There's lots of rooms in our house that nobody uses. Will you, Jenny?"

Devin froze, waiting for Jenny's answer.

"I don't think so, Amy."

"But why not?" Amy protested. "You could marry my popie, and—"

"Jenny," Devin called sharply, stepping through the doors onto the grass, unreasonable anger and fear warring within him. In his haste to see Jenny suffer, he'd never given thought to what would happen to Amy when he forced Jenny from the house. The closer the two of them became, the more Amy would be hurt. "I don't believe I'm paying you to loll around on the lawn with my daughter. Don't you have work to do?"

Stung by his harsh words, Jenny scrambled to her feet. "I'm sorry, Devin. I needed a break, and Amy and I decided to come outside. We were waiting for Harriet to bring us some refreshments."

"I'll have them sent to the workroom," he stated, his uncompromising tone leaving no room for argument. "Amy, you should be doing your exercises."

Amy's large, mossy eyes began to fill. "Mrs. Filbert had a dentist appointment, so we did them earlier."

"Then go to your room and rest. Jenny and I have some things to discuss."

"Yes, Popie." Amy limped off, head bowed, emitting a loud sniff as she disappeared through the veranda doors.

"Devin, was it really necessary to be so hard on her? It was my idea to come out here, not Amy's. If you're looking for a whipping boy, use me." Jenny glared at Devin's stony face. What on earth had set him off this time?

"She's *my* daughter. I don't appreciate you telling me how to raise her, nor do I appreciate you filling her head with nonsense about white knights and castles in the air. Amy devises enough fantasies on her own."

Anger boiled in Jenny. "What's wrong, Devin? Afraid she'll see the chinks in her *popie's* armor, or maybe the tarnish?" Fed up with his attitude over the past few days, his snarling at everyone, his unreasonable bad temper, Jenny challenged him with her tone as she blundered on. "Take it from me, Mr. Montgomery, every girl needs a few dreams before the reality of life steps in and she discovers there are no silver linings in cloud nine."

"Is that what happened to you?" Grabbing her shoulders, he pulled her toward him until their laboring breath was all that separated them. "Did you try to trample everyone before they could get to you? Is that why you put so little value on the happiness of others?"

Confusion distracted Jenny from her anger. Every time she and Devin exchanged heated words, he managed to say things she didn't understand. Bewildered, she stared into his hard eyes. "I don't know you at all. Is this what fame has done to you? If it is, I liked you better when you were a struggling writer—before..." She stopped just short of blurting out something that had gnawed at her since she first learned of it.

"Before what?" he ground out, fighting the urge to devour her with kisses, to return to that other time, that other place, to—

A soft breeze lifted a strand of her hair, passing it over his cheek with the gentlest of caresses. With it came her scent and a deluge of forgotten memories, insignificant little things: the sound of a cricket through the bedroom window, the snap and crackle of dried leaves under thrashing bodies, the fragrance of freshly brewed coffee shared under a full moon, the caress of her arched foot on his bare leg.

Ironically, these details shattered his calm more than any of the other recollections he'd encountered, bringing his memories to life with a clarity that threatened to distract him from her unfinished sentence.

"Before what? Before you ran out on me? Before you...?"

Jenny jerked from his grasp, glaring at him. "Before you put your daughter in a children's home."

He took an unsteady step back. "I did *what?*"

"Did you think I'd never find out, Devin? Were you so intent on not being saddled with a family that you allowed your only child to spend four years in a home so you could travel the globe writing books?"

Devin stared at her, dumbfounded.

"Let me tell you something, Mr. Montgomery. I've grown to love Amy. Don't count on me to enforce your idiotic orders. Amy can spend as much time with me as she wants." She turned and stalked to the door, stopping and spinning back to him. "And I'll tell you something else. If she were my child, she wouldn't have spent one second away from my side."

Chapter 6

In the days following the incident outside the library doors, Devin seemed to change. Jenny caught him watching her constantly, assessing her every move, paying undue attention to her every word. Her nerves were stretched beyond endurance. She wanted nothing more than to scream at him, "What is it? What are you looking for? Tell me, but for the love of God stop this dissecting silence."

His temper had grown so short, even Amy avoided him when she read the signs. He began to look drawn, as if he weren't sleeping well. Often, when Jenny and Amy were together, he would just stare at them for long, silent periods of time, then suddenly stand and stalk from the room. Living under the same roof had become akin to sharing a dwelling with a rumbling volcano.

As a result, Jenny took to closeting herself in her workroom. Taking her meals on a tray, she concentrated on finishing her job and getting away from Claymore as soon as possible.

Torn between what she'd come to accept as a legitimate worry on Devin's part over the potential damage to Amy from the continued strengthening of the growing bond between her and the child and her desire for Amy's company, she reluctantly excluded Amy from the workroom, as well. Consequently, the hours dragged by, and her aim of completing the job suffered.

Many times she would rouse herself from daydreams of Devin or Amy to find that precious time had sifted away like sand through an hourglass. It seemed that no matter how often she reprimanded herself for wasting time, she would lapse back into her thoughts.

By the time four days of isolation had passed, she nearly flew from the stool to answer the welcome intrusion of a knock on her door. Opening it, she was surprised to find Devin and Amy standing in the hall. For a moment, she could do nothing more than drink in the sight of their smiling faces.

"Popie's taking me to a Cajun fair, and we want you to go, too." Amy's bright eyes danced with excitement.

After all Devin's efforts to make it clear to her she was an employee, Jenny's hesitation came automatically. This invitation had all the earmarks of a family outing. She glanced at Devin.

"That's if you'd like to," he added.

Was this man exhibiting an almost boyish nervousness the same man who'd read her the riot act about wasting time he was paying for?

"I don't know," she finally said. "I have a lot of work to do here." She gestured toward the crude beginnings of a tiny spinet on the workbench.

"It can wait."

Jenny's wide-eyed gaze locked with his. "But—?"

"I believe, Miss Tyson, that you're on the clock, so to speak."

Surprisingly, his words were accompanied by a playful grin.

"Yes, but—"

He raised a hand to halt her words. "Then I should be able to dictate what I am paying you to do."

"Yes, but—"

This time he stopped her by grabbing her wrist and pulling her into the hall. He turned the lock on the door and closed it. Planting his hand at the small of her back, he gave her a gentle shove down the hall toward her bedroom. "No more buts. You have fifteen minutes to change. We'll be waiting in the car."

With her back still to them, Jenny could hear the metallic clanking of Amy's brace as she jumped up and down and laughed in delight. "It worked, Popie. We finally got her out of her room. But why didn't you tell her how worried we were about her being lonely?"

Amy's words were quickly admonished by Devin's whispered "Shush." Swallowing hard, she pivoted slightly and watched father and daughter disappear down the stairs. She felt foolish, but she couldn't stem the flow of tears Amy's statement produced. It was the first time since he'd come back into her life that Devin had shown her one ounce of compassion.

Feeling her spirits lighten, she hurried to her room and exchanged her work clothes for stone-washed jeans, a white camp blouse and sneakers. Running a comb through her hair and applying a fresh coat of lip gloss, she grabbed a cardigan and headed for the stairs.

Two hours later, the three of them were strolling leisurely down a footpath leading past the houses, churches and shops of Acadian Village. On the ride there, Devin had explained how the historic structures had been moved from their original locations to rest beside the sleepy bayou as a reproduction of an authentic Cajun community.

Amy, who'd made the trip before, had added the aside that this trip would be more fun with Jenny along.

"Last time, Popie was talking to everyone, gettin' his stuff for his book, and I had to sit and wait for him. I was bored. Popie said next time we could bring a baby-sitter for me."

Jenny's heart sank. Her bright happiness at being included in their day dimmed. Devin hadn't really wanted her company. She'd been asked to go simply as Amy's baby-sitter. Once more she'd been relegated to the status of employee. She jumped when his hand covered hers where they had been clenched in her lap.

"That's not why I asked you along."

Before she could stop her next words, they tumbled from her pale lips. "Why *did* you ask me, Devin?"

He avoided supplying an answer by becoming absorbed with the fact that Amy hadn't fastened her seat belt. He pulled the car to the roadside and turned to his daughter. "Sit back, Amy, and put your seat belt on."

Amy's lips screwed up in a pout. "Do I have to? Jenny doesn't have hers on," she pointed out.

Wordlessly Devin reached across Jenny, brushing the underside of her breast with the back of his hand. His gaze flew to her face. "Sorry," he mumbled, grabbing for the end of the belt and drawing it across her lap. With a decisive click, he inserted the metal tongue into the buckle and sat back.

"She does now."

Now, an hour later, guiding Amy over the protruding roots of a giant oak tree, she could still feel a tingling where his hand had touched. Recalling his sharp intake of air just before he'd slipped the buckle together, she wondered if the accidental contact had affected him as strongly as it had her.

Devin stopped before the shop of a basketmaker. "I have to talk with these ladies for a while. Do you want to come in and look around?"

Jenny wanted to say yes. Not only was she reluctant to be parted from his company, but she was also interested in hearing what the crafts people had to say. However, Amy had other plans.

"Jenny, can we go see the flowers while Popie's talking?"

Torn between her desire to stay near Devin and the wish to please Amy, Jenny hesitated.

"Please, Jenny. Please," Amy begged.

Devin touched her hand, his palm warm against her skin. "It's okay. You'll love the Around-the-World Gardens. If you still want to go in here, we can come back later, when I've finished."

She was certain she imagined the faint wistfulness in his smile.

"I'll be about an hour. I'll catch up with you then. Have fun, you two."

She was still staring at the door through which he'd disappeared when Amy tugged on her hand impatiently.

Devin shoved the small notebook containing his research data into a pocket of his khaki shirt and hurried toward the gardens, unaccountably eager to catch up to Amy and Jenny. As he walked briskly, he thought about the question Jenny had asked in the car—the question he couldn't find an answer to even now.

Why *had* he asked her along? Had it been merely to provide Amy with a baby-sitter, as she'd assumed? Or had there been another reason? Lately, his thoughts about Jenny had been a tangled mass of contradictions. One minute he wanted her, the next he was reminding himself of his plan to make her suffer.

Since her revelation on the lawn, it had only gotten worse. How could she have accused him of putting Amy in the children's home, when she knew who was responsible? It made no sense, but then, his well-thought-out revenge, and the reasoning behind it, had begun to show some gaping holes.

At first he'd convinced himself she'd said it to cover for her own abandonment, but he'd watched her, listened to her, when she was around Amy. She displayed all the natural aptitudes and instincts of a mother. She didn't give the impression of a woman who would walk out on a child. Then, when she locked herself away in her workroom to do exactly what he'd ordered her to do, he'd missed seeing her around the house.

When Amy suggested the possibility of Jenny going with them to the fair, he'd fairly leapt at the opportunity to spend a few hours with her.

What in hell was happening to him? Had he completely lost his mind? Was he beginning to feel compassion for a woman he should hate, a woman who would never feel anything but contempt for him once she learned the truth?

He rounded the corner of the gift shop and came to an abrupt halt. Jenny was sitting on the grass, looking like the Pied Piper of Hamlin. Amy rested in the place of honor on Jenny's lap. Enclosed in a circle of children, their rapt attention on her, she was telling them a story. He stepped behind the cover of a bush and listened.

"And when the white animals asked Zak to paint them and their colorless island with the same bright colors in his pants and shirt, Zak opened his magic lunch box. What do you suppose he found?" she asked.

"What?" came back a chorus of young voices. "What did he find?"

"Why, paint, of course, and paintbrushes."

Amy clapped, and soon the other children joined in. Devin's gut tightened into a painful knot when Jenny showered them with a beautiful, spontaneous smile.

"But Zak grew sad."

"Why?" Amy asked.

"Because he didn't have nearly enough colors to paint everything as it should be." Jenny kissed Amy's cheek before going on. "So he sat down to think. And while he thought and thought and thought, a white frog began to jump up and down. Frogs always think better when they jump, you know. But the frog jumped so hard, he lost his balance and knocked over all Zak's paint cans."

The children's smiling faces melted into frowns of concern over the spilled paint. Ironically, Devin felt concern himself. Inexplicably, he wanted Jenny's story to have a happy ending.

"As the paint ran together, Zak jumped from his seat on a big white mushroom and shouted, 'Hurrah, now we have all the colors we'll need. Look,' he told the white animals, 'see how the paint has mixed together and is making newer and brighter colors. I shall be able to paint all of you, and have enough left over for the trees and flowers, too.'"

Devin never heard the end of the story. He was too busy recalling the color Jenny had brought to his drab life years ago, and, to his chagrin, was doing again. Her obvious love for Amy was slowly erasing the black hate from his heart and replacing it with—

"Popie, Popie!" Amy came limping toward him. "Jenny told us a story about..."

"I heard, Scamp," he replied, his gaze fastened on the woman who seemed to draw children to her like bees to a sweet treat.

"Popie, wasn't it a wonderful story?"

Devin nodded dumbly, his eyes locking with Jenny's over the heads of the children crowded around her. The blue eyes gazing back at him sparkled with a happiness he hadn't seen since their time in Tennessee. But it quickly vanished, clouding over with a poignant sadness, and... God, was that fear? Was that what he'd done to her? Had he, with his thirst for revenge, reduced her to looking as she had when she lived with her drunken father? He felt sick.

"Popie, can we get a drink?"

Shaking away his upsetting thoughts, Devin took Amy's hand and walked toward Jenny. "Sure, Scamp, but first we'll have to rescue your...your friend from her admirers." He felt himself blanch at the knowledge of how close he'd come to letting Amy know that Jenny was her mother. Rattled by the thought of how disastrous that would have been, he forced a smile as they drew near Jenny.

Amy released his hand and began pushing her way through the throng of children clamoring for another story. When she'd nearly reached Jenny, she crumpled to the ground.

Devin and Jenny started toward her, but a Cajun woman who'd came to collect her child got there first.

"Oh, no, *petite,*" she crooned in a soft Cajun accent, helping Amy to her feet. "You okay, *hein?*"

Amy looked at her pink jumpsuit. "I'm okay, but my pretty pants are all dirty."

Being closer, Jenny reached Amy before Devin. She squatted next to her, brushing the dirt from the child's clothes. "There," she said. "Good as new. Are you sure you're okay, Scamp?"

Amy's head bobbed up and down. "I was coming to get you."

Brushing a stray wisp of hair from her cheeks, Jenny cradled Amy close to her, thankful she'd suffered nothing more than a smear of dust on her clothes and a slight scare.

"Leetle ones need mommas," the Cajun woman said, smiling down at them. "You see, me, I got four leetle ones. Always wanting momma's arms, *hein?*" She patted Amy's head, smiled at Jenny and took the hand of the little boy at her side and walked away. *"Adieu,"* she called over her shoulder.

Frozen into speechlessness, Jenny stared after her. Her heart lay in a knot of pain inside her chest.

"Is she all right?"

Devin's voice roused Jenny from her agony, only to plunge her into the depths of apprehension. Had he heard the woman? Did he wonder why she hadn't denied being Amy's mother? Did it show on her face that she'd give her life to make thc woman's words true?

She finally forced a reply from her lips. "She's fine. Just shaken, and a bit dirty." Hesitantly she raised her eyes to look at his face. Concern for his daughter was all she saw. She suddenly felt more alone than she'd ever felt in her life.

It wasn't until an hour later, when they shared a lunch of Cajun gumbo and Amy dozed nearby on the grass, that Jenny's fears were realized. He had heard.

"I don't claim to be an expert in children's behavior, but I think they'll accept any familiar, open arms when they're scared."

Looking up from the contemplative study of her untouched lunch, Jenny nodded. "You're probably right." Her troubled gaze returned to observing the task of moving her food around with her plastic spoon.

Devin looked back to his full bowl and realized he mirrored Jenny's preoccupation with the arrangement of the food. He hadn't been able to think of anything but the Cajun woman's statement. Had her innocent words started alarms ringing in Jenny's head? Was that why she'd been so thoughtfully silent ever since?

The notion brought bile rising in his throat. Suddenly the idea of Jenny discovering his deception terrified him. Why? Why was he now trying to avert the very thing he'd planned on not so long ago?

The answers hit him like an out-of-control truck. Seeing Jenny hurt would tear him apart. He vividly recalled the sharp twinges of pain he'd experienced each time one of his barbed statements struck a nerve, the hurt in her eyes when he'd blithely consigned her to the kitchen for her meals, the disillusionment when he'd used his ownership of the building housing her shop to keep her at Claymore.

When had he become this monster who got pleasure from someone else's pain? All of a sudden Devin didn't like himself at all, and he had no idea what had prompted this abrupt change in his thinking.

While the Cajun woman's words had disturbed her immeasurably at the time, Jenny came to view them as no more than a stranger's mistake. Because she had rushed to Amy's side and Amy had accepted her consolation, the woman had assumed Jenny was her mother. After all, aside from their hair coloring, Amy bore no resemblance to her. On the contrary, she was the picture of Devin.

What did haunt her was this puzzling change in Devin. When they'd arrived home, he'd invited her to share supper with him and Amy in the dining room and made it perfectly clear he expected her to take all her meals there in the future.

When she questioned him about it, he'd smiled.

"Spending all my meals taking part in conversations with a five-year-old grows old fast. I need the company of an adult who can discuss something besides dolls, dollhouses, and the latest addition to Barbie's ever-expanding list of necessities."

Then, much to her consternation, they'd spent the meal in a silence broken only by Amy's sleepy yawns.

He'd further surprised her by suggesting she get Amy ready for bed, since it was Mrs. Filbert's night off and he wanted to organize his research notes while they were still fresh in his mind.

He was beginning to be about as predictable as a summer storm—one minute she basked in the warmth of a man who bore a strong resemblance to the one she'd once loved, the next he became the changeable, temperamental stranger who'd brought her to Claymore.

But while these things bothered her, she carefully avoided digging too deeply into the possible reasons for them. The last time she'd tried to find out what made Devin Montgomery tick, she'd walked into a mess that had haunted her for years.

One week later, Jenny was still riding the emotional merry-go-round when the ride turned treacherous. The weather turned nasty, and a chill wind holding the promise of rain blew through the windows. Jenny had gone to the workroom, intent on putting the finishing touches on the scrollwork on the tiny spinet, the last piece to be made for the music room.

Her back to the door, she heard the hinges squeak ominously. "Come in, love," she called, intent on her work. "You're late. I expected you a long time ago."

"I'm sorry. If I'd known you were waiting for me, I would have come much sooner."

Jenny froze as the deep, rich tones of Devin's voice swept over her. Her hands forgot their task, barely mindful enough to hold on to the small piece of furniture.

"Devin. What a surprise. I thought you'd gone into the city."

He came to stand next to her, leaning his slim hips against the edge of the workbench, close enough to watch her. "I thought I'd see if you might like to take the ride with me. We could stop at your shop, and you could give Belle your list in person. Then we could grab lunch somewhere before coming home." He carefully removed a wood shaving clinging to the fine hairs on her temple, brushing her skin lightly.

The touch of his fingers sent Jenny's heart racing. Quickly she laid aside her project and stood, moving away from him. "I don't know," she said, hedging. "I have a lot of work to do here." Were her ears deceiving her, or was he actually seeking out her company?

He captured her arm in a gentle grip before she went two feet. "Jenny, it's just a ride into New Orleans, and lunch. I promise I'll behave."

Was that humor she heard in his voice, genuine humor? "Is Amy coming with us?"

"No. Do you need Amy to chaperon? Don't you trust me?"

"Should I?" Her blue eyes bored into his, looking for a motive for his seemingly innocent proposal. A fire smoldering deep in their mossy depths reached out and warmed her.

"Why don't you come with me and see for yourself?"

His challenge rocked her precariously balanced emotions. Suddenly, she wanted to go, to tempt fate, to forget the pain and loneliness of the last years.

Don't do it, Jenny, an inner voice warned. *The last time you played this game, you got hurt irreparably. Can you afford another heartbreak?*

But heartbreak only comes when your heart is involved, she argued.

Isn't yours?

No. No. She felt nothing for Devin, nothing. And she was still saying that when her skin suddenly came to life under the slow caress of his finger as it slid down her cheek and outlined her lips. *Don't let me feel,* she begged. *Please, don't let me feel.*

It's too late, Jenny. You already feel more for this man than it's safe to admit.

"Sam?"

Her gaze flew to his face to find his mouth scant inches from hers. His breath tickled her skin. His eyes devoured her. His lips gobbled up her protest.

Without offering even token resistance, Jenny felt her body molding into his, her arms encircling his neck, her fingers diving into the silky hair at his nape. Lord, but she loved the textures of Devin. She lo—

She froze. Springing away, she looked up at him as if he'd grown horns and a tail. No. It couldn't be happening again. She'd been so careful, fought so hard, been so determined not to—

Excusing her actions by claiming a sudden onset of nausea, Jenny managed to convince Devin to go to New Orleans without her. She needed time, time to come to grips with the trap she found herself enmeshed in. Sitting next to Devin, alone, in the confines of a car, was not the way to do it.

Most of the remainder of the day she spent sorting through her mind, trying to find out when it had happened. By late afternoon, she still had no answers. Early evening found her descending the stairs, strolling blindly out the door, and taking a seat beneath a willow, seeking the concealment of the branches, like a mouse looking for its hole. She needed quiet, a place to think, somewhere to hide.

Twilight had come early, with the aid of the darkening sky. Vaguely she recalled a weather forecast warning of a squall coming in off the Gulf.

A small part of her acknowledged the faint flashes of lightning on the horizon and the low growl of accompanying thunder. The larger part of her mind focused on the indisputable fact that she found herself head over heels in love with Devin Montgomery—again. Or had she been fooling herself all this time, and had never fallen out of love with him?

It would explain a lot of things—her unmanageable thoughts, her inability to control her body's reaction to him, that bottomless feeling that always accompanied his entrance into a room where she was.

How could she stay here now? How could she leave? Could she bear the pain of a one-sided love again? Her head began to pound in time with the increasing strength of the thunder. Tears welled up in her eyes, overflowing her lashes to blend with the soft sprinkle of the first raindrops. Miserable, she lay down on the bench and curled into a ball, clutching her middle with crossed arms. Suddenly her fabricated stomach upset had become real. Curtained by the powerful birth of a summer storm, she prayed for death of her reborn love.

The shop bell tinkled softly as Devin stepped into The House of Miniatures.

"Devin," Belle called in greeting, glancing behind him.

"Jenny's at Claymore," he explained, "feeling a little under the weather. I think she's been working too hard." Reaching into the breast pocket of his tan sports jacket, he withdrew a folded sheet of paper and handed it to Belle. "She wants you to order this list of things for Amy's dollhouse."

Belle glanced at the paper, laid it aside, and looked back at Devin. For a time, she remained silent while he toyed with a miniature replica of a red wagon, drawing it back and forth across the top of the display case, appearing to be in no great hurry to leave.

"Was there something else?" she asked finally, her bright eyes taking in the way he started when she spoke.

Pushing the tiny wagon aside, Devin stuffed his hands in his pockets and glanced at Belle. "Belle, why did Jenny open this shop?"

A wide grin split Belle's face. "Kids. She told me once she'd never get married and have her own. I guess this is her answer. By being in a business that draws kids like flies to honey, she gets to share everyone else's."

Devin found Belle's answer less than satisfying. It wasn't what he'd wanted to hear, expected to hear, needed to hear. She should have said Jenny's motive was money, but she hadn't. Instead, she'd said the one word that would add to the pile of questions he'd already accumulated.

"Have you talked to her since she came to Claymore?"

Belle frowned. "Every day. Why?"

"Has she mentioned Amy?"

"Every day. In fact, once we get past the business, she talks of nothing but Amy and you."

Running his fingers through his hair, he rearranged the riotous tumble he'd created in the car by torturing his normally well-groomed black waves. Nothing made sense anymore.

Distractedly he bid Belle goodbye and started from the shop, pausing next to Jenny's castle and staring at it thoughtfully. Everything had been fairly clear in his mind—with the exception of a few unanswered questions—until the day he found Jenny and Amy on the lawn looking at the clouds, the day Jenny knocked him off his high horse by throwing her accusation about him having put Amy in that home. Now, none of the round pegs fit in the suddenly square holes.

Hours later, after walking the streets to end up on Jenny's bench in Jackson Square, he was no closer to the answers than when he'd left Claymore.

If Jenny hated kids enough to give up her infant daughter, why had she chosen to make her life's work in an occupation that guaranteed her close association with them? Why was she so fond of Amy, and where had this idea that he was responsible for what had happened to Amy come from? As far as Jenny knew, Amy was just another kid, no one special. There had to be some small piece of the puzzle he was overlooking, but try as he might, he couldn't pinpoint it.

Wearily, just before twilight, he walked back to his car and headed for Claymore. Somewhere on the long drive, he realized why he'd done this about-face concerning Jenny, why he'd suddenly started talking himself into considering her innocence.

As much as he declared otherwise, as much as he'd pushed it to the back of his mind, as strongly as he'd fought against it, and as many other names as he wanted to give it, he still loved Jenny. With the acknowledgment of his feelings came the realization that he might have misjudged her, and worse that he might have killed any chance of winning back her love.

He still hesitated, wondering if his desire to see her unblemished had gotten entangled with the love he felt for her. Did he want her innocence so badly he had built a case to substantiate it in his imagination?

He began sifting through the tangle in his mind for facts. Jenny loved Amy. He'd have to be blind not to see that. Jenny had put herself in a position to be in touch with children daily. She'd admitted to Belle that she loved children, but would never mother one of her own. And unless she was planning on playing him for a fool again, she was doing a damn good job of trying to hide her feelings every time he got within two feet of her. Was that the attitude of a woman who ran out on a man, who deserted a child?

He slammed his palm against the wheel. Nothing jibed. What he knew and what he saw and felt were in direct contradiction to one another.

Purposefully he dug into his memory of the day he had visited Dr. Hines in North Carolina and learned he had a four-year-old daughter.

"Mr. Montgomery." Dr. Hines greeted him in a cheery voice accompanied by a firm handshake. "Please," he added, motioning him to a cracked brown vinyl, straight chair.

As Devin took the proffered seat, the doctor seated himself behind a massive desk. Glancing around, Devin tried to block out the smell of alcohol and stale cigar smoke by looking over the unkempt, less than modernly equipped medical office. Abruptly he brought his attention back to the doctor who'd penned the mysterious message summoning him to this backwater North Carolina town.

Dr. Thomas Alva Hines, as the yellowed framed diploma above his head declared him to be, looked as if he'd stepped out of a TV role as Dr. Zorba on an old rerun of "Ben Casey, M.D." The unruly shock of white hair atop his head stood out in various directions, hinting it was seldom visited by a comb, and even then not with any serious intent. Blue eyes twinkled back at Devin from beneath full eyebrows, overlooking cherry red cheeks and a bulbous rum-blossom nose. His mouth, too full for the rest of his features, contrarily fit the image of the short, chubby man dressed in rumpled, ill-fitting black trousers, off-white frayed shirt, string tie and black vest.

"Drink?" Dr. Hines asked, motioning to a bottle marked Formaldehyde that he extracted with practiced ease from a medicine cabinet.

"No, thanks," Devin said politely, looking skeptically at his choice of drinks.

Noting Devin's wry glance, the doctor grinned. "Don't let the label fool you. I drink nothing but Jack Daniel's. Sure you won't have some?"

Devin shook his head and watched in amusement as Dr. Hines sloshed two fingers of Tennessee's best in a water glass, capped the bottle, took a long swallow and placed the glass firmly on the desk. "Jacob Clinton."

Devin blinked. "I beg your pardon?"

"Jake Clinton," Dr. Hines stated, as if Devin would recognize the nickname more readily.

"I'm sorry. I don't know any Jake or Jacob Clinton," Devin explained patiently, cursing himself for not asking more questions before he made this trip for nothing, and wondering to himself if the old man had slipped a gear. "I don't believe I've ever met a Mr. Clinton."

"'Course you haven't, boy. Never will, either. Old Jake died a month or so back. I just wanted to see if the name rang a bell."

"I'm afraid I don't understand what I have to do with all this," Devin replied in complete bewilderment.

The doctor refilled his glass and leaned back, his chair squeaking ominously under his weight. "You will, you will." With maddening slowness, he pulled a copy of an anatomy book from a shelf to his right. Opening it to a cavity carved in the pages, he extracted a fresh cigar and nipped off the end with his teeth, spitting it onto the floor at his side. "Have to keep my pleasures hidden from Iris, my secretary. Thinks she's my mother. Has a nasty habit of dumpin' my bourbon and smashin' my cigars when she finds them."

"Dr. Hines," Devin began, his patience wearing tissue-thin, "I don't have much time, so if we could get down to why it was so urgent that I come here . . . ?"

"Certainly, my boy. I don't often get a chance to just sit and chew the fat. You'll pardon my bad manners."

It wasn't his manners that were driving Devin to distraction, but his constant evasion of the subject. He had the feeling the doctor was playing for time to size him up. "No problem," Devin lied. "But could we take care of whatever made you contact me?"

"Your daughter."

Sitting bolt upright, mouth agape, Devin stared at the man as if he'd taken leave of his senses. "My what?" Devin swallowed hard. "You must have me mistaken for someone else."

"You Devin Montgomery?"

"Yes, but I don't have any children. Good grief, I'm not even married. I'm a folklore author. Are you sure it's me you're looking for?"

Dr. Hines leaned two chubby forearms on the cluttered desk and pinned Devin with eyes full of wisdom. "Now just calm yourself, boy. I know blame well who you are. And yes, I'm sure I got the right man. You were the one that got Jake's granddaughter pregnant and ran off to New York City."

Springing to his feet, Devin leaned forward, planting his hands firmly on the edge of the desk and looking the doctor in the eye. "I repeat. I don't know any Jake Clinton, *or* his granddaughter... whatever her name is. I'm—"

"Tyson. Jennifer Tyson," the doctor supplied. "You might want to take a look at these," he added, pulling a Bible and a sheet of paper from his top drawer. "It's the girl's birth certificate, and the Clinton family Bible."

Devin looked down at the paper and read his name listed as father and Jenny's as the mother of Rebecca Clinton. His face blanched, and then his legs buckled. He flopped backward into the chair. His gaping mouth snapped shut.

"Want to reconsider that drink?"

"I..." Devin cleared his throat and tried again. "I believe I will."

Dr. Hines grinned and found a glass that looked suspiciously like an eye cup and filled it. He handed it to Devin and frowned as he gulped it down, blinking and coughing as the bourbon seared its way to his stomach.

"You better start from the beginning," Devin squeaked when he could breathe again.

Between gulps of bourbon and puffs on his cigar, Dr. Hines related his story in his shorthand-style speech.

"Met Jenny a month after she come to Jake's. Nice girl. Never could figure why she just up and ran off after the baby came," he mused. "Anyway, the night the youngster was born, Jake said there wasn't time to call me. Delivered the baby himself, but she said she didn't want it. Asked Jake to get rid of it for her. Jenny ran off a week or so later." Dr. Hines clicked his tongue and shook his head, mobilizing his head of hair into a bizarre, uncoordinated dance. "Never made sense to me. She didn't impress me as the thoughtless type. Seemed eager to have the baby." He sighed and leaned back in the chair.

"Her ma died tryin' to raise Jenny alone. Maybe Jenny was just plum scared." He roused as if from a daydream. "Oh, well, guess there's no second-guessing people, specially kids."

Devin missed most of what came after Jenny not wanting the baby. Black rage roared in his ears.

"Jake said the baby needed a name, so he called her after his wife, Rebecca. Said you could change it to whatever you like better."

"Where is the baby now?" Devin asked in a voice he didn't recognize as his own.

"I placed her in the Asheville Children's Home." He went on quickly when he saw Devin's heavy frown. "You gotta understand, boy, Jake was near eighty-five. He couldn't see to a baby."

Devin nodded. The chill of the words *children's home* clung to his bones like an early frost, summoning memories of a lonely little boy with no friends and no family.

"Anyhow, Jake visited her regular, but when he got sick and knew he was goin' to meet his Maker, he asked me to help. By the time I got there, ol' Jake was workin' on borrowed time. He barely had enough life in him to tell me about you and Jenny and ask me to make sure you came and got the girl."

"How did you find me?"

"Jake said Jenny talked about you bein' a writer, so I went to Mabel Johnson at the Asheville Library. Knew who I was talkin' about right off. She looked up your publisher's address for me." He paused to pour another drink. "You gonna take the girl?"

"Absolutely," Devin replied, without a moment's hesitation.

The doctor smiled. "Thought you would."

"One more thing," Devin added, shaking the doctor's offered hand. "I didn't know about the baby. I didn't even know she was pregnant."

The shock of hair moved like a field of wheat with an erratic breeze blowing through it. "I believe you, boy." He stood, slid his arms into the black jacket hanging on the hat tree, and turned to Devin again. "Now, you come with me, and we'll go get her. You'll need my statement to verify you're her father."

A bolt of lightning crisscrossed the sky in front of the car, bringing Devin's attention back to the road. As much as he analyzed it, there wasn't a scrap of evidence in what he remembered that could change his mind. Yet it was changing.

Rain cascaded down the windshield as he steered the car into the drive at Claymore. The headlights played over the rose garden, and he caught a faint movement of a light color flashing through the shrubbery. Shutting off the engine and pulling the collar of his jacket around his neck, he bolted from the car to investigate. Rounding the corner of an azalea bush, he came face-to-face with a sopping-wet Jenny.

Casting a disapproving glance at her dripping shorts and blouse, he grabbed her arm, yelling to be heard above the pounding of the rain. "Good God! What in the name of hell are you doing out in a storm like this, and half dressed?"

Through the falling rain, Jenny blinked up at him, his words an echo from the past. Her large, frightened eyes bored into him as she realized they'd come full circle, back to the beginning.

Never weighing the consequences, Devin scooped her up in his arms and headed for the house.

Chapter 7

Devin set Jenny's feet on her bedroom floor. Loath to let go, he retained his hold on her hips. "You'd better get out of those clothes," he said, trying to block out the images his words conjured up, his gaze roaming over her wet face and dripping hair, his voice rasping from his throat.

She nodded wordlessly, returning his appraisal's heat with the same yearning look.

"Want some help?" Though he tried to make the question light and teasing, it held the unmistakable flavor of an erotic suggestion.

To Jenny's chagrin, the answer stuck in her throat. She continued to gaze up into his mesmerizing eyes. Dear God, what was she going to do? She wanted him with a power that staggered her, but the old fear of rejection hovered close by.

Stung by what he read in her eyes, Devin released her and backed away. "I'd better change, too."

"Yes," she whispered, feeling the chill on her wet body now that his warmth no longer shielded her.

Flashing her a half smile, he turned on his heel and strode through the connecting door and into his room. Closing it, he leaned against the cool wood and squeezed his eyes shut, waiting for the fires of his desire to burn down, waiting for the pull urging him to go back and take what he'd seen offered in her eyes to ease.

"What do you do now, Montgomery? And don't say go to bed. There's not a hope in hell of you getting one second of sleep tonight."

His gaze flew to the blank computer screen. Work. He'd bury himself in the revisions Dave was crying for. Impatiently he peeled his soaking clothes off, toweled himself dry and drew on a pair of sweatpants. Shutting out all thought that didn't pertain to his newest book, he padded to the desk, tore the plastic cover from the computer and threw on the switch. Maybe if he got the revisions in before deadline, he'd be able to talk them out of that damn TV interview.

Jenny stared fixedly at the closed door. Was she ready to spend another night tossing and turning, knowing that the one person who could quench the hunger burning its way through her insides lay just a few steps away?

Too cowardly to consider the alternative, she removed her sodden garments. Toweled dry, she slipped a lacy white gauze nightgown over her head and climbed into the big, empty bed, attempting not to think about how quickly he'd dismissed her when she heard the faint clicking of the computer keys from next door.

But try as she might, the constant clicking drummed on her nerves. She could feel the need for him growing inside her like a swelling sea, battering her resolve, washing over her common sense. With each click, the longing grew, reaching out to her, until it swamped her like a helpless little boat before a hurricane. He was so close, so very close.

She had only to walk through that door. But if she did, what awaited her on the other side? Heartbreak, loneliness, pain?

Fighting against it, she reminded herself over and over of the last time she'd seduced Devin Montgomery, and how she'd suffered immeasurably for it. For every second of pleasure, she'd endured years of agony. She'd have to be crazy even to consider opening herself up to a repetition of that.

Turning onto her side, she pulled the extra pillow over her head to shut out the intrusive clicking. Five minutes later, she shifted to the other side. The need grew, moving from an ache in her throat to a burning in her core.

The bed coverings weighed her down. She threw the tangled blankets from her body and slipped from the bed, her thin nightgown clinging to her damp flesh. She shook it loose and began to pace. The sound from the next room continued, uninterrupted. She paced faster, trying to outrun her pounding heart and the incessant clicking of the computer keys.

You're blowing this out of proportion. You'll be fine, she told herself stalwartly. *Just don't think about it.*

Devin paused, stared at the screen of the computer, held down the delete button and watched as line after line disappeared. Out of the three pages he'd managed to wring from his brain, perhaps one could be salvaged, and that only if he rewrote it.

His mind refused to concentrate on anything but the woman next door. This self-enforced celibacy only magnified his awareness of her, rendering him brain-dead when it came to anything else. A picture of her standing there, the wet fabric of her clothes clinging to every curve, silver drops of moisture shining on her skin, stayed with him. The de sire he'd seen in her eyes taunted him, dared him. But *was* it desire he'd seen?

Damn! It seemed that everything that happened lately was designed especially to drive him mad. Sharing meals with her was like having splinters slid under his fingernails. He felt like a high school kid, stealing glances at her while she aimed her attention at Amy. The need to touch her, hold her, had blossomed in him so strongly that his insides were twisted into knots of denial. Sitting through the entire meal without screaming his need resembled a form of ancient torture fashioned to test his endurance. By the time each meal ended, he dashed from the room to keep from grabbing her and dragging her off to a bed—any bed.

"Damn!"

A faint sound from her room attracted his attention. The realization of what might be causing her restlessness brought a smile to his lips. So she was having her own problems sleeping. He listened quietly for the telltale squeak of the bedsprings. When he heard her leave the bed, and the rhythmic squeak of the floorboard told him she'd begun pacing, he began hitting keys at random. The speed of the pacing increased. He stopped. The pacing slowed. He began again. The pacing sped up. His carefully guarded control snapped.

Before he could talk himself out of it, he turned off the computer, opened the connecting door and stepped through, closing it softly behind him. Then he saw her. After one glance, he knew he couldn't turn away again. She was stunning, sensual, breathtakingly sexy, everything he'd searched for in every woman of his acquaintance and failed to find.

A lamp on a night table illuminated the room with a soft amber glow and haloed her in its golden light. Devin's wide chest moved spasmodically. His hands opened and closed, aching to touch the body silhouetted beneath the sheer white lace nightgown. Her light perfume twined around the silence, weaving a spiderweb of erotic thoughts.

Jenny had been holding her breath since the sounds of the computer ceased, staring at the door, somehow knowing he would walk through it. When the door swung open, she'd exhaled, only to catch her breath again at the sight of Devin in sweatpants slung low on his bare hips. His rumpled hair broadcast his state of agitation. A hunger identical to the one burning in her was reflected in his eyes.

For a moment, they stared at each other, each devouring the sight of the other's near-naked body, all thought of betrayal, rejection and revenge far removed from their fevered minds.

Jenny licked her lips and nearly collapsed at the sound of his throaty growl. Her flesh came alive under his penetrating gaze.

"I can leave, or I can stay, Sam. But if I stay, if I touch you, you won't be getting back into that bed alone, and you won't be sleeping any sounder than you were."

Emotion clogged her throat. He'd left the choice to her, put the decision in her hands. Did she really want this? *Yes!* her heart screamed. *Yes!*

"Please..."

Devin held his breath.

"Please... don't go," she finally whispered, too weak to continue the war with her nerves.

In one long stride, Devin closed the space separating them, clasping her to him. His mouth covered hers, sucking up her passion like a starving man. Her heat singed him through the fragile fabric of the nightgown, scorching his hands as they traveled over her.

"I told you long ago you were a woman," he whispered against her neck, "but I was wrong. You were a girl then. Now, Sam, now you're all woman."

"Devin," she pleaded, her labored breathing telling him what she couldn't with words.

Placing a finger under her chin, he raised her face and saw the moisture on her cheeks. With the pad of his thumb, he wiped each tear away. He cradled her face in his hands and kissed her mouth to still her trembling lips. "From now on, Sam, no more tears."

Tightening her arms around his neck, she pulled his mouth back to hers, but he denied her.

"Sam, if you aren't ready for this, stop me now. If we wait a minute longer, I won't be able to let you go and walk back into that room alone."

She pulled back to look into his smoldering eyes. "If you go back into that room, it won't be alone."

Sweeping her into his arms, he carried her to the rumpled bed and laid her down, pulling the tangled sheets to the foot. With a wry laugh, he grinned down at her. "If I'd waited much longer, you'd have hung yourself in this mess."

She opened her arms to him. "If you'd waited much longer," she purred, nestling against him as he slipped in beside her, "I'd have come after you." Her admission brought a stirring of more powerful emotions.

"And when you got me," he whispered, his lips closing over her earlobe, "what would you have done with me?"

"Seduced you." Her voice hummed across the flesh of his throat.

"Like this?" His hand cupped her breast and kneaded the pliant flesh. She arched toward him. "Or this?" He pulled the shoulder of her nightgown down to bare a breast and suckle its engorged tip. His tongue swirled around it. She writhed beneath him in response. "Or maybe this?" With one deft movement, he pulled her gown from her body. His hand began to stroke her heated core with fingers that remembered exactly how to stoke the fires of her passions.

"Devin, please..."

He kissed her, long and deep, while his hands and mouth continued their quest to tease and inflame.

"Not yet, Sam, not yet." Though his words denied them both, the days of waiting, wanting, took their toll. He couldn't deprive either of them of the pleasure a moment longer. Leaving her with a whispered promise of return, he raced into his room and fumbled through the night table until he found the small foil packet he sought. Ripping it open impatiently, he donned the protection. In seconds, he had slipped back into the bed beside her.

Settling between her legs, he moaned as he entered her heat.

Jenny dug her heels into the mattress, raising herself to receive him. Her hands clutched at the hard muscles of his back. Her head rolled from side to side.

"Come on, Sam," he encouraged, "make those little sounds I remember. Don't hold back."

His words banished any reservations she might have had. Coherent thought vanished, replaced by wanton need. She ran her hands over him, purring deep in her throat. Possessed by a wild abandon, she thrashed and twisted, meeting him thrust for thrust.

Devin had been trying to go slow, to be gentle, but when he felt her response, his restraint went up in flames. He paused for breath and felt her muscles contract around him, begging him for more. He obliged. The world came apart. Wave after wave of pleasure washed over him. Her breath caught. He knew she neared the top, and he joined her to soar over the peak with her.

His body shuddered, and he clung to her. Only she could make him feel this suspension of life and the crashing reality of rebirth. Only his Sam could make him feel as if his insides had been torn from his body—and love every minute of it.

Moments, hours, perhaps days, passed. They lay sated, spent, entwined in each other's arms.

"Witch," he mumbled into her hair. Breathing deeply of the fragrance of honeysuckle clinging to her, he crushed her to him and slid his leg between her thighs.

Cuddling closer to his warm, naked body, she rubbed her face against the downy mat of hair on his wide chest. How she wished she was a sorceress. She'd brew a potion or intone a spell to keep him here in her arms forever.

With the satiation of her body's need for Devin, Jenny became aware of a new need making itself known, one that until this moment, she'd never before considered. She wanted to tell him about their child, share her grief with the one person in the world who might understand the emptiness she'd carried within her for so long.

"You're very quiet," he said, nuzzling her hair with his chin, then dipping his mouth to kiss the top of her head. "You aren't having second thoughts, are you?" He held his breath in dread.

She shook her head, luxuriating in the caress of his silky chest hairs on her skin. "No. No regrets." At least not yet, she added silently.

"Then why the thoughtful silence?" He hugged her close. Somehow he sensed he was about to be robbed of the peace and serenity that had been growing inside him.

"I was thinking...." She paused. How did a person introduce the subject of a lost child? She swallowed the threatening tears clogging her throat. "I was thinking about our baby," she blurted out.

Devin went deathly still, barely daring to breathe. Did she know? Had she guessed? "Our baby?" he asked cautiously.

"You've never asked about it. Why?" God, please don't let him say it was because he didn't care. The idea brought the threat of a new onslaught of tears. This time, they gathered in spite of her efforts to hold them at bay. Surreptitiously she brushed at them with her hand.

Devin waited, breathing a sigh of relief that she couldn't see his face. "I never knew there was a baby." He told the half-truth in the hope that she would continue to talk and, in doing so, clear up the tangle of mystery surrounding Amy.

Levering herself up on her elbow, Jenny searched his face. "But the letters. I told you in the letters."

Letters? Devin's interest was piqued. "What letters?" he asked, his broad forehead furrowing.

"The ones I sent from my grandfather's house. I went there after our fight. I thought you didn't want me. I wrote nearly every day, but you never answered," she finished, her voice cracking.

"I didn't answer the letters because I never got them, Jenny."

"But Gramps sent them." Was he lying? She looked into his mossy eyes and found stark honesty staring back at her. "But you must have gotten them," she insisted, in spite of herself. "Unless..."

"Unless what?"

"Unless you left Tennessee before they got to you."

"Perhaps, but they would have been returned to you, in that case." He framed her face with his hands. "Jenny, is it possible your grandfather didn't send them?"

The thought had been lurking at the back of her mind, but she had been vehemently denying that her beloved grandfather could have done anything so heartless. With Devin putting it into words, she had to face the fact that it was a distinct possibility. The pain of betrayal sliced into her.

"Jenny, forget the letters. What were you going to tell me about our baby?"

The idea of her gramps betraying her in such a cruel way, combined with the thought of her baby's death, robbed her of all composure. Lowering her head, she pressed her face to Devin's bare chest and retched up her story, allowing the grief to overflow the banks behind which she'd kept it safely contained. The deluge that came as a consequence tore from her throat in agonizing sobs.

Stunned, Devin found himself unable to console her. This was definitely not one of the explanations he'd expected. Despite the contradictory proof sleeping on the other side of the house, Devin was convinced that the sobbing woman in his arms believed her child was dead. This kind of horrible grief couldn't be a masquerade. Her tears were real; he could feel them hitting his bare flesh. Her shudders were real. He could feel the entire bed vibrate with the force of them. Her agony was real. He could feel it being torn from her body, could feel it in the pain that etched itself in him.

At the same time, he knew their child lived. It made no sense. Unless, for some reason, Jake Clinton had wanted her to believe her child had died at birth. But what about the story Dr. Hines had related to him about the words of a dying man? But Clinton could have told him anything and been believed. He had, after all, been the only one in attendance at the birth, besides Jenny. Could he have spent all this time hating Jenny for something she had had nothing to do with—something she had known nothing about?

Hines had said Jenny had run off after the baby's birth. That much made perfect sense. If she thought her baby dead, why would she stick around to be tortured by the memory? From what he'd observed of Jenny with Amy, and of her growing love for a child she believed mothered by another woman, there wasn't a way in hell she'd willingly give up her own child.

A new dilemma popped up to leer at him. If all this supposition was based in truth, then he'd done Jenny a terrible injustice. She'd never deserted their child. Self-revulsion rose up to blind him. He was no better than that bastard who'd played with Jenny's happiness. Thank God he'd found out the truth before he added his misdirected revenge to her heartbreak.

Her sobs had subsided into fitful sniffles. The shudders were gone. She lay placidly on his chest, drained. He felt a compelling need to banish her pain for good, to shield her so no one could hurt her again.

"Jenny, our baby didn't die. She's alive. Amy is our baby," he whispered, smoothing the tangled hair from her face. When she didn't react, he gently shifted her off his body and gazed down at her. She was sleeping.

No matter, he told himself as he nestled her in the crook of his arm. There's always tomorrow to tell her. For now, he'd let her sleep and hold her through the night.

Oh, yeah, a little voice nagged, *and she'll fall down on her hands and knees in gratitude and thank you for keeping Amy's identity to yourself for all these weeks. How do you plan on explaining your way out of that?*

Devin groaned, feeling the bite of the double-edged sword of vengeance. If he told Jenny about Amy, she'd probably end up hating him, but he couldn't see that he had a choice. The longer he kept it a secret, the harder it would be to tell her, and the worse the repercussions would be. Tomorrow. He looked forward to it with all the enthusiasm of a condemned man.

The odor of freshly sanded wood filled the workroom. Jenny turned a tiny spindle in her hand as she cleaned a miniature Chippendale chair with a tack cloth in preparation for staining. Her eyes sparkled; a bemused smile curved her lips.

A warm glow blanketed her as she recalled the precious hours of the past night. Devin had awakened her to make love to her again, as though he couldn't get enough of her, and she'd responded in like form. He'd already been inside her before she came awake enough to answer her body's urgings.

As the recollections of the night spent in Devin's arms passed through her mind, inevitably she came to the things they'd talked about afterward. Although there were still questions—questions that required answers, if they were to build any kind of relationship out of the ashes of yesterday—she felt relieved at finally having shared with him the facts about their baby.

She'd made so many mistakes about Devin. If he hadn't received her letters, she'd been hating him for something he'd had no control over. She still had trouble believing Gramps wouldn't have mailed her letters, especially since he'd urged her to write them, but what other explanation could there be? Why hadn't he given them to her, if they'd been returned? And if they hadn't been returned, what had happened to them?

She sighed and shrugged. The letters didn't matter now. The damage had been done. So much damage had been done. Would the wounds they'd inflicted on each other ever heal? Or had the six years of festering infection made that impossible? Had the pain killed all the feelings Devin had had for her?

Could they ever trust each other again? It suddenly occurred to her that the one element lacking in their relationship all those wasted years ago had been basic trust. If she'd trusted Devin and his love enough, she would have waited through eternity for him. Not only had she not allowed him to explain why he didn't want to marry her, she hadn't had enough faith in what they had to see that neither of them could exist as a whole human being without the other.

She wasn't even sure there was a relationship to heal. Last night could have been attributed to no more than lust brought on by propinquity on Devin's part. She'd made the mistake of reading too much into their relationship once before, and she wouldn't do it this time.

But could he have made love to you with such passion if there wasn't something there? she asked herself.

Her hands stilled. She stared blindly at the work she'd done on the miniature chair. Devin had said nothing last night to lead her to believe there was anything more between them than there had been the day she walked into Claymore. He hadn't even expressed any sorrow about their mutual loss of a child.

The eagerness with which she'd anticipated seeing Devin today dissolved into trepidation. She set the unfinished chair aside and clasped her hands tightly in her lap to stop their trembling. What would she say to him? What would she do? How could she look him in the eye, remembering her wanton behavior of the night before—with a man who more than likely cared nothing for her as anything beyond a willing bedmate?

Looking around her at the completed miniatures on the workbench, and the ones Amy had already placed in the dollhouse, she experienced an overwhelming sadness. She was nearly done. Earlier, she'd checked the list of furnishings Devin had given her when she first arrived at Claymore. Almost all of them had been completed, with the exception of the pieces for the master bedroom. She'd left them for last, needing Catherine Clay's diary to get the measurements.

Steven Clay's specially commissioned bed and armoire were all that remained. How long would it take to complete the master bedroom? Another week? If she worked slowly, she could stretch it to two weeks, but no more than that. Very soon, she'd have no excuse to remain at Claymore, to remain with Devin and Amy.

Devin opened his eyes slowly. Images of the night before raced through his mind. A satisfied smiled spread over his face. Steeped in the satiation of having spent the night in the arms of the woman he loved, his body came to life as if that night had never been.

How he'd wanted to remain at her side all night to celebrate the sunrise of a new day with her, a new future as a family. The risk of discovery by Amy was the only thing that could have driven him from her side and back to his lonely bed.

Thoughts of Amy cooled his heated body. When he recalled Jenny's anguished telling of their baby's death, her despondency over his apparent desertion, her desperate attempts to find him and right their lives, he could—

The truth hammered into him with all the force of a crippling blow to his midsection. What he'd believed to be Jenny's abandonment of their child had been nothing more than an excuse to assuage his male pride.

If she had run out on their child, she'd had good reason: a young girl faced with the task of raising a baby alone, the knowledge that her mother had died doing just that. Those things should have occurred to him, and would have, if he hadn't been blinded by his own selfishness.

But they hadn't. For four years he'd lived with the pain and humiliation of having the woman he loved walk out on him without a word. During that time, he'd fed the festering wounds of his ego, allowing them to grow way out of proportion. Learning he had a child had been nothing more than the steam valve that let the poison escape. But even more unforgivable was his use of the child he'd professed to love and protect as a tool to gain his ends. In his haste to humble Jenny, he'd never considered the damage he would do to Amy by depriving her of the mother she longed for and needed.

In doing so, he'd perpetuated the crime against Jenny, too. She'd already lost so much of Amy that she'd never get back: her first tooth, her first words, her first step, her first smile. And he'd been prepared to rob her of still more.

In short, he'd played God with all their lives, and now, perhaps losing Jenny in exchange for righting the wrong would be his payment for his selfishness.

Sick with himself for seeing his mistakes too late, he crawled from the bed, slipped on his jeans and crossed the room to the connecting door. He'd wake her, this time. He had to rid himself of this gnawing shame and guilt for hurting the two people he loved most in the world—and hope he didn't lose them both as a result.

Devin stood in the open doorway, watching Jenny work, while his heartbeat resumed a normal rhythm. When he awakened and gone into her room to find her gone, he'd panicked. Had last night been too soon for her, after all? Fear more intense than any he could ever recall had clawed at him, dogging his steps as he hurried to find her.

"Jenny."

At the sound of his voice, she turned hesitantly and looked into his eyes. For a moment, she searched his face. Apparently finding what she sought, she flew into his arms.

Relief washed over him, chasing the cold fear from his heart. No regrets. His mouth clamped over hers.

"You taste good in the morning," he whispered between kisses.

"It's not morning yet. The sun's not even completely up."

"God, Jenny," he groaned, tightening his hold. "I couldn't find you. I was afraid..."

She pulled away a fraction, just enough to see into his beautiful eyes, and stopped his words with a finger to his lips. "I missed you after you left me. I couldn't sleep, so I came here." She suddenly realized how her unexplained disappearance six years ago must have hurt him, but before she could say anything, he pressed a hungry kiss to her lips.

He kissed her once more before steering her toward her workbench. "How's it going?" he asked, tucking her close against his side as they walked, searching for the right words to begin his confession.

Although it served as a diversion from what he had to do, it was an unnecessary question on his part. Her workroom had been a regular stop for him each night before he went to bed during the past weeks. Often he'd just sat there for hours, absorbing her presence, wondering, asking himself the same questions over and over, groping for answers.

"I'm getting close to being finished. Belle has the curtains and bed coverings ready, and Harry said the wallpaper should be in sometime this week."

He detected the note of sadness in her voice. Was it reluctance to leave? His blood sang through his veins, giving him a hope he desperately needed to latch on to.

"Perhaps," he said, turning her in his arms, "I can find more work for you." His teeth nibbled at her bottom lip.

She returned his nibbles with light butterfly kisses, savoring his sultry suggestion. "Will I be required to demonstrate my talents?"

"Oh, most assuredly. I can't hire you without a proper review of your skills." Pleasure at the darkening of her eyes to a deep cobalt blue as she imagined what his job interview would consist of suffused him. *Tell her!* his conscience prodded mercilessly. *Don't wait any longer!*

For a second, she held back. What would this job be that he joked about so lightly? Would she just be a bed warmer, or would she have a real share in his and Amy's lives? To her shame, she knew she'd accept whatever he offered.

Be careful, Jenny. You're falling into the same trap—assuming too much, reading into his words and actions things that might not be there.

But he's here in my arms, saying things that mean he doesn't want me to leave. And, God help her, she didn't want to leave, not after last night, not after they'd finally begun to bridge the chasm that had separated them for too long.

Perhaps she was on a collision course with pain, but she'd become powerless to apply any brakes. She'd continue on her suicidal emotional ride, and take the consequences, whatever they might be. Loving him so much didn't leave many alternatives.

"I see you get the idea." He wiggled his eyebrows, his forced smile a villainous leer. "We really should get started. This could be a long, exhausting interview."

"I certainly hope so, boss," she whispered, her voice growing husky. She offered her mouth to him in a brief kiss. "Do you always conduct middle-of-the-night interviews?"

"It's not the middle of the night," he said, stealing another kiss. It felt so good to play with words the way they used to. No more weighing each one. No more wondering—just for a while longer. Lord, give him a few more minutes of holding her, loving her.

"It is for the other people sleeping in this house."

He looked around. "They are sleeping, aren't they? Even Amy is still asleep."

She could read his thoughts, and they coincided with hers exactly. "Uh-huh."

"Shouldn't we do something about it?"

"Want to wake them up?" she asked teasingly.

"Good God, no. I had something in mind for us."

"I thought you said we couldn't be found together in one bed. If we do what your lecherous mind is suggesting, we will."

"Trust me," he said.

"With my life," she replied, her face becoming serious. And she did. For the first time since she'd met him in the Tennessee pine forests, she had total and unquestioning trust in him.

Swallowing the acrid taste of his guilt, he cupped her face in his hands and stared deeply into her eyes. With his heart, he promised, "I'll hold that life with all the care of the most fragile crystal." Emotion rose up and prevented more words passing his lips. He knew what she was offering him, and it was a gift more precious than his own life—a gift he neither deserved nor had earned. What would he do if she didn't forgive his deception? How would he survive without holding her again, loving her again?

Suddenly he knew he had to love her one more time before she walked away—and she would walk away, he was as sure of it as he was that their child lived and breathed. His throat closed, and he blinked against the burning in his eyes.

The moisture gathering in his eyes surprised her. She'd never seen Devin cry before, and it did strange things to her insides. Standing on tiptoe, she kissed away the tears rolling down his cheeks. "I should have trusted you all those years ago. I should have known you wouldn't hurt me intentionally."

Guilt rose up anew to choke off his air with its vile taste. He had to tell her about Amy. Every minute he postponed it put their happiness at greater risk. "Jenny..." he began.

"No." She stopped him with a finger across his lips. "No more words, Devin. I want you to make love to me. Save the words for later."

Grateful for the reprieve, fearful that his confession would destroy this new and delicate bond between them—as fearful as the coward he called himself, he allowed her to silence him. Without another word, he walked to the open door, closed it and turned the key in the lock, then walked back to her and pulled her into his arms.

They made slow, exquisite love on the floor of her workshop, unmindful of the sawdust and clutter surrounding them. Nothing mattered but the moment. Neither of them thought beyond the circle of their arms. Everything else got washed away on the tide of passion.

Hours later, Devin entered Jenny's room to find her bathed and dressed. He looked her over slowly while she pivoted for him.

"Blue does wonderful things for your eyes," he said, approving of her choices of white slacks and a sky blue silk blouse.

"Thank you, sir," she said, taking in with pleasure the rolling muscles beneath his green shirt and the way his tight jeans hugged his perfect buns. Lord, but he was the most bone-jarring specimen of manhood she'd ever seen.

"Come here," he growled, holding out his arms to her. "You know we have to talk," he told her as she nestled against him.

Jenny raised her head and nodded, apprehension making the movement slow and jerky. "Does this mean I failed the interview?" she quipped, her voice cracking with the dread building inside her.

"No. You passed with flying colors." He only hoped he'd be as lucky. Although he'd tried to inject a lightness he was far from feeling into his remark, the knotted fear in his gut kept him from his goal.

Taking her hand, he led her to the workbench, cleared away a spot and lifted her onto it. He positioned himself between her knees, his hands remaining on her hips, hoping the physical contact would help him tell her about Amy. He could feel the tension in her body against his palms.

"Jenny, there's something we need to get straightened out between us before this goes any further."

The lump that had risen in her throat refused to allow her to swallow.

"Last night, when you told me about the baby..."

"Popie, are we gonna get a baby?" came a sleepy voice from just below them.

Devin released Jenny, bent and scooped Amy's pajama-clad body into his arms. She squirmed toward Jenny, holding out her arms to be received. Jenny took her and settled her on her lap.

He cringed as he watched Amy burrow into Jenny's shoulder, her little arms encircling her mother's neck. As much as the picture should have elated him, it didn't. His heart filled with a desolation he hadn't felt in over five years—the wasteland left behind after losing Jenny.

Chapter 8

"I love pancakes," Amy said, shoveling the last of her third helping into her mouth.

Jenny laughed and wiped a dribble of syrup from the little girl's chin. "You'll burst wide open if you eat any more." She glanced at Devin. He'd seemed so preoccupied ever since they left her bedroom, almost sullen. "You're doing a lot better than your popie," she added, sending a questioning look at Devin. "Is there something wrong?"

He shook his head and offered a weak smile. "I guess I lost my appetite." He studied Jenny, noticing something new about her. The sadness that had seemed to cling to her like tree lichen was missing. She held her shoulders back, and the old sparkle lit her eyes. This new glow had transformed her.

Shivers raced down Jenny's spine. She dragged her gaze away from Devin, uncomfortable with this change from the lighthearted man who'd made love to her with such passionate intent amid sawdust and wood shavings.

"I wish you were my mommy," Amy announced out of nowhere, shocking the two adults out of their pensive moods.

Jenny could feel Devin staring at her, but she couldn't meet his gaze. She couldn't bear to see the anger Amy's innocent request might bring to his eyes. Not today. Not when the smallest glimmer of hope existed that her crazy world was finally righting itself.

"Finish your pancakes," she said, avoiding any reply.

"Would you be my mommy, Jenny?"

Devin cleared his throat. Listening to this child beg for her mother tore chunks from his heart. He couldn't do this to either of them a minute longer. "Jenny, I have to speak to you, alone."

A chill coursed through her.

"Can we talk later, Devin? I really have to get back to work."

"No. We have to talk now." Damn. He was going about this in fine fashion. Scaring her wasn't what he'd had in mind. "Please," he added, gently.

Jenny rose. Her knees wobbled. She gripped the edge of the table. Dread wrapped its cold hand around her heart.

"Mr. Montgomery?"

"Yes, Harriet?" he said impatiently. He dragged his attention from Jenny to his housekeeper.

"There's a long-distance call for you from New York. It's your agent, Mr. Schaefer."

"Thanks, Harriet. I'll take it in the library." He stood, then glanced back at Jenny. She looked so frightened. He took her shoulders and kissed her firmly. "I'll be right back. Don't go away."

She smiled weakly, sat down and watched him disappear into the house.

"Do you love my popie?"

Amy's candid question jolted Jenny back to reality, leaving her floundering for an answer. Honesty seemed her only choice, especially in view of what had just transpired.

"Yes, Amy. I do, very much."

A whoop of joy issued from the little girl. She jumped down from her chair and lumbered in her uneven gait around the table to crawl into Jenny's lap. Wrapping her arms around the small body, Jenny kissed the top of her head and cuddled her close.

"You didn't answer before. Will you be my mommy?"

Ah, the persistence of youth. Jenny considered her answer very carefully. "I don't know, Amy."

Amy leaned back to look into Jenny's eyes. "But you said you love Popie." Her little chin dropped. "Then you don't want to be my mommy 'cause you don't love me."

"That's not true. I do love you, but..." How was she going to explain this to a five-year-old, when she couldn't provide an explanation for herself? "Sometimes there are things that stand in the way of other things," she replied lamely.

"What things?"

"Grown-up things, Scamp. Things adults don't always understand. It's very hard to explain." She smiled through watery eyes, her happiness of early this morning growing dim.

"It's compli...compli..." Amy sighed.

"Complicated," Jenny finished for her, having grown quite accustomed to aiding Amy in her choice of grown-up words.

"Yeah," Amy agreed, snuggling into Jenny's shoulder.

Jenny was amazed at how much Amy had come to mean to her, and how quickly. She seemed to be an extension of herself. The pain of the loss of her own child didn't seem quite so sharp, with Amy's love to cushion the edge.

"Jenny?"

"Yes, Scamp?"

"I love you."

Tears rose to Jenny's eyes, and emotion clogged her throat. "I love you, too, Amy."

"Dave," Devin said cheerfully. "What's up?"

"Evidently not you," came the terse reply snapping through the telephone. "Have you forgotten you were supposed to be on a late flight to New York last night?"

Devin swore under his breath and raked a shaky hand through his hair. "Yes. As a matter of fact, I did forget." Doing this TV interview had been the last thing to cross his mind in the past seventy-two hours.

"I've rebooked you on a flight for late this morning. The taping's not until three. You can just make it."

Cold despair washed over him. "I can't leave now, Dave. There are personal things going on that demand I be here."

"Dev, I'm really sorry if life isn't treating you as well as it could, but unless it's a death in the family, the publishers aren't going to relent. I warned you before that this wasn't a multiple-choice assignment."

An idea formed in Devin's mind. "Mind if I bring someone along?"

A heavy sigh issued from the receiver. "You can bring the New Orleans Saints with you, if you can find a plane to put them on. Mardi Gras just got over yesterday, Devin. Every seat is booked coming out of New Orleans and Baton Rouge. Yours was the last one on that flight. As it was, I had to do some fast talking to get the airlines to sell me a standby seat." He cleared his throat uncomfortably. "By the way, if anyone should ask, your aunt Emma was very old and very sick. Her passing was a blessing in disguise."

Devin pulled the receiver from his ear and glared down at it. Placing it against his ear again, he barked back at Dave, frustration robbing him of all patience with Dave's dry sense of humor. "What in the name of hell are you babbling about? I don't have any relatives—you know that. Who's Aunt Emma?"

"Well, dammit, I had to tell them something. Otherwise they wouldn't have given up the seat, and you'd be in deep trouble."

"It's too bad you went to all that trouble. I won't be on the flight." He listened as a deafening silence drifted back to him from New York. "Dave, did you hear me?"

"Yeah, I heard." Dave sighed. "Look, my friend, I'm gonna level with you. Read the fine print in your contract. It obligates you legally to cooperate fully with any and all promotional activities your publisher deems beneficial for the good of the book. It doesn't say a damn thing about family emergencies. You're already two months overdue on your rewrite deadline. Don't aggravate Big Brother any more."

"What you're saying is that I don't have a hope in hell of getting out of this interview." Devin could hear the defeat in his own voice.

"You got it. The contracts with the network are already signed. To put it bluntly, unless you want your posterior dragged into court and your pants removed by the New York State legal system, you'll be on that plane. It's up to you." Dave hung up.

Cursing vehemently, Devin slammed the receiver into the cradle. He glanced toward the veranda. What a hell of a mess, he thought, hearing the light laughter floating in through the open doors. Life was far from fair, but then, hadn't he learned that at the ripe old age of four, in the first of a long line of foster homes?

He returned to the veranda to find Jenny and Amy cuddled close together. Before he made his presence known, he recorded the picture to comfort him in the days ahead.

Damn! How could he have forgotten the interview? It had been his intention to call Dave and pressure him into getting him out of it, but with all that was going on, it had slipped his mind.

He wanted so much to clear up the secrets looming over their happiness, but he had to be on that plane. Dave had made that more than clear.

At the same time, he knew he needed time to tell Jenny. He didn't want to drop his bomb on her, and then desert her to handle it on her own. He wanted to be there, to hold her and guide her through it, to help her understand. So, once more, it had to be shelved until a later date. Damn you, Dave Schaefer!

"Hey, you two, did you miss me?" he asked, with a false brightness only Jenny detected.

"Bad news?"

"Yes and no," he said, sitting down and replenishing his coffee. "No, because my newest book is almost ready to hit the stores. Yes, because I have to fly to New York this morning for a TV interview."

Jenny's stomach dropped.

Amy's head shot up from Jenny's shoulder. "I want Jenny to stay with me."

"I want Jenny to stay, too," Devin said, looking at her over Amy's dark head. "Please?"

She suddenly saw him as a vulnerable man, pleading for her compliance, like a small boy requesting special permission from a parent. This parting seemed to be affecting him as strongly as it was her.

She leaned forward and took his hand in hers. "I'll stay," she promised, unconsciously adding her love with her eyes.

Devin raised her hand t[illegible] and pressed a kiss into her palm. "Help me pack?"

"Me too!" Amy cried, s[illegible]ing from Jenny's lap and starting for the door.

"I'm afraid not." Mrs. Filbert intercepted her. "You need to bathe and dress, Amy. It's nearly nine o'clock, and you're still in your night things."

Amy looked at her father. He smiled and shrugged helplessly. "I'll see you after I pack, Scamp. Go along and make yourself beautiful." He winked.

"Oh, Popie." She giggled, taking Mrs. Filbert's hand, already running down a list of possible outfits.

The two smiling adults turned to each other. Merriment vanished from their faces. The pain of the separation to come had already taken root and reflected from their eyes. Without a word, Devin took Jenny's hand and drew her after him into the house and up the stairs to his room.

"You have to pack," she reminded him as he turned the lock on the bedroom door and pulled her into his arms.

"Later."

She didn't argue. She held on to him as if her very life depended on it. And it did, she realized with a jolt. Before Devin reentered her life, she'd merely existed from day to day in the little world of her shop. Even when they butted heads, she'd felt more alive than she had in years. Last night meant more than the reuniting of their bodies. It offered indisputable proof of how closely their lives were still entangled. This separation had come too soon. They needed more time together to strengthen the fragile bonds.

"How long?" she asked when she could tear her lips from his. His answer frightened her, but the need to know propelled her beyond her fears. She'd been too long without him already. A minute away from Devin stretched before her like an eternity.

"I'm not sure." He kissed her again. "Jenny, I don't wan to leave. There's so much I have to tell you."

She shook her head. "Not now," she whispered. "Just love me, and come back soon."

Burying his face in the perfumed abundance of her hair, he clutched her close. He knew she was recalling a time when he hadn't come to her.

"I'll be back as quickly as is humanly possible." The words were superfluous, but they both needed to hear them.

"That won't be nearly soon enough," she murmured, sliding her hands under the hem of his sweater.

He pulled her down onto his bed and kissed her. Everything about their lovemaking this time took on a poignant urgency. Their kisses were deeper, longer, more passionate, flavored with desperation. Their hands went on forays, memorizing everything they touched. Bodies joined with such tenderness that mutual tears marked their climax.

Amy waited at the bottom of the stairs. She'd finally settled on an apricot dress abounding in ruffles and lace. Matching ribbons held her dark hair in ponytails on either side of her head.

"Am I beautiful enough, Popie?"

Scooping her into his arms, Devin kissed her pink cheek soundly. "You are always beautiful enough, Scamp."

"Am I as beautiful as Jenny?"

His eyes traveled from Amy's jet black hair to her mother's. He compared the perfectly matched arched eyebrows, the slightly upturned noses. To him, it would be impossible to believe that anyone but Jenny could be Amy's mother.

"Yes, Amy, just as beautiful as Jenny." He smiled at Jenny over Amy's head.

Jenny's heart turned over.

"You'll be late, Mr. Montgomery, if you don't leave now."

Harriet's reminder came like a splash of cold water. He kissed Amy once more before setting her on her feet. Picking up his briefcase, he turned to Jenny and memorized her face.

"Take care of my girls," he said. "I'll call you every night."

Unable to speak, Jenny nodded, accepted his hard kiss and followed him to the car.

"Devin," she called as the car began to pull away, "I need Mrs. Clay's diary." The words mixed with the dust swirls in the drive.

Oh, well, she thought, if I don't have the diary, I won't be able to finish until Devin comes home. The idea of an excuse to prolong her stay with Devin, and of all that free time to spend with Amy, brought a smile to her face.

The rest of the day stretched before her like a yawning abyss. Amy was doing the therapy she'd been allowed to postpone due to Devin's departure. Afterward, she'd be exhausted, and would sleep for a time. Until dinner, Jenny was left to her own devices.

She decided to stain the last pieces of furniture for the dining room. As she skillfully smoothed the rough edges of the wood, her mind drifted back to a time when she'd been fascinated by her grandfather's fingers doing much the same thing.

Momentarily she fought the recollections, not wanting to think about him, about what he might have done to her, to Devin, to their child. Eventually, as she knew they would, the memories had their way.

* * *

"Glad to have you here, girl," Gramps said, holding open the screen door so that Jenny could pass into the old farmhouse.

"I'm not sure how long I'll be staying. Probably until I can find a job and a place of my own." She dropped her suitcase beside the worn sofa.

"You'll stay till the little one comes," he said, matter-of-factly, picking up the suitcase and going down the hall to the back of the house.

"But how—?"

He cast a smile over his shoulder. "Don't know how I know. Knew your grandma was in the family way before she did. It's just something the good Lord lets me in on."

Jenny hadn't seen him since she was five, and his advancing age had shocked her when he picked her up at the bus station in his battered old pickup truck. She hadn't expected him to look his eighty-four years.

The door he'd disappeared through opened and closed, and as he approached her, she reassessed her earlier conclusions. His gnarled hands were shoved inside the bib of his worn overalls, but the wrinkles spiderwebbing his face revealed the toll of time. The sun had weathered the bald spot on the top of his head, turning it a leathery tan to match his face, making the fringe of ivory hair around the outside look like a misplaced halo.

His sloe eyes held the fatigue of many years of backbreaking toil, the sadness of lost loved ones, and the wisdom of a lifetime, but the softening effect of the laugh lines around his mouth told her those years also had held large quantities of shared happiness with those around him. His bent shoulders, bowed under an invisible burden of loneliness, seemed to have straightened some with her arrival.

"You'll have your ma's old room. It'll be easier than climbin' the stairs in a few months." He came to a stop in front of her and took her face in his hands. "It'll be good to have someone in there. Been empty too long." He gazed at her for a long time, his eyes glazed with unshed tears. "Lord, but you're a picture of her when she..." His callused hands fell to his sides. He stumbled past her and out the door.

During the first few days, Jenny tried not to think about Devin. Little by little, however, she found it impossible to keep him from her thoughts. She should have let him explain, instead of allowing the hurt to drive her away. If nothing else, he deserved to know about his child.

"Write him a letter," Gramps finally said after seeing her mood worsen by the day.

"I'm not sure he'd want to hear from me."

"Never know unless you try" were his final words on the subject.

When she handed him the first of many letters to mail, his only comment was a half smile and a curt nod of his head.

Following the string of unanswered letters and her fruitless trip back to Tennessee to find Devin, she cried her heart out in his comforting arms.

"You stay here and have the baby," he crooned as he rocked her shuddering body. "Your old gramps'll make sure ain't nothin' ever hurts you agin."

Once in a while, after that, she'd see him staring at her with a mist of tears filling his eyes. She began to wonder if he regretted his decision to let her stay.

Finally she couldn't stand it any longer. "Gramps, I can leave, if you want me to."

His gnarled old hand closed over hers. "Now what gives you the idea I want you to leave?"

"Sometimes I see you looking at me."

"Child, that's only 'cause you remind me so much of your ma."

During the months that followed, she faced some hard truths and began to plan a life for her and her child, without Devin and away from the farm.

"I'll raise my baby alone," she told Gramps that evening while she dished up their supper. "We don't need anyone."

It didn't take a college education to understand that Devin wanted no part of her or their child. She'd been an amusement for him while he was stuck in the dull mountains writing a book. Sharing the responsibilities of caring for a child was not something he had wanted to do. She'd have done well to remember that, instead of being certain she could change him simply by loving him.

Gramps said nothing, just looked at her for a long time. Seeming to come to some decision, he patted her hand and left the house, not returning until after the sun had sunk behind the hills.

The sound of Amy's laughter drew Jenny from her sad memories. She felt grateful, in a way. Her hands were trembling, and beads of moisture dotted her forehead.

"Jenny, Jenny," Amy called, hobbling into the room in her broken gait. "Mrs. Filbert says, if it's all right with Harriet, we can have dinner in the gazebo. It'll be like a picnic." She danced around Jenny, her excitement bubbling forth like a busy fountain.

"I'm terribly sorry, Miss Tyson," the old Scottish nurse said, hurrying into the room, winded from her chase. "I tried to tell Amy not to disturb you, but when she gets a bee in her bonnet, there's no stopping her. She slipped out before I could catch her."

"It's okay, Mrs. Filbert. I'm done here for the day." Mrs. Filbert raised an eyebrow and retired from the room with a disapproving huff, obviously convinced Jenny was spoiling the child. "Now, about that picnic..." Jenny raised her eyebrow in a perfect imitation of Mrs. Filbert.

Amy collapsed in a fit of giggles.

An hour later, they were sitting on a blanket on the floor of the summer house, finishing the remains of fried chicken, potato salad, and juicy slabs of peach cobbler. Jenny listened with rapt attention as Amy described in great detail how the gazebo would be decorated for her upcoming birthday party.

"Popie says we can put up streamers, and there will be fairy lights in the trees. I want a zillion trillion balloons," she cried, standing up and spreading her arms as wide as she could. Sitting down again, she clutched her hands to her chest and swooned. "It's going to be a wonderful party, Jenny."

"I'm sure it will be, Scamp, but tell me, who's going to blow up all these balloons?" Jenny asked in mock seriousness, popping the last bite of cobbler into Amy's mouth and wiping her fingers on a napkin.

Amy chewed thoughtfully and swallowed. "My popie. He can do anything."

"You really love him a lot, don't you, Scamp?"

"More than anybody in the world, 'cept you." She stopped for a minute. Her eyes shone like two pale green stars. "Do you think Popie would let me invite your friends from the shop, Jenny?"

Jenny scooted over next to Amy and pulled her into her lap. She wrapped her arms around Amy's warm body and inhaled the little-girl scent of her skin. "We'll just have to ask him, won't we?"

Amy sighed wistfully, leaning back against Jenny. "I really wish you was my mommy."

I really wish I was, too, Jenny thought.

"Jenny, what's wrong? You look so funny."

"Nothing, sweetie," Jenny replied. "Now, back to these zillion trillion balloons. I don't think even your popie can handle that many. How about fifty?"

"Okay," Amy conceded. "But they have to be all the colors of the rainbow."

"Why?"

"'Cause they're happy colors." Amy smiled up at Jenny. The young woman's heart skipped a beat.

"When is this big event, anyway?" Jenny prodded, tickling Amy under the chin.

"In two weeks," she said proudly. "June seven."

Pain stole Jenny's breath as if a dagger had been plunged into her chest as she calculated the passage of time. Her baby had been born on the seventh of June, too.

Later, alone in her room, waiting for Devin's call, Jenny thought about the ironic twist of fate that allowed Devin's second born to share the same birthday as their dead child. She thought about Amy celebrating her birthday in a children's home. Would they at least have given her a cake?

So many times she'd wanted to ask Devin about why he'd put her there, why he'd left her there for four years, and so many times she'd held back the words. But she made up her mind that tonight she'd ask.

The phone rang, startling her from her thoughts. She laid aside the book she'd been attempting to read and reached for the receiver.

"Hello."

"Hi, Sam."

Warmth washed over her at the sound of his deep voice.

"Hi."

"How're things on the home front?" he asked.

"Okay. Amy and I had a picnic in the gazebo tonight. Confidentially, I don't think Mrs. Filbert approved." Her voice became low and husky. Her mind was far from the picnic with Amy, drifting back to the short interlude in Devin's room before he'd left.

"Probably not," Devin replied, his voice, as well as his thoughts, matching hers. The woman was a witch. From hundreds of miles away, she could still reach out and snare him in her web. "She doesn't approve of Amy wearing trousers, as she calls them. She says it's not ladylike. But she's a hell of a good nurse. Been with me ever since..."

"Ever since you brought her out of the home?" The silence on the other end of the phone line walked over her, like the footsteps of a restless ghost.

"Yes. But how did you know about that?"

"Amy. We were talking about her room one day, and she let it slip."

He remembered the day. He hadn't heard what they were talking about, but the guilty look on Jenny's face had spoken volumes.

"Devin, why did you put her in the home? Was it your answer to not dragging her around the country with you?" She tried to keep the sharp edge from her voice, but failed miserably. This was a child, his child, and she hated the idea with a passion.

"I didn't put Amy in that damn place," he ground out.

"Then who? Her mother?" Another drawn-out silence came to her. Was he going to remind her again that she was an employee and that this was a family affair?

"Jenny, this is not the time or place for this. I promise when I get back I'll tell you everything."

She squeezed her eyes closed to ward off the feeling that there was more to this than just an inopportune time for a discussion.

"Okay?"

She agreed stiffly. "Okay."

"Sam, please don't be angry with me. I promise, when I come home, we can talk all you like. We'll sort out all the misunderstandings. Now tell me about your day."

Jenny relaxed purposefully. She was pushing for information that really didn't concern her, and that he had promised to talk about when he got home. Besides, the day had dragged as she waited for his call, and she wasn't going to squander one more moment of it with things that could wait until he returned to be sorted out. "We planned Amy's birthday party," she said brightly. Silence drummed back at her from his end. "Devin, are you still there?"

"Yes, honey, I'm here," he said quickly, wondering if the date of Amy's birth had meant anything to her. "I'm sorry, something distracted me. A birthday party, huh? What tortures were assigned to me?"

Jenny laughed, clutching the casual endearment close.

"God, I love to hear you laugh."

She swallowed her heartbeat. "I'm afraid she wants you to blow up a zillion trillion balloons." She shifted in the bed.

Silence.

"Where are you?" he asked, knowing the answer.

The laughter left her voice. "In bed."

"Damn," he cursed softly. "What are you wearing?"

She raised the blankets and looked down at her plain cot-on nightdress. "See-through lace, black, slashed to my high," she said teasingly.

He groaned and cursed again.

"Shouldn't you be getting some sleep?" she asked coyly, mothering a grin.

"After your description of your nightgown, I doubt if I'll leep again until I'm back in your bed."

"Well, you did ask, and if all you plan on doing is sleeping when you get home, I'll tell the truth. I have on an old ankle-length white cotton gown, with part of the hem coming loose and a torn piece of lace at the neck."

Silence.

"No good. The black one is already embedded in my imagination." He laughed, his voice deep and throaty. Jenny was a woman made for black lace, warm, dark nights, satin sheets, and wild lovemaking. "God, woman, I miss you."

"Me too," she replied in a whisper.

"I talked to Dave Schaefer today. He says they'll only need me here for a couple of days. I can come home anytime after that."

"How's it going? Are you a TV celebrity now?"

"Don't even mention that TV thing. I hated every minute of it. But let's talk about you. I can't wait to be back at Claymore."

"I'll be here," she promised softly.

"In bed, in that black thing?"

"I don't own a black lace nightgown, Devin."

He growled into the phone. "We'll have to remedy that. I'll buy you every sexy nightgown I can find." He was quiet for a second. When he spoke again, his voice had lost all its playfulness. "Sam? I will be back. Please, remember that, and we'll discuss this mess about Amy then—that's a promise, too."

"I'll remember."

"Speaking of remembering, I forgot to give you Mrs Clay's diary before I left. Will you be needing it before I get back?"

She chuckled. "Changing the subject?"

"It's either that or a very sleepless, very painful, very long night... alone."

The loneliness of her own bed squelched all inclination to tease him further. "I'll probably need the diary before you get here. I think I can start the master-bedroom furniture tomorrow."

He laughed. "Now who's changing the subject? It's in the library, in the bottom right drawer of my desk. You shouldn't have any trouble recognizing it. It's a plain black leather-covered book."

"Devin?"

"Yes?"

"About what I asked before, that business about Amy? I'm sorry. It was really none of my business."

"Don't give it another thought," he said quickly. "Well, I gotta go. See you in a couple of days." The connection went dead.

Jenny hung up the phone slowly. She'd sensed a change in Devin's attitude, but she couldn't put her finger on when or why it had come about. Turning out the light, she slid down in the bed and closed her eyes, but they popped open again. He'd seemed almost eager to cut their conversation short. Why?

Chapter 9

The following day, bored with the late-morning meeting with his agent and publisher, Devin began thinking about his conversation with Jenny the night before. God, but she had sounded sexy. He smiled as he remembered the way she'd tried to change the subject, deriving a certain pleasure from knowing he could do that to her over a long distance phone line.

He just wished he hadn't panicked when she started talking about Amy and the home and virtually hung up on her. Paranoia was making him overly cautious. There wasn't any reason to think she'd find out anything until he could tell her. Amy's birth certificate and the—

He sat bolt upright in the chair. What had he done? If Jenny looked in his desk drawer, she'd find a lot more than the Clay diary. As if a snapshot had been thrust in front of him, he could see the diary lying on top of the Clinton family Bible, where he'd stuck it days ago. The Bible that held the notation marking Amy's removal to the orphanage. The two volumes were almost identical. What if she took the wrong one? Ice coursed through his veins.

"Excuse me, gentlemen," he blurted. Leaving the stunned men behind, he rushed into the outer office. "Miss Daniels, please call my home for me. It's very important." His blood pounded in his temples. *Please, let me be in time.* He could feel Jenny slipping through his fingers.

The secretary dialed and listened. She replaced the receiver. "I'm sorry, sir, the line is busy."

"Try it again," he ordered, then softened the command with "Please."

She dialed again and waited. As she replaced the receiver, she shook her head.

"Devin?" Dave Schaefer had followed him into the outer office, his face masked in concern. He'd seen that same look of desperate frustration on his client's face once before—the day he came back from Tennessee. "What is it?"

"An emergency at home," Devin explained, starting for the door. "I have to leave. Please call the airport and get me on the first flight to Baton Rouge."

The flight had taken forever. The airport had grounded the original plane with mechanical difficulties. While the ground crew did a flight check on the second plane, Devin called home. This time the phone rang and rang, but there was no answer. He hung up and dialed again. As the last of several rings died out, his flight was called. Damn! If only Dave had been able to book a ticket into Baton Rouge, he'd be nearly home. By the time he drove from New Orleans to Claymore, precious hours would have elapsed.

The New Orleans airport teemed with tourists arriving in and leaving the Crescent City, clogging the airport's access road. His car overheated, idling in stop-and-go bumper-to-bumper traffic with the air conditioner running. Twilight covered New Orleans by the time the lights of the city faded from his rearview mirror.

Doctor Hines's voice haunted him as he drove like a madman toward Claymore. *It's the girl's birth certificate and the Clinton family Bible.*

"Rebecca." Devin said aloud the name Jake Clinton had given Amy at birth. If Jenny found the Bible, maybe she wouldn't put two and two together. Belatedly he wished he'd put the Bible back in the safety deposit box along with the birth certificate.

"Who are you kidding?" He spit the words out into the gathering darkness, slamming his fist on the steering wheel. "Jenny's no fool. All she has to do is read the father's and mother's names." Devin's heart dropped to somewhere below his kneecaps. His only hope was to get to Claymore before she went in search of the diary. The car leapt forward.

The unnatural silence of a house normally ringing with Amy's laughter and constant chatter disturbed Jenny's concentration. She gave up trying to work. Hoping the soft breeze off the river would ease the throbbing in her temples, a result of missing lunch and spending three-quarters of an hour on thc phone with a supplier, assuring him he'd be paid if her shipment was sent C.O.D., she headed for the veranda.

Amy had gone with Mrs. Filbert to shop for birthday-party decorations. Jenny would be alone for hours.

Missing Devin and his daughter made her uneasy. Even though Devin had been loving and gentle since the night he found her in the rain, she still had no guarantee that her place in his life came with any permanent status. Finding her thoughts depressing and the solitude of the empty house increasing her restlessness, she decided to make her daily phone call to Belle earlier than usual.

"Hello, House of Miniatures," Belle's winded voice announced.

"Hi, Belle."

"Good Lord, girl, don't you have anything to do but bother me?" Jenny laughed. "Bit early for you to be calling, isn't it?"

"I was at loose ends."

"He's still in New York, I take it."

With the use of her usual bone-gnawing techniques, Belle had managed to pry a little of the information about what was happening between Devin and Jenny from her close-mouthed boss during their phone conversation the previous day.

"Yes, he's still in New York, you old busybody." Knowing Belle and Harry worried about her gave her a warm feeling of family. "How are things in the Crescent City?"

A pause hung over the conversation while Belle tried to settle herself on Jenny's stool and ended up standing, leaning her elbows on the glass countertop.

"We're fine. We took two house orders after I spoke to you yesterday."

"Wonderful. What kind?" Jenny crossed her fingers, hoping this meant her business was recovering from its slump, and that she'd be able to pay Devin back the extra money he'd included in the deposit. Surviving the separation from him, if that was what was to come, would be hard enough. The last thing she needed was to be indebted to him in any way.

"One is for a log cabin. It's for a little fella who's real upset 'cause his mama won't take him to Texas to fight Indians. I guess this is in the way of a substitute."

Jenny laughed.

"The other's for an overbearing mother with a spoiled brat on her hands."

Clearly recalling the type, Jenny sympathized. They wanted the best at the cheapest price. More often than not, they were the ones who wanted to buy the castle and refused to take no for an answer. "What did she order?"

"A turnabout."

Jenny straightened in the leather chair. "Can Harry do a turnabout?" She remembered her first try at that style of dollhouse. A bit more complicated than the conventional house, it was mounted on casters, so that it could be swung around. One side depicted a certain period of history and its architectural style, while the other side depicted another. She explained in detail to Belle how it was done.

"Harry will muddle through. Don't you be worrying about him. If he can handle me, he can handle anything." Belle chuckled. "Now, young lady, enough shoptalk. How's your handsome boss and his darling daughter?"

"They're both fine. Amy's shopping with her nurse for the gala birthday party she's planned for herself."

Belle could hear the loneliness in Jenny's voice. "How're you coming with the dollhouse furniture?"

Jenny sighed. "It's nearly finished. All I have left to do is the master bedroom."

"Since you're almost done, you'll be coming home soon." For someone who'd fought tooth and nail not to go to Claymore, she sure didn't sound like she was in any hurry to leave. Belle waited for a reply.

"I guess so," she said after a long pause. She didn't want to get into the whys and wherefores with Belle. It was just too new to discuss. Besides, she wasn't all that sure a relationship existed between her and Devin beyond her wistful imagination. His references to that elusive job that would keep her at Claymore were vague at best.

"I have one question. Do you love him?" Belle waited.

"Very much," Jenny admitted softly.

Belle exhaled. "Then don't rush back here. Harry and I have everything under control. You stay there and concentrate on the Montgomery family."

Jenny's throat filled. "Thanks, Belle."

"My pleasure. I even got Harry going to the market for my pralines, so we're all taken care of."

They chatted for a few more minutes before saying goodbye. About to get up and go in search of Harriet to see about her missed lunch, Jenny remembered the diary. She might as well save herself a trip later and look for it now.

The bottom drawer slid open easily. The plain black leather book Devin had described was on top. She congratulated herself on the ease with which she found it and removed the book. A similar book lying beneath it caught her attention. Oh, great, she thought. They were both old, both black, both covered with leather, the one difference being the piece of yellowed paper tucked between the pages of the book still in the drawer. Which one was the Clay diary?

She laid the first book aside and took the second one from the drawer. Inserting a nail at the paper marker, she flipped the book open. The curly letters at the top of the page read Births. Beneath it were listed names in various styles of handwriting.

She scanned the names. Suddenly she jolted to a stop. She knew that name very well.

Jennifer Samantha Tyson, born March 1, 1970, to Laura Clinton and Lester Tyson

She read on, her heart beating wildly, wondering vaguely why Devin had her family Bible, but too caught up in her reading to question.

Rebecca Jennifer Tyson, born June 7, 1988, to Jennifer Samantha Tyson and Devin Montgomery

Tears blurred the page. She'd had a girl, and Gramps had named her after his wife. The child's having an identity drew Jenny's pain from its hiding place. While she remained a nameless creature, it had been easier to bear. Now the hurt went beyond bearing. It tore at her, lacerating her heart. The whole nightmare took shape again. She wiped impatiently at the blinding tears.

Carefully she turned the yellowed pages. A note jammed between the next page caught her eye. She opened it and read the words scrawled in Dr. Hines's illegible script.

Rebecca—Asheville—Home of the Little Sisters of Mercy—June 7, 1988—T. A. Hines, M.D.

An address followed, but Jenny never read it. The words telling her Rebecca had been taken to the home the same night as the baby's death drew her attention. Why? Not for burial. Gramps had shown her the tiny grave and marker next to her grandmother's in the family cemetery behind the house.

She began to shake, nearly dropping the book. Placing it on the desk, she stared at it as though it had come alive. Her stomach knotted. Her head felt light. Her vision blurred and darkened.

"Now, Jenny," she told herself, "get yourself under control."

She took a deep breath, wiped her cold, sweaty hands on her jeans, and picked up the book. Slowly she read all the information again, fighting against acknowledging the facts as they fell into place.

Questions kept hammering at her, over and over. Why would Gramps have taken a dead baby to the convent? Unless... An idea began to form, an idea so preposterous even she couldn't believe it. Had her baby lived?

Frantically she tried to organize her thoughts. Bits and pieces of things teased at her mind. She looked at the Bible again. Quickly she paged back to the flyleaf. In Gramps's childish handwriting, the words *The Clinton Family Bible* glared up at her.

Abruptly, one thought insinuated itself ahead of all the rest. How had Devin gotten her family Bible? She felt like a white mouse in a maze, clawing her way to the answers, able to smell them, but unable to reach them.

"Okay," she told herself, "relax. Think this out."

The leather chair protested under her as she shifted her weight. She swung it to face the desk and the open Bible. Impatiently she swept the Clay diary to one side and pulled the Bible in front of her. Slowly she read each passage once more. The futility of her task nearly overwhelmed her before a thought struck her.

Jumping to her feet, she raced from the library and up the stairs, stopping at the doorway to Amy's room. Slowly she inched toward the cabinet housing the tiny carved bears and released the latch. The click scraped across her nerve endings like fingernails on a slate blackboard. *This is a real long shot,* she told herself.

Her hand shook. She reached for one of the figurines and drew back as though burned. Sucking in a deep breath, she slid her hand inside the cabinet and retrieved a tiny white pine bear. With great care, she turned it over and searched the bottom for the sign to confirm her suspicions.

On the bottom of one tiny paw, she found a small *C* etched into the wood. It was her grandfather's hallmark, the same mark he put on all his finished carvings.

Like a zombie, she placed the animal back on the glass shelf and removed another and then another, until she'd inspected each one. Each bore his hallmark.

For a long time, she remained in front of the cabinet, staring at the figurines behind the glass. Snippets of barely remembered conversation played in her head, chasing each other like autumn leaves in a brisk wind.

...at the children's home...

"My name is Amy, but I have two names."

"My grampy carved them for me."

Amy's birthday, June seventh...

How could she have been so blind? Amy was her daughter. For a moment, she stood very still, absorbing the miracle, letting it sink in. Then she laughed out loud as happy tears streamed down her cheeks. She threw back her head and shouted, "My baby is alive!" She felt light enough to float around the room.

Devin. She had to tell Devin. Their daughter was alive and right here in this house. She made a mad dash back to the library but came to a screeching halt with her hand resting on the phone. Devin had known all along. That was why the Bible was in his desk. He'd known, and he hadn't told her.

Crushing reality pricked her buoyant mood with its sharp talons, sending all her joy in her discovery crashing around her. Devin was out for revenge. He cared nothing for her. He'd fabricated the dollhouse job just to get her into his house, with the intention of humbling her. When that hadn't worked, he'd changed tactics and become the attentive male, wooing her with his charm, making sure she fell in love with him before he dealt the final crushing blow and sent her away from them—alone. A gut feeling told her she'd hit upon the only explanation for his sudden appearance in the shop and his acquisition of the building housing her shop. They were the clubs he'd needed to hold over her head.

Beneath all his subterfuge was the desire to give her everything she'd always longed for, only to snatch it back, leaving her with even less. Everything began to make horrible sense—his determination to bring her to Claymore, his slow, deliberate seduction, his need for her promise to be there when he returned, his evasiveness about who had put Amy in the children's home. He'd done it all just to make sure she wouldn't run off and cheat him of his final victory.

All her strength drained from her. She dropped into a chair like a rag doll. Amy was hers. But in finding her daughter, she'd lost the man she loved.

Her hand fell on the open Bible. With a fingertip, she traced the awkward lines of her grandfather's writing. Terrible memories threatened to rise to the surface. She had no strength to fight them off. Slowly she allowed herself to be ambushed by her emotions, to go back, back to the night of Amy's birth.

The day was hot, not surprising for June. Her pregnancy had been difficult, and her hands and feet were swollen with retained water, despite the pills Dr. Hines had given her and the care she took with her diet. Shoes had become a luxury she no longer could manage. Instead, she shuffled her large frame around shod in her grandfather's slippers. The tent-like dresses, once belonging to her grandmother, had replaced her own clothes months earlier.

Late afternoon found her settling her ungainly bulk in her favorite rocker on the front porch, the intermittent breeze cooling her flushed skin. An unreasonable restlessness tugged at her, and the oppressive heat only seemed to intensify it. Closing her eyes, she passed the frosty glass of lemonade she'd carried out with her across her forehead. The cold glass felt heavenly on her hot flesh.

"You okay, girl?" Gramps asked, gently touching her shoulder.

"I'm fine. Just hot." Words took energy, and the expulsion of energy made her hotter, so she kept her explanation simple. "It seems I pray all day for the cool nights, and when they come, I can't wait until morning." Further explanation of her restless nights would be wasted on him. She knew he heard her thrashing around, beleaguered by dreams, calling Devin's name.

The old man studied her closely before turning back to his work.

Jenny watched with envy as her grandfather began carving on a piece of pine. Because of her swollen fingers, she'd had to give up the pastime she'd learned to love. But she recalled with pleasure how easily she'd caught on to his teachings, and how good she was at it. When she had no longer been able to hold the knife, she'd missed it.

His rheumatic fingers handled the block of wood for some time before he made the first cut, searching for the identity of the animal encased within it. Jenny had scoffed at this belief as no more than another hill fancy—until she began to carve.

Each day, Jenny thanked God for Gramps. Through him, she'd garnered a new strength to see her through this time, to face Devin's abandonment.

"You're a good man, Gramps," she told him. Sighing, she laid her head back to catch the breeze, resting her glass on the top of her mounded stomach. The glass wobbled in her hand.

"That little one's mighty anxious to get out in the world," Gramps said with a chuckle, catching the movement of the glass.

She shifted the glass and rubbed a hand over her swollen belly.

"Thought any more about what you'll do after it's born?" He put the knife to the wood and made the first cut.

"It seems I've thought of little else. I'll need a job to support us. I guess that means moving to Asheville." As much as she hated leaving Gramps, she couldn't bring herself to stay there and live off him. Besides, a baby needed things, things it wouldn't get on Gramps's run-down farm and limited income.

The old man kept silent, his balding head bent over his work.

"Oh!" She sat up straight, clutching the rocker's arm.

"You okay, girl?" His blue eyes centered on his granddaughter.

"Just a crick in my back," she said, breathing deeply, rubbing at the offending ache and settling back.

A few minutes later, the sound of the glass smashing against the floor brought the old man to his feet. He laid his knife and the wood aside, walked calmly to Jenny and took her hand.

"It's time," he announced, and helped her to her feet, leading her inside the house to her bed.

Without another word, he went about preparing for the birth of his great-grandchild. When pains weren't ripping through her back and abdomen, Jenny observed his methodical labors.

"Shouldn't you call Dr. Hines?" she managed to ask after a particularly painful contraction.

"No need. 'Sides, it's too early yet, and he's out of town."

"But the baby's gonna come—" she cried, frightened for the new life.

"Jenny, I delivered your ma and your uncle Charlie, rest their souls. There ain't no reason I can't take care of this."

She relaxed. Gramps's frail appearance had always belied his inner strength. He'd lived through the deaths of his beloved Rebecca and their two children. Any man who could do that could deliver her child.

"I trust you, Gramps."

He glanced at her and quickly turned away to rip a sheet into pieces, his eyes troubled.

The pains grew progressively worse, tearing at her insides like some trapped wild creature. It went on for hours. She screamed for Devin, but all she ever heard was Gramps's soothing voice. She pleaded with Gramps to get Devin and bring him to her, but he never came.

In the early hours of morning, when the pain had become unbearable, she blessedly lost consciousness.

Late the following day, she awakened, and Gramps told her the baby had strangled on the umbilical cord. The pain of the birth had been bad enough, but the agony of her baby's death went all the way to her soul.

"What was it?" she whispered hours later.

"Now, ain't no sense in you knowin' that, Jenny," Gramps said, his eyes reflecting his sadness. "It ain't gonna bring it back, and it ain't gonna hurt any less with the knowin'." He took her hand and patted it. "Leave it be, girl. The babe's being looked after by God's own."

The phone stopped ringing just as Jenny roused herself from her memories. She started to reach for it but pulled her hand back. A few minutes later, it rang again. This time she made no move to answer it. She had no desire to talk to anyone. Soon the incessant ringing ceased.

Jenny stared blindly at it. Then the front door opened. Amy! Quickly she stuffed the paper marker between the pages of the Bible, closed it and replaced it in the drawer.

"Jenny! Jenny!" Amy's excited voice rang out through the empty house, wrapping around Jenny in a new way.

"I'm here, Scamp," she called.

How could Devin have done this to her? How could he have kept Amy's identity from her? Had he ever planned on telling her? And Gramps... God, she didn't even want to think about what he'd done. The pain was too excruciating to bear.

As she walked from the library, she schooled her features into a smile and removed all traces of the tears she'd shed in the past hours.

Squatting in anticipation of Amy vaulting into her arms and wrapping her limbs around her, Jenny gathered Amy to her chest, holding her tight, burying her face in the mop of hair that was so like Devin's and her own.

"We got rainbow balloons and streamers and a clown. Mrs. Filbert says it will be an auspicious 'casion."

"Auspicious occasion," Jenny corrected softly, choking back tears. "Where's Mrs. Filbert?" she asked, too brightly, glancing behind Amy.

"She's waiting in the car. She has an appointment to get her hair curled, and she wanted to make sure you were here before she left." Amy wiggled free of Jenny's embrace. "Let me go so I can tell her it's okay. I have lots of stuff to show you, too." She squirmed until Jenny released her, and then limped down the hall to wave to the waiting nurse and gather her treasures from where they were waiting by the front door.

For the next hour, Jenny dutifully oohed and aahed over the purchases. Having trouble concentrating on Amy's words, she hoped she was suitably impressed by the description of the cake to be constructed for the occasion. Through it all, her brain kept repeating, *This wonderful child is my daughter.*

Having run down at last, Amy cuddled into the circle of Jenny's arms amid the litter of tissue paper and balloons.

"Scamp..." Jenny said.

"Mmm?" Amy's voice was muffled with sleep.

"You told me once what your name means, but you said you had two names."

"Uh-huh."

Jenny held her breath. At last, the final proof. "What was the other one?"

"Becca," came her daughter's sleepy reply.

The bath foam sent the delicious aroma of honeysuckle into the heated room. Amy scooped up another handful of bubbles and blew them into the air. Several landed on Jenny's leg and popped.

Just like my dreams, she thought, rubbing her fingertip over the dark circle the bubble left behind on the denim. God, she had to stop thinking about it right now. Every time she did, tears gathered in her burning eyes. Undoubtedly the discerning little girl playing in the bathtub would soon notice and begin firing a barrage of unanswerable questions at her. And the last thing she wanted was to have to explain to her daughter that the child's beloved popie was a deceitful liar.

"I'm glad Mrs. Filbert isn't here," Amy chirped, popping another bubble. "She never lets me play in the bathtub. And she never lets me use bubble bath. She says only grown-up ladies use perfume in the tub."

"Then this will be our secret," Jenny promised, determinedly plastering a smile on her lips. "And since this is my bathroom and my bath foam, you can play until you shrivel up."

Her mind tripped to all the baths she should have given her daughter, and all the millions of other everyday things out of which she'd been cheated—first by Gramps, then Devin. Neither of them would ever know the extent of the heartache they'd caused.

She quickly corrected that last thought. Devin knew. Devin knew, damn him to hell. He knew, and he relished every painful moment she suffered. What in God's name had she done that was bad enough to deserve what he'd had planned for her? He hadn't cared enough back in Tennessee to be this cruel. But she couldn't think what else...

Could he possibly believe she'd put their daughter in the children's home? Before she could give it more thought, Amy's voice cut in.

"Jenny?"

Shaking herself mentally, she peered down at Amy.

"Yes?"

"Are you mad at me for blowing bubbles on you?"

Jenny slid from her perch atop the vanity and knelt next to the tub. "Of course not. What ever gave you that idea?"

"Well, a minute ago, you looked real mean. And Mrs. Filbert always gets very angry when I splash her."

Cautioning herself to keep a tight wrap on her thoughts until she was alone, Jenny kissed Amy's cheek. "I was just thinking about something that made me mad, but it wasn't you. You can splash me all you want."

"What were you thinking about?"

As much as she loved her daughter, Amy's never-ending curiosity was often a trial. "Nothing, Scamp. Just something that got broken," she added, hoping the lie would stem the flow of questions.

"Can you fix it? Will Popie be mad?" Amy's eyes, so like her father's, grew large and bright. "It seems like Popie's always mad lately."

"No, it can't be fixed," she said, realizing it hadn't been a lie, but a reference to the condition of her heart. "And I don't think your popie will be mad. It wasn't anything he wanted." Forcing a smile, she dipped her hand into the water to retrieve the washcloth. "Lean forward, and I'll wash your back." Amy did as she asked. "Let's talk about your birthday party. Do you have all the invitations written?"

Amy shook her head vigorously. Her soaking hair sprayed water over Jenny and the bathroom floor as if she were a wet puppy. Jenny squealed, threw the washcloth into the air, and flopped backward hard on her rump.

Amy flashed Jenny an impish grin where she lay in a puddle of warm, soapy water. "Baths are fun with you."

Pulling herself up, Jenny scowled playfully at her. "They won't be if we get any more water on the floor and it leaks through the ceiling." She spread a towel to absorb the puddles before taking up the washcloth and resuming her task of bathing her daughter. "But if you don't tell, I won't," she added, close to Amy's ear.

Amy giggled and contented herself with poking at the remaining bubbles. She grew quiet. Jenny had seen this before. Usually it meant her little brain was careening down a new path, gathering questions to baffle some poor unsuspecting adult. This time was no exception.

"Jenny, do you believe in angels?"

The hand smoothing the cloth over Amy's pink skin slowed. "I don't know, honey. I never gave it much thought."

Again Amy became silent. This wasn't a thoughtful silence. Obviously something was bothering the child. "Amy?"

Raising her serious eyes to Jenny, Amy asked, "You won't laugh at me, will you? Mrs. Filbert said I was being foolish."

Taking Amy's shoulders, Jenny turned her to face her. "I'd never, ever laugh at anything you told me, unless you wanted me to."

Amy threw her arms around Jenny's neck and squeezed. "I love you."

Unmindful of the water seeping into her clothes from Amy's body or the growing pool forming beneath her knees, Jenny hugged her close, relishing the feel of her daughter's warm little body snuggled against hers. "I love you, too." She blinked against the gathering moisture that had hovered just below the surface of her eyes all afternoon. "What do you want to know about angels?"

Amy settled back into the water, automatically extending her arm for Jenny's attention. "Well, Reverend Mother at the home says my grampy is an angel now. Do you think if I pray real, real hard, God would let Grampy come to my party?"

Swallowing the lump that had taken up residence in the middle of her throat, Jenny wiped at the tear rolling down her cheek. She didn't want to talk about him, think about him, but it was impossible to avoid it without pricking Amy's curiosity.

Thankfully, before Jenny had to formulate a reply, Amy began talking again. "Reverend Mother said Grampy had a special place in heaven, 'cause he was so special here on earth. Do you think that's true?"

"Why was he so special?" she managed.

The child furrowed her forehead and raised her splayed fingers. Ticking off each finger, she began to enumerate her grandfather's virtues. "'Cause he made all those bears for me. 'Cause he came to see me every Wednesday. 'Cause he was my friend. And 'cause he told me all about my mommy and my gramma." She dropped her hands and busied herself molding a mound of white foam in her lap.

Jenny's hands stilled. "Stories about m—your mommy and gramma?"

"Yeah. My Grampy said my mommy was beautiful, and she loved me a lot. I asked him to bring her to the home, but he said she went away, and he didn't know where to find her. But he said if he knew where she was he would bring her to me. Why do you 'spose she did that, Jenny?"

The child's words hit Jenny solidly in her heart. She wondered if Amy's recollection of the old man's words was accurate, or was just what the child had wanted to hear? She knew well Amy's tendency to create fantasies out of her active imagination. Could this be just another one, or had Gramps tried to find her?

"Jenny?" Amy turned to look at her. "Why do you 'spose my mommy went away?"

Clearing her throat, Jenny choked out an explanation. "I...I... Maybe she... I'm sorry, Amy, I don't know. But I'm sure she must have had a very good reason to leave you."

Amy shook her head and grew sullen. "Popie says she didn't want to be a mommy, and he guessed she didn't love me." Amy reached for Jenny's face, framing it in her small hands. "Do you think that's true?"

Wordlessly Jenny shook her head, wondering how Devin could be cruel enough to tell a child such a lie. "No, Scamp. I know she must have loved you very much, and she wanted to be your mommy more than anything else in the whole world."

A brilliant smile streaked across Amy's face. "Me too. I'm sure I got put in that home by mistake."

From a child's lips to God's ears, Jenny thought.

With Amy bathed and tucked into bed for the night, Jenny took her shower, slipped into an ivory gown and robe, collected the Bible and wandered into the sitting room. She curled up on the couch and thought about her grandfather making weekly trips for four years to see his great-granddaughter. Easing a troubled conscience, no doubt, she surmised callously.

Well, Devin wouldn't have that problem. He obviously had no conscience, if he could devise such a heartless plan. But his plan had one flaw. Her hand caressed the cover of the book on her lap. He'd made a disastrous mistake by leaving the Bible where she could find it.

She'd stay at Claymore until he came home, but only because Amy was there. Once he returned, she'd go back to New Orleans. The worry about losing her business no longer entered her mind. It hadn't taken much thinking to figure out it never had been in jeopardy. Devin had other quarry—her peace of mind and possession of their child. However, in the end, she'd be the winner, because she'd surrender neither to him without a fight.

Chapter 10

Darkness had descended when Devin pulled into the drive at Claymore. Despite the lone light burning in the sitting-room window, a disturbing quiet hung over the house, as if it were deserted. Fear threatened to choke him. Guilt ate at his insides. A dark, stifling fog of foreboding stole over him. Had she found the Bible and returned to New Orleans without waiting to hear him out?

As he walked through the big front doors, he prayed he was wrong. Tension drained from his stiff muscles when he stepped into the sitting room and saw her curled up on the sofa. His whole body reacted to the picture of her hair spread out behind her head like a dark velvet fan, her body molded by a pale ivory negligee and peignoir, but when he spotted the Bible clutched to her breast, his heart sank.

She stirred, alerted to his presence by his sharp intake of breath. Sitting, she stared at him for some time before she spoke. "I didn't expect you so soon, but it's just as well you're here." The stony expression on her face told him that hours had passed since her discovery of the Bible, hours she'd used to gather the strength she would need for this confrontation.

Her control amazed Devin—or *was* it control? He looked closer at her. Her eyes were large pools of pain, surrounded by the evidence of the tears she'd shed, but there were no tears now. Before him stood a statue, cold and lifeless, impenetrable, devoid of any emotion.

Words escaped him. What could he say? What explanation could he offer? *I'm sorry I didn't tell you our baby is alive, and you've been living with her, laughing with her, loving her, for weeks?* He collapsed into a nearby wing chair and buried his face in his hands.

She laid the Bible on the table between them and raised her cold eyes to study his bent head.

Devin looked up. "Jenny, I—"

"No, Devin. There's no need to explain. I found it this morning, and I've had plenty of time to think. Little by little, I've pieced most of the story together. What I don't know doesn't matter. What I *want* to know is, when did you plan on telling me—that is, if you ever did?"

He shuddered at the ice in her voice and wished for the warm, loving woman he'd left behind only yesterday. Having already made up his mind to be totally honest with her, he took a deep breath and waded into the explanation he knew would only drive her farther from him.

"In the beginning, when Dr. Hines—"

"Dr. Hines?"

"Yes. He wrote me to come to Eden right after your grandfather died." He paused, waiting for her reaction.

Steeped in icy silence, she stared through him.

"Jenny." He extended his hands in supplication. "You've got to understand. I thought you'd left me because I couldn't make a commitment, because you wanted a way out of the hills and I wasn't providing it. I thought you didn't want our baby and put her in that children's home. I wanted you to suffer for that, to hurt, to pay for giving Amy to strangers." He dropped his hands. "God help me, I had no idea what your grandfather had done until—"

"Until the night you charmed me into taking you into my bed?"

"No!" He jumped to his feet. "It wasn't like that, and you know it!" he snapped.

"Do I?" She shook her head. "Never mind. Go on. What changed your mind? Was it my pitiful confession?"

Her cold eyes bored into him. "I'd begun to have doubts before that, but I couldn't make any sense out of it until that night. I knew then, I'd misjudged you all along." He took a step toward her, desperate for her to believe him.

"Jenny, honey, I tried to tell you the night I came to your room, but you fell asleep. Then I planned on telling you the next morning, but I got called away. By that time, I'd also realized I'd used the circumstances around Amy to cover my real reason—my hurt pride."

"I could have forgiven that. I could have forgiven the convenient excuses you've always had at the ready for anything you did. What I can never forgive is your theft of the time I could have had with my daughter." She searched his face for something to crack the awful cold encasing her heart, something to erase the knowledge of the betrayal of one of the only two men she had ever loved and trusted. There was nothing.

"I would have told you about Amy, I swear," he said, reaching for her and flinching away when she neither moved toward nor away from him, but looked at his hand as if it were contaminated.

"When Devin? When? When she graduated? Or when she got married? How much of my child's life did you plan on stealing from me before you told me?'' she asked, in a hushed, chilly monotone.

He paced the length of the room, running a hand through his hair. Loosening his tie, he ripped it from his neck, throwing it to the floor. ''You've got this all wrong. I would never hurt you.''

''Not now,'' she said flatly. ''Not ever again.''

In the long hours while she waited for him, she'd had time to think and had figured it all out. It all fit so nicely: the loving phone calls, his entreaties to her to remain at Claymore. But the hardest to bear was his seduction of her. She'd taken him into her bed and given him all she had to give, while he'd laughed at how easily he'd won. The shame was overwhelming, the pain excruciating.

Her controlled calm scared the hell out of him. He wished she'd scream, stamp her feet, hit him. Anger would be preferable, and far easier to deal with, than this constrained reserve. At least then he'd know she felt something.

''I suppose the old man who lied to me and took *Rebecca* never meant to hurt me, either.''

''I can't speak for him, but no, I don't think he did. Perhaps he felt he did what he thought best.''

''Best for who? Himself? Me? You? Amy?''

He came to stand before her. ''God, Jenny, believe what you must about him. I understand that, but try to see that what I did, I did because I hurt.''

She sprang from the couch, the icy calm imprisoning her emotions melting under the heat of her sudden rage. Slapping his hands away, she skirted him and went to stare out the dark window.

''I hurt, too, Devin, worse than either of you will ever know. I'd lost the one man I loved beyond my life, and our child, in nine short months. Don't think for a minute I didn't hurt. It never seems to stop hurting." Her arms curled around her in an unconscious effort to ward off the pain.

"You weren't the only one hurting, Jenny," he ground out, suddenly blinded to her anguish by the memory of his own pain.

"Don't expect me to feel sorry for you, Devin."

His fist slammed the tabletop. A Dresden vase wobbled and fell, sending rainbow-colored bits of porcelain across the rug. "Dammit! I don't want your pity. I never wanted your pity. I want your love and your trust."

A cold, brittle laugh issued from her. "You had both at one time, until you threw them in my face, until I discovered your deceit. For a man looking for trust and love, you have a damn funny way of achieving your goal. So spare me the details of your *pain.*"

Her words cut through him like a knife. He'd never known Jenny to be anything less than understanding. Dammit, he'd counted on that when the time came to tell her about Amy. "No. No, I won't. It's about time you heard what your selfishness did." He wrenched her around by the shoulders to face him. "You damn near killed me when you disappeared from my life without a word. Doesn't that count for anything? Do you know what it feels like to die a little at a time, to bleed to death through your heart?"

Fat tears rolled down her cheeks. "Shattered hearts don't bleed, Devin. They just explode inside you and leave an empty, aching hole."

"But the empty space fills with anger, Jenny. When Dr. Hines told me I'd had a daughter for four years I never knew about, and you gave her away because you didn't want her, I experienced more anger than I'd ever known before in my life. It choked me until I had to find somewhere to vent it."

"And that's where I came in. It didn't matter that an old man had deprived us of our child. All that mattered to you was your sick, misdirected revenge," she whispered.

The torment in her quiet voice broke through Devin's anger as nothing else could have. He pulled her to him, but he might as well have had his arms around a tree. She neither pulled away nor leaned into him. His arms fell to his sides. She turned to face the window. "I would have been there, if I'd known. You have to believe that." He forced himself not to touch her. "Why didn't you come to me, instead of leaving?" he asked, unwilling to admit to the truth of her accusations.

Her head swiveled to face him. "Because you'd made it quite clear that marriage wasn't a part of your plans for the future. You didn't want to be encumbered by a family. You had your career." She turned from him and continued to stare into the darkness. "I thought I'd wronged you, so I wrote those damn letters, begging you to forgive me, to think about our child, to let you know I'd settle for whatever crumbs of a relationship you'd offer me. It took eight weeks of pleading and humiliating myself for me to realize you didn't care. Even then, before I finally gave up, I went back to Tennessee. But you were gone."

"Jenny." He placed his hands on her shoulders. "I waited. I had no idea why you'd left or where you'd gone. I never got those letters. I told you that. Your grandfather must not have mailed them," he said, grasping at any hope he could to put an end to this. "I swear, I never got them."

"So you say." She pulled free. "Why didn't you come looking for me, if you loved me so much?"

"I did. Your father said you ran away. I didn't believe him at first, but when I saw your things were gone, I didn't have a choice. I tried to get him to tell me where you'd gone, but he wouldn't. So I checked the bus station, but the agent couldn't, or wouldn't, remember seeing you." He'd never known such frustration in his life. He had to find a way to get through to her.

"That shouldn't have stopped you." Her words sliced through the room the way her X-acto knife cut through a piece of soft balsa. "You had no trouble finding me a few weeks ago."

"Private detectives cost money, money I didn't have," he said, his eyes focused on her reflection in the window. "Back then, I was lucky if I ate. Hiring a private detective was a dream I couldn't afford. I could only wait. And then I told myself I didn't care, I could live without you. But it was a lie."

"Too bad. The one you hired this time had no trouble. Oh, yes," she added when he flinched, "I figured that out, too. But don't kid yourself—lack of money wasn't your only excuse back then. If you really cared, you would have found a way." Turning to him, she studied his face for a time, as if searching for the truth. Finding nothing to satisfy her need, she walked around him to sit on the sofa.

Devin suddenly felt deflated. Had he been so shallow back then? He remembered saying he'd have sold his soul to find her. He also remembered the emptiness, the utter loneliness, he'd experienced, and how he'd existed in a daze for months after she left. There had been anger, pain and even tears, but none of that could compare with what she must have gone through, believing her child dead and its father oblivious of them both.

"I love you, Jenny," he said, coming back to sit near her and take her cold fingers in his. "I'm sorry for everything."

"So am I, Devin, so am I." Fatigue weighed her down. She was tired of the lies, the deceit, the arguments that led nowhere. She slipped her fingers from his. "I'm going back to the city in the morning. I'll take Mrs. Clay's diary and finish the furniture in the shop." When he would have spoken, she stopped him with a raised hand. "Don't insult my intelligence more by repeating your fears about the diary leaving the house, or the threats about the money. I have a safe in the shop. The diary will be kept there whenever I'm not consulting it for measurements. As for the money... I'll pay you back anything you paid beyond the cost of the job. You can't manipulate me anymore. There's nothing left to threaten me with."

"I don't give a damn about the diary or the money. I want you to stay and help me straighten this out. Keep the damn money!" he exploded.

"For services rendered?" she returned acidly, trying not to think about the time she'd spent in his arms.

Defeat settled over Devin, smothering further argument. "What will I tell Amy?"

"I'm sure you'll think of something. You've become quite good at tall tales. Isn't that what they pay you for?" She rose and moved to the doorway. Keeping her back to him, she spoke low, but firmly. "I don't want to disrupt Amy's life any more than necessary. She can stay here for now, but when I get back to New Orleans, I'm consulting an attorney. I plan on suing you for custody of my daughter."

"Sam, please," he whispered, hoping the endearment would break through to her. He felt his heart tear from his chest when his impassioned pleas fell on deaf ears.

"No, Devin. I'm not Sam. I'll never be Sam again. She's truly dead now. You killed her when you decided to keep my daughter's identity from me."

As she climbed the stairs, she never looked back. Had she done so, she would have seen Devin crumple before her eyes. Not only had he lost Jenny, but there was every chance she'd take Amy, too.

* * *

"Sit," Belle commanded, pointing to the chair situated near the workbench in the back of the shop.

"Belle, I..."

"I said, sit." The sternly issued command left no room for argument.

Several days had passed since Jenny had returned to New Orleans, days during which she'd offered no explanation for her sudden appearance. The Masons had asked for none. But in the interim, Jenny had changed. She'd become quiet, sullen, and increasingly irritable. She'd almost stopped eating entirely, as was evident in the noticeable shedding of pounds she couldn't afford to lose. Work had become a buffer against reality. She dived into it with a vigor that exhausted Belle to watch. Allowing her this respite had Belle's nerves stretched to the breaking point.

"Harry's at the dentist. The shop's closed. There's no one to disturb us. Talk," Belle commanded. Settling her girth on a chair to Jenny's left, she folded her arms over her chest and waited.

"There's nothing to say," Jenny said with downcast eyes.

"You've been walking around here like a ghost with no home. You've taken on the work of ten people. How can you sit there and tell me there's nothing to say?" Belle took Jenny's hand in her chubby fingers. "When we came to work for you, you reminded me of a beaten dog. I could never figure out what happened to suppress that spirit that sparkled in your eyes from time to time. That beaten look's there again, but worse this time.

"You've become like my own over the past couple of years, so you'll have to forgive me if I exercise a mother's curiosity and pry. Harry and I care about you. Neither one of us can spend another day watching you tear yourself apart, a little at a time."

Jenny looked at Belle with watery eyes.

"Come on, honey, tell old Belle what's troubling you, and we'll see if we can't work it out together." She patted the slim, cool fingers lying across her palm. "Harry says there's a rainbow in every storm, all you have to do is look for it."

Suddenly the burden became too overwhelming for Jenny to shoulder alone. She knew if she didn't share it with someone she'd go quietly mad.

"Amy Montgomery is my daughter."

The words gouged a path through the silence of the stuffy little room. For once, the inimitable Belle was speechless. Never would she have guessed that this had caused Jenny's depression.

"From the beginning," she said encouragingly.

Starting with the real reason for Devin's commissioning her to do the dollhouse furniture, Jenny related the events leading up to her unannounced return to New Orleans. Leaving out nothing, including the night she'd spent in Devin's bed, she concluded with her plan to sue for custody of Amy.

"And what about Amy?" Belle asked quietly. "What do you think this court battle will do to her?"

"I want my daughter with me. I was robbed of her infancy. I'll not be robbed of her childhood, too," Jenny countered hotly. She didn't want to drag Amy through court, but Devin would never give her up willingly.

"Doesn't she have some say in this? She seemed to love Devin very much. What will it do to her if you take her away from him?"

The same thought had plagued Jenny night and day. "She'll get used to it. She'll see him whenever she wants. I'd never keep them apart."

"And you think that'll compensate for her broken heart?"

Jenny rose and walked away from Belle. "Belle, please. I thought I'd get some compassion, some understanding, from you. Instead you've taken Devin's side."

"No." Belle jumped to her feet and grabbed Jenny's arm, spinning her to face her. "If I've taken sides, I'm on Amy's. She has two parents she loves a lot. Her parents love her. But the one thing they're overlooking is, they love each other, as well. There must be a compromise that won't tear this child's heart out. She deserves to have both of you, not her mother part of the year and her father on holidays. Jenny, honey, you've got to search your heart and make peace with your granddad and Devin and yourself, before you shatter all their lives, and yours, too."

Jenny's shoulders sagged. "Devin doesn't love me, and I don't think I'll ever forgive him, or my grandfather. They took something irreplaceable from me." Hot tears rolled down her cheeks.

Gathering the young woman to her ample bosom, Belle rubbed her back. Her gut feeling told her Jenny was wrong about Devin not loving her. "We'll figure this out. Seems to me, if you're looking to untangle this mess, you should start at the beginning."

Sniffing loudly, Jenny accepted Belle's offered handkerchief and sat. "I've tried to understand, tried to work it out, until I think my head will burst."

"Honey, you're never going to understand the things someone else does unless you hear it from the horse's mouth." Belle sat across from Jenny, holding her hand.

Her sad blue eyes, puffed and red now, turned to the older woman. "I don't understand. I talked to Devin, and all he could tell me was more lies."

"Lies? Are you sure they were lies? What about those letters?"

"What about them?"

"If they were sent and he didn't get them, where are they? Come on, Jenny, you're an intelligent woman. Stop selling yourself on Devin's guilt, and look at this with some perspective."

"He probably has the letters tucked away in another drawer somewhere," she replied scathingly.

"You're selling yourself a bill of goods. You want Devin to be guilty. Maybe you want to punish him, maybe not, but you're working awful hard to make him the bad guy. I think he's as much a victim as you."

Jenny stared at Belle, aghast that she could say something so preposterous. "Devin, a victim?"

"Yes, a victim. He had something stolen from him, too. He lost you and his child. He just happened to find her a little earlier than you did."

"But why didn't he tell me right away? Why?" Sobs were wrenched from her as she relived the pain of his betrayal. She buried her head in her hands, trying to fight against Belle's corkscrew logic.

"He said he tried." Belle gave Jenny a moment to get control. "Jenny, give him the benefit of the doubt."

"He lied to me, Belle. He allowed me to believe Amy was another woman's child."

"And you've been completely honest, I suppose—about everything."

Thinking back, Jenny recalled the lies she had told Devin. But they hadn't been meant to hurt Devin, only to deter him, to protect her. *Were they?* a small, persistent voice asked. *Didn't you try to make him see how little he meant to you, how little you needed him and a child in your life? Weren't you trying to hurt him?*

Taking satisfaction from Jenny's thoughtful silence, Belle waited.

The hurt would no doubt be excruciating, but Jenny knew in her heart that she'd never have a moment's peace until she found out what had happened the night of Amy's birth. Gramps couldn't tell her, but the man who'd signed that sheet of paper in the Bible might be able to. Dr. Hines.

"Belle, I'm going upstairs to pack. Call the airport and get me a seat on the next available flight to Asheville, North Carolina."

"North Carolina? Jenny, the old man's gone. What do you expect to find there, besides a lot of painful memories?"

Jenny stopped halfway across the floor and pivoted to face Belle. "The truth, Belle. I'm going to find the truth."

Devin fingered the old Bible Jenny had overlooked when she made her hasty exit. In the beginning, when Dr. Hines had given it to him, he hadn't wanted to look at it, sure it would compound the raw pain of Jenny's betrayal. But he'd finally read the words that helped damn her. Last week, he'd taken it from the safety deposit box and he'd read them again, looking for the answers to the questions that had plagued him.

Now he read them one more time, through the eyes of a man who'd destroyed everything and everyone he loved because of pride. Throwing the book on the desk, he stood and began pacing the length of the library.

The last days had been an ongoing nightmare. Aside from being constantly assailed by his own guilt, and living with the fact that he'd probably lost Jenny forever, he'd had to contend with a weeping child who didn't understand adult logic. Nothing he had said or could say pacified Amy as to Jenny's sudden departure. Not a night had passed that Amy hadn't cried herself into a fitful sleep, wanting her friend to return.

Once the misunderstanding about Amy's stay in the children's home had been cleared up in his mind, all he'd ever wanted was to tell Jenny the truth. It didn't take a rocket scientist to figure out that he'd screwed up. He should have woken her and told her that first night. Or had he still been trying to salve his pride? Had he still been making her pay for walking out on him?

He'd gratefully accepted every obstacle to his confession, allowing Jenny to deter him, putting off the moment of reckoning, knowing in his heart what the result would be—that he'd kill any hope of ever winning Jenny's love again.

Every time he lost Jenny, a piece of his soul was cut away. He'd nearly bled to death the first time. Terror of it happening again had sealed his lips. Instead of inflicting the fatal wound on himself, he'd sliced Jenny open. And he'd been right to be afraid. When the truth won out, he'd lost her again.

"Damn!" Anxious, frustrated fingers clawed through his tousled hair, working their way down to massage the stiff muscles at his nape.

Sweet, innocent Amy had ended up caught in the crossfire of their emotional struggle. She, more than either Jenny or himself, didn't deserve the hell that they had subjected her to—that *he* had subjected her to.

The last thing he wanted was to face Jenny in a courtroom and do battle for their daughter. Amy would have suffered immeasurably by the time their attorneys finished dragging the dirt of their relationship through the legal system. He swore he'd do anything to see that Amy would never be exposed to that.

To prevent it, he had to convince Jenny to change her mind, to make her understand, to bring her home. He started for the door, pulling his keys from his pocket, and changed his mind. Amy and he were alone in the house. Mrs. Filbert would return soon. He'd wait. Frustrated by the delay, he threw himself down behind the desk and stared at the phone. Did he dare call and give her time to leave? No, she wouldn't run anymore, not with Amy here. He reached for the phone, picked up the receiver and dialed.

"Jenny?" he said, when a female voice answered.

"No. This is Belle Mason. Miss Tyson is out of town for a few days. Can I help you?"

"Where did she go?" He tried desperately to keep the anxiety out of his voice.

Belle hesitated. "I'm sorry, Devin. I can't tell you that."

"Why? Belle, I have to talk to her."

"Leave her alone, Devin. She needs time to come to grips with this. Can I give her a message?"

"No. No message." He was still holding the receiver to his ear when he heard the decisive click of the severed connection.

Chapter 11

Jenny maneuvered the rental car off the road and onto one of the many lookouts dotting the Blue Ridge Parkway. She told herself it would have been a sin not to stop at one of them and admire the grandeur of the Great Smokies, but in her heart, she knew it was really to delay coming face to face with another piece of her past.

The car door swung open and gravel crunched beneath her sneakers as she alit and ambled to the railing along the four-thousand-foot drop. Pulling on her cardigan to ward off the chill of the late-May breeze, she looked out over an endless sea of mountaintops. Cloaked in a hazy fog, their bluish crags piercing the clouds, their feet anchored deep in the rich Carolina soil, the mountains seemed to stand in brooding silence—listening to the wind whispering tales of the immigrants who'd settled there.

Why had she waited so long to come back here? Why never even a postcard to a lonely old man, to say she was okay? In the beginning she could blame the still-fresh pain of the memories the place held, or even the meager salary she'd earned waiting tables at the Café du Monde in the French Quarter. Her salary had been barely enough to provide her with life's necessities, much less bus fare.

And as the years sped by and the sharp edges of the memories softened into a blunt ache, the shop had become the focus of her life. To her shame, she'd deliberately pushed the tiny Blue Ridge Mountain hamlet and everything in it—including her grandfather—from her mind.

The familiar silhouette of Grandfather Mountain, to the north, told her she was nearing the small town of Eden and the truth behind her grandfather's lies. She shivered. As much as she longed to know the cause of what had happened on that hot June night six years ago, she dreaded it, as well. Loving her grandfather as she did, she knew in her gut that what she'd learn in Eden would destroy that love.

In the days since she walked away from Claymore, she'd begun to see Devin's reasoning. Knowing how bitterly she'd come to view what she saw as his desertion of her and their child, she also knew that, under the same circumstances, she'd have longed for a piece of his flesh, too.

But her grandfather hadn't had bitterness and hatred as a motive for his actions. That was what made the forgiving impossible.

Both she and Devin had been victims, as Belle had pointed out, victims of an old man's betrayal. A small part of her still rebelled at thinking of him in that light. She'd trusted him. Turning off that trust entirely was difficult. The time had come to find out what had motivated him, if indeed it was anything more than the ravages of age on his mind.

Sighing, she slipped back into the car. On the seat beside her, a paper bag held a book she'd purchased in the airport. Tracing her fingers over the edges, she used it as a talisman to give her the strength she needed for what lay ahead, and the reassurance to face it. Starting the car, she pulled it onto the road, heading resolutely north to Eden.

The town of Eden had a new face. Shops selling ski apparel and equipment to skiers who frequented Devils Mountain, Sugar Mountain and the other nearby slopes, dotted Main Street. Every now and again, Jenny glimpsed a familiar building, but the business it housed had taken on a new name. A part of her mourned the quaint little town of her memories.

Main Street was quiet. The Singing on the Mountain festival wouldn't take place for another few weeks, when the ski season came to an end. Jenny had loved that restful time when the town lay in wait for the next onslaught of tourists who would descend on it for a brief taste of the Appalachian way of life.

Leaving the main thoroughfare, she turned into Franklin Square and parked in front of a newly painted turn-of-the-century house. A sign—DR. T. A. Hines, M.D.—swung from a bracket on one of the porch posts. While she sat staring at it, the front door opened and an aged Iris Harrison helped a young mother and her four children down the stairs.

Iris waved goodbye to them, glanced in Jenny's direction and pivoted back toward the house. She'd gone halfway up the brick walk when she turned, the skirt of her crisp white uniform swirling around her legs. The nurse's sharp eyes zeroed in on Jenny. For a time, she studied her. Then with a curt shake of her salt-and-pepper head, she continued up the stairs and disappeared inside the house.

Jenny watched her go. Her gaze remained glued on the front door long after it closed behind Iris. She half expected the nurse to come out and demand she come inside.

Jenny's fingers gripping the steering wheel; she lowered her forehead against the cool, smooth plastic. Minutes passed while she gathered her courage around her. Finally, she straightened, plucked her purse from the seat, smoothed the collar of her blue silk blouse and reached for the door handle. Pausing for a second, she ran her hand over the airport bag containing a copy of Devin's latest book and got out.

The smell of antiseptic, stale cigar smoke and Iris's gardenia perfume filled the waiting room. Jenny wrinkled her nose and looked around her. The office hadn't escaped the effects of modernization. Along the wall where the overstuffed chintz-covered settee had stood, a wood-and-aluminum bench was surrounded on all sides by brown molded plastic chairs. The frayed brown rug had been replaced by beige indoor-outdoor carpeting that matched the ivory silk draperies. A huge Boston fern Iris had babied for over twenty years filled the bay window.

"So it was you," came Iris's high-pitched voice from the other side of an opening cut in the far wall. "Thought so, but figured you'd come in on your own, if you had a mind to." Iris obviously remembered her furtive departure after Amy's birth and hadn't forgiven her for it.

"Is Dr. Hines busy?" Jenny asked, not in the mood to explain her past transgressions, a part of her praying he couldn't see her, the other part wanting to finish with this and put it behind her.

Iris consulted the appointment book. "He's free for thirty-five minutes." She pointed her finger in the direction of a door marked Office. "He's waitin' for you. Told him I thought you'd be in, after I saw you sittin' out front in your car."

"Thanks." Jenny walked toward the door Iris had indicated, smiling to herself at the way the doctor's nurse had picked up the abbreviated speaking style of the man she'd worked for most of her life.

"Jenny! Couldn't believe my ears when Iris said you were here." The chubby doctor pushed himself from his creaking chair and skirted the desk to embrace her. Pulling back to arm's length, he let his gaze drift over her casual jeans, blouse and sneakers. "You look like one of them tourists." He grinned and winked, guiding her to the chair fronting the desk.

"I feel like one," she admitted, sitting and crossing her legs as he took his recently vacated seat. "Everything's so different."

"Yup. We're a growin' town they tell me. Hear tell someone's puttin' in a McDonald's." He shook his head. "As if the town wasn't stuffin' itself with enough cholesterol already. Damn fast food. Don't know why the people're in such an all-fired hurry to kill themselves." Noticing her lack of attention, he leaned his forearms on the desk. "What brings you back, girl?"

"My baby," she said, studying his reaction closely.

"You're about a year too late. The girl's father came for her. No one knew where you went. When old Jake died, his last request was that the girl go with family." He glanced at her. "You did know Jake passed on, didn't you?"

She nodded. "Devin told me."

The fact that he could detect no remorse in her tone or her features disturbed the old doctor. As he recalled, she and Jake had been pretty close. "It probably ain't none of my business, but...in for a penny, in for a dime..." he mumbled. "Why'd you run off, girl?"

"I had to get away." *Far away,* she amended. God, she didn't want to talk about this. It hurt too much. She didn't even want to think about it.

"Away? Jenny, you'd just had a baby. Most women feel a responsibility for the life they've brought into the world. They stick around to look after it."

Jenny's head snapped up. His words brought back the full force of the pain she'd felt the night Gramps told her the child had been born dead. She fought to control it, allowing bitterness to take its place.

"Not when she's been told the baby was dead," she countered, staring into the twinkling blue eyes assessing her from across the expanse of scarred, water-stained, cluttered mahogany.

"Where'd you get a damn fool idea like that?"

Slowly, painfully, Jenny related her story, including the disintegration of her newfound love for Devin.

When she'd finished, Dr. Hines looked at her over steepled fingers. His evaluating gaze took in every detail of the mature young woman facing him with dry eyes, pursed mouth and ramrod-straight posture. She'd changed from the timid woman-child Jake had brought to him for a checkup. Life had hardened her, sharpened the soft edges of childhood.

"I want you to understand what I'm about to tell you ain't 'cause I aim to make excuses for what Jake did." The old doctor leaned toward her over the cluttered surface of the one piece of furniture Jenny could clearly remember. "I'd known Jake for most of our lives, fished with him, broke Sunday bread with him and Rebecca, worshiped with him. But when your ma was born... well, I don't ever recall seein' a happier couple.

"Laura was the daughter him and your gramma had waited for all their married lives. When he brought her back in that pine casket, he was a different man. Part of him died along with her. I didn't recognize my old friend anymore. A stranger who never smiled, never laughed, never—" His voice broke. He cleared his throat before going on.

"Then you came along, lookin' for all the world like your ma come back to life. Jake was like a new man. I don't know what happened that night. Don't know as how I want to, either, but I think Jake... Well, he talked to me once about what was gonna happen to you and the young'n after it was born. He was worried, no doubt in my mind. I think maybe his imagination got the best of him. I think he saw his Laura leavin' him again, but this time he could do somethin' 'bout it to stop it from endin' the same way."

Feeling as if her heart were being squeezed in a tight fist, Jenny took a deep breath. "What part did you have in all this?"

"Jake brought the baby to me. Said I was to place her somewheres, he didn't want to know where. Said you'd changed your mind 'bout keepin' her. I believed him." He noticed the skeptical look Jenny studied him with, and sat back sharply. "Hell, girl, he was my best friend. Never lied to me before. Had no reason to doubt him."

"My daughter has told me about an old man who came to see her every Wednesday." The old doctor nodded, but she went on. "I believe he was my grandfather."

"Never heard you call him that before," the doctor commented. "Always called him Gramps. Them your city manners?" he asked gruffly.

"Please answer my question." Jenny needed no one pointing out the gulf that now existed between her and the man she'd called Gramps.

"That'd be Jake. He came here a few weeks after he dropped her off and asked me for the address of where I took her. Heard tell he went there every week till he got too sick. That's when he came to me again."

Holding her hand up to stop him, Jenny shifted in her chair. "I know what happened after that. What I need to know is what happened the night of the baby's birth."

"I can't help you there, but maybe this might have some of them answers you're cravin'." Shuffling through the bottom drawer of his desk, he pulled forth a yellowed envelope with her name on the front in her grandfather's handwriting. "Jake asked me to see you got this if you ever came back to these parts. Said it was important." The only sign she showed that the letter affected her was the slight trembling of her fingers as she took it from him.

Gingerly she ran her fingertips over the faded ink, unmindful that Dr. Hines had risen from his chair and shrugged into his perennial black suit jacket. Grabbing the black bag on the examination table, he strode to her side. "I gotta go out to the Miller place. Gracie's havin' a right painful bout of arthritis. You stay here as long as you have a mind to. I'll tell Iris to leave you alone." Patting her shoulder, he left the room, closing the door firmly behind him.

Carefully Jenny laid the letter on the corner of the desk, smoothing its worn edges. On shaking legs, she stood and moved away, eyeing it from the other side of the room. Did she want to know? If she left it unopened, she could claim his actions to be the result of senility, or hardening of the arteries, or... But if she opened it...

A thousand butterflies took flight in her stomach. Her palms beaded with moisture. Her throat closed. Her mouth felt as if a desert wind had blown through it. Her mind fought a fierce battle with her common sense, urging her to leave the letter unopened. What good would an explanation do? What was done was done. No amount of excuses could erase years of heartbreak. No amount of apologies could make his betrayal hurt less.

Yet you'll never rest easy until you know, her common sense countered. *The only way to end the nightmare is to read the letter.*

With tentative fingers, she slid it from the desk and inserted her nail beneath the flap. The years had dissolved most of the glue. It opened easily, with a crackle as brittle as her nerves.

The sheets slipped from the envelope. She slowly unfolded them to reveal the carefully written letter from her grandfather.

Jenny,

If you're reading this, you know what I did. You probably hate me. Lord knows you have every right to. I ain't never had much book learnin', but I'm gonna try to explain.

When your grandma and I had your ma, we was nearly past the childbearin' age. It was like God had picked us out special to be givin' this miracle of a little baby girl. I loved both my kids, but, Lord, I never loved anybody but your grandma as much as I loved Laura.

While she was a youngster, she tagged after me and your grandma like our shadows. We took her fishin', 'n' hikin', 'n' picnickin'. We taught her the names of the wildflowers 'n' the trees, 'n' where the squirrels hide their nuts for the winter. I even taught her to swim in the creek behind the house.

We ain't never had much money to speak of, but Laura was our own little treasure. Havin' her around, your grandma used to say, was like havin' the sunshine livin' inside our house.

Even though Laura'd been sickly from the time she was born, we never regretted havin' her for one minute.

When she was sixteen, a carnival came to town. Laura begged us to go, so we got your grandma's egg money together and gave it to her. She was so happy, she laughed and skipped all the way down the lane. The next night, she went again, even though we didn't have any more money to give her. She got all dolled up in her best dress, brushed her hair till it shined and off she went. The carnival stayed in Eden for a week, and she went every night.

The last night, a car pulled in front of the house, and Laura got out. There was a man with her, Lester Tyson, one of the carnival workers.

She told us she was in love with him, and he wanted her to go with him and marry him. We tried to talk her out of it, but she wouldn't listen. Said if we didn't let her go, she'd run off as soon as we was asleep.

She left that night, wavin' out the car window, lookin' happier than I ever see'd her. A year later, three months after her seventeenth birthday, she sent us word she'd had you. Five months after that, I brought her home to be laid to rest beside your grandma.

Seems Lester had left the carnival for another job in Tennessee. He got hisself fired for bein' drunk after only a few weeks work. Frail as she was, Laura got a job and worked until you was born. After she had you, she went back to work to feed you, still sick and worn out from the birthin'. Pneumonia set in, and she died before the doctor could get to her.

When you told me you was gonna take care of the baby alone, all I could see was Laura's coffin sittin' in the hole out back, and I knew right then I'd never rest easy unless I stopped you from doin' what your ma did. So I took the baby and told you it died.

I knowed a few weeks later I'd done wrong, but before I could make it right, you'd run off. Since her pa had returned all your letters unopened, and I burned them to keep you from bein' hurt more, I didn't know how to find him. There was nothin' I could do but leave her in the children's home with the nuns. I couldn't take care of no little baby. I wanted the tyke to know she wasn't alone, so I visited her once a week.

You'd be proud of her, Jenny. She growed into a right purty, smart little thing, just like her ma.

I'm not askin' for forgiveness; it ain't my right to have it. I just wanted you to know I didn't mean to hurt you. Lord, girl, I loved you as much as I did your ma. It near tore my heart out to see you sufferin' like you was. I hope you can understand that.

Gramps

Like a zombie, Jenny folded the letter and slipped it back into the envelope. Cramming the letter in the bottom of her purse, she left the doctor's office.

Several hours later, her rental car bumped its way up the driveway to her grandfather's house. Aside from looking more weathered and run-down, the house looked exactly as it had the day she left. The front porch, with the two empty rockers, sagged drunkenly. The railing, resembling a child's gap-toothed grin, clung tenaciously to the porch posts. Clumps of knee-high grass grappled for survival with overgrown weeds.

Gravel crunched beneath the tires as she maneuvered the car over the rutted surface. Applying the brakes, she turned off the engine and sat quietly looking at the place she'd called home for almost a year of her life.

With a jolt, she realized that this was no more home than her little apartment in New Orleans was. Home was now a white castle on the banks of the Mississippi, hundreds of miles from here, with Devin and Amy.

Her gaze shifted to the door, and she imagined she could hear the protesting squeak of its rusty hinges as her grandfather stepped through it and onto the porch, block of wood and carving knife in hand. Resolutely she shook away her fancies and emerged from the car.

Moving around the fender, she approached the disintegrating steps with measured tread, as if she were walking on ice. She knew the hinges would squeak when she opened the door to gaze into the darkened interior. Dust motes danced in the rays of sunlight filtering through the grime on the windows. A thick layer of dirt and dust covered everything. Other than that, it looked as if her grandfather had stepped out for a moment and would return presently.

The floorboards protested her weight as she made her way into the kitchen and to the back door. Wiping a circle of glass clean with her fingertips, Jenny peered out at the hill, which was crowned with a neat row of white crosses, four large, one small.

Gripped by an overwhelming urge to race up the hill and snatch the smallest one from the earth, she twisted at the rusted doorknob with all her strength.

Her feet were starting up the grade when she arrested her flight. What good would it do, besides helping her vent some of the anger and frustration bottled up inside her? Stepping back to flat ground, she cast one last glance at the crosses and headed to the house. In a strange way, the little cross no longer marked the resting place of her child. Her heart told her it marked the death of something else, but its exact meaning remained, tantalizingly, just beyond the edges of her mind.

For the next hour, she wandered around the house, touching the table where Gramps had discovered her talent for carving, putting into motion his favorite rocker by the hearth, cradling his pipe in her hand, fitting her fingertips into the indentations his fingers had worn in the bowl.

Tightening her fingers around the pipe, she gave way to the tears that had threatened since she read the letter.

"Gramps," she cried, falling to her knees and resting her face against the smooth wood of the rocker. "How could you? What gave you the right to decide our lives, to play God? It was my choice to make, mine and Devin's. And because of what you've done, I may have lost everything again. I'll never forgive you—never."

"You sanctimonious son of a—"

Devin hit the desk with his fist, almost enjoying the pain in his knuckles. A minor twinge, in comparison to what he'd inflicted on Jenny. No matter how he tried to dress it up, it boiled down to one glaring fact—he'd been concerned for nothing but Devin Montgomery's petty revenge, and to attain it he'd kept silent about the things that mattered.

If he'd only told her right out, back there in Tennessee, why he didn't think marriage was a good idea, all this could have been prevented. "Silence!" he growled, striking the desk a second blow. His silence about Amy's birth had made Jenny believe another woman had taken her place in his heart and bed.

Because of his damn silence, he'd put her through the agony of hearing her own child beg her to be her mother. Worst of all, because of his silence he had added weeks to what already had been years of pain that only a mother who had lost a child to death could understand. No wonder she couldn't forgive him—he was finding it damn hard to forgive himself.

Not only Jenny had been hurt by his closemouthed attitude. Amy's right to know her mother had fallen by the wayside because of his selfishness. He'd broken his daughter's heart by keeping her mother's love from her.

That, however, was one wrong he could try to right. And there was no time like the present, he decided, striding toward the door.

Mrs. Filbert intercepted him. "Mr. Montgomery?"

"Yes? What is it, Mrs. Filbert? Can't this wait?"

"No, sir. It's Amy, sir," she said, wringing her hands. "I've looked everywhere, and I can't find her."

Devin's gut snarled into a tight ball of stark terror. He calmed himself and thought about the problem as rationally as he could. "Have you checked Miss Tyson's workroom?"

"No, sir." The nurse moved into the room, her starched uniform crackling like stiff paper. "It's locked. I assumed Miss Tyson locked it before she left."

"She did. She was always careful about keeping Amy away from her tools unless she was with her, but you and I both know, if Amy wants to do something bad enough, a locked door won't stop her."

The old nurse nodded vigorously. "Aye. She's a clever one. That she is."

"I'll check the workroom. If you don't hear from me, you'll know I found her."

"Very well, sir." She started to leave, but stopped, turning her worried eyes to him. "You don't think she's run off, do you, sir? She's been that upset since Miss Tyson left."

"No, Mrs. Filbert. Amy's impetuous, not foolish."

The nurse smiled weakly and left. Devin got the extra key to the workroom from his desk drawer and started for the stairs. He wished he felt as sure as he'd sounded when he calmed Mrs. Filbert. Amy had been so distraught over Jenny's sudden disappearance, even he hadn't been able to cheer her. Suppose she had taken it into her head to go to New Orleans to find Jenny? His blood ran cold at the prospect.

The door to Jenny's workroom was locked. Inserting the key, Devin opened it noiselessly.

Amy sat before the dollhouse, on Jenny's stool, her good leg tucked beneath her, the one with the brace dangling free. He watched in silence as she moved the pieces of furniture around haphazardly, totally unconscious of her actions. When Devin stepped to her side, he could hear her muffled sobs and see the sheen of moisture covering her cheeks.

"You shouldn't be in here alone, Scamp," he said gently.

"I know."

"How did you get in?"

"I used the extra key." More tears rolled from her shimmering eyes.

Devin smiled at his lovely daughter. She was so much like her mother, his heart tore wide open with pain. Bending, he scooped her into his arms and took her place on the stool, seating her on his lap.

Very softly, he began to tell Amy who Jenny was and why she had left.

"A long time ago, when I was just a young man, I fell in love with a beautiful girl. She loved me, too. We made a baby together, but I didn't know it. She went away before she could tell me. When she had the baby, they told her it was born dead, but it wasn't. They took it to live with some nuns."

"Like me?"

"Yes, Scamp. In fact, that baby was you, and Jenny's your mother."

Amy's eyes grew large.

"She didn't know that until the day before she left here." Devin cleared the emotion from his throat.

Her face clouded. "If she knew she was my mommy, why did she leave? Doesn't she love me?" Fat tears rolled anew down Amy's cheeks.

Devin hugged her close. "She loves you very much, Scamp. But I'm afraid she's very angry with me for not telling her she was your mommy."

"Why didn't you tell her, Popie?"

"It's hard for me to explain. All I can say is, I thought it best to wait. I didn't want to hurt her."

"Popie, if she loves you and she loves me, why did she run away? Why didn't she stay here and let you explain?"

"Jenny's a little mixed up right now, sweetie. She needs time to think." He kissed the top of her head and wished it were that simple.

"Why can't she think here?" she cried, the tears increasing.

"Because she needs to be by herself."

"Popie, bring her back!" Amy wailed, her distressed sobs causing her little body to quiver. "Bring my mommy home, Popie!"

Devin cradled her close in his arms. "I'll try," he promised fervently. "I'll try real hard, Scamp."

"Tomorrow, Popie! Bring her home tomorrow!" she cried, cradling his cheek in the palm of her little hand.

"Maybe not tomorrow, but soon, real soon. I promise."

Amy's distraught state brought back with crystal clarity the first agonizing months after he'd taken her from the children's home. She'd been almost five, and terrified of the big man who said he was her daddy.

For weeks, she'd cried for her grampy and the sisters. Devin had showered her with gifts, toys, clothes, pets, outings and attention. She'd scorned it all. The tears had continued to flow like a never-ending rainstorm.

Devin had racked his brain for a solution. What had that pitiful old man given her that he wasn't? He wasn't used to children, but he'd vowed to learn and win his daughter's love and acceptance.

In retrospect, he could laugh at his own stupidity, but back then, it had nearly been his undoing. His battle had gone on, his buying sprees had become more extravagant. Amy's indifferent acceptance had continued until he realized all she wanted was his unconditional love.

The day it had finally all changed—the day he'd bought the house, a permanent home for Amy—began to run through his mind. At the time, he'd told himself the house was for Amy and him. But now he readily admitted what he couldn't see past his heartache to admit back then—that he'd bought a castle for Jenny, with the dream that she would one day live there with them.

"Scamp," he said suddenly, looking down into the tear-streaked face of his child. "Do you want to help me bring Mommy back?"

Her expression brightened as if a thousand lamps had been turned on at once. "Oh, yes, Popie! Can I?"

"You certainly can," he said, squeezing her. He didn't bother to correct her, because for once she was right—she was able. "You run and get your crayons and paper, while I clear a spot for us to go to work."

"Are we going to carve something, Popie?"

"Yes, Amy, we sure are." When Amy had disappeared out the door, he added, "We're going to carve out a life for all three of us."

Chapter 12

Jenny sat on a low stool in front of her castle, her fingers curled tightly around an object in her lap, her eyes trained on the two tiny figurines in the throne room. Carefully she placed the small princess on the stairs at their feet.

Since her return from Asheville three days before, she'd slept little, eaten only because Belle insisted, and driven herself with something akin to superhuman endurance to finish the little dark-haired replica of Amy. During that time, she'd had opportunity to rethink a lot of her previously drawn conclusions about Devin, herself, and Gramps.

She'd judged Devin through a mist of bitter anger and hurt, unwilling even to consider his side of the story. In her heart, she had to admit Belle was right. She'd wanted to hurt Devin as badly as he'd hurt her, and she hadn't cared to what extent or how—just that he should feel the agony she'd lived with for all those lost years of Amy's childhood.

And dear old Gramps. His motives had been exactly the opposite of hers. He'd tried to prevent pain, and in doing so had caused her more than she'd ever known. She was slowly learning to forgive him, but it was coming hard. *Perhaps,* she thought, *in the years to come, when it doesn't still ache so much, I'll be able to.*

"Looks just about perfect to me," Belle said softly, coming to stand behind her and place a hand on her shoulder.

Patting Belle's hand, too choked to speak, Jenny continued to stare at the little family.

"Neither of them meant to hurt you, Jenny." The long silence Belle had imposed on herself while she waited for Jenny to come to terms with what she'd learned on her trip was broken.

Jenny nodded. "I know that now."

"They loved you. When we love someone, it goes hand in hand with hurting them sometimes. Even though we don't mean to, it happens."

Gramps had said something similar to that, but at the time, it had seemed inconceivable to Jenny. How could you deliberately hurt someone you loved? The answers had come slowly and painfully. She had managed to hurt both Devin and Gramps, and had labeled it love.

Instead of leaving Tennessee so abruptly, she should have gone back to Devin, told him about the baby and accepted his love on any terms. But she'd tucked her injured pride in her suitcase and turned her back on him. And when she'd finally seen how foolish she'd acted, had she come back to Tennessee? No. She'd sat in North Carolina, nursing her pride, and writing those pitiful letters. Even the bus trip home had come long after it should have. God, what an idiotic, spoiled fool she'd been.

Convenient excuses were the words she'd thrown in Devin's face when he tried to make her see the obstructions he'd come up against in trying to find her. He at least had reasons for his failure. She had no such crutch.

And Gramps. It tore at her to think how she'd repaid his love by sneaking off like a thief in the night, never telling him where she was or going back to see him. Had she done that, all this additional pain could have been avoided.

"Here's the mail," Belle said, interrupting her introspection.

Jenny accepted two white envelopes from Belle. The longest one bore the return address for the attorney she'd contacted her first day back from Claymore. She laid it aside, making a mental note to call him and inform him his services wouldn't be needed after all. Why take Amy away from the father she adored and add to everyone's heartache?

Fingering the smaller square envelope, she checked for a return address and found none. A question written clearly on her features, she looked over her shoulder at Belle.

Belle gave a noncommittal shrug.

"It's probably my invitation to the miniatures expo in Chicago," she decided, pulling the flap open. "I've been thinking about going this year. You and Harry could watch the shop for me, and it would give me an opportunity to get away. It might be just the distraction I need to get my mind off—" Her nervous chatter came to an abrupt halt when she saw the front of the card.

The invitation was hand-drawn and covered with rainbow-hued balloons. Each one held a letter to spell out It's a Birthday Party! The center of a gaily frosted birthday cake proclaimed the name Amy in a child's scrawled handwriting.

Her heart somersaulted. She'd completely forgotten Amy's birthday party. The party they'd planned together.

It took a moment before she could open it to read the time, date and place Amy had printed inside. Her eyes misted. Next to the Place was printed Jenny's Castle. At the bottom was an additional note.

> Please come! We miss you terrible. It will be an auspicious occasion. We love you.
>
> Love, Amy

Below Amy's name was another signature in a very familiar script—Devin. Tears welled in Jenny's eyes and slipped past the lids to fall on the paper. The carefully printed words blurred.

"Are you going?" Belle asked quietly.

"I don't know," she whispered past the lump filling her throat. Could she go and see them and perhaps have to walk away? She wasn't at all sure she had the strength for it. Did she have the right to expect their forgiveness?

"You'll break her heart if you don't."

"I could send her a gift and tell her I'm sick."

"And do you think a present will take your place? Is that all you think she wants from you?" Belle huffed her disapproval. "It appears to me the only present that child wants is her mother. It also appears Devin might join her in that wish." She moved away noiselessly.

Swinging around to deny it, Jenny caught a glimpse of the woman's dress as it disappeared behind the workshop curtain. *She sure can move fast for a woman of her size when she wants to.*

But she's right, as usual, she admitted grudgingly. For so many years she'd made presents for other children's birthdays and only dreamed of celebrating one with her own child. Now God and Devin had made that possible. Fool! The opportunity she'd always dreamed of teased at her fingertips, and she busied herself making excuses not to take advantage of it.

Her heart cried out to her child and the man she loved. She needed them with a desperation far beyond anything she'd ever known. Her entire body ached with the wanting.

Suddenly, a clear picture of the little white cross on the hill came to mind. She knew instantly what it symbolized—the death of the misunderstandings standing between her and Devin.

Limp with relief, she realized the fear that had made her back away from a confrontation with Devin and Amy was not of seeing them, but of not being able to get over the past, of not having recaptured Devin's love.

But she remembered his avowal of love in the midst of that terrible argument before she'd left Claymore. At the time, she'd thought he said it purely to keep her there. Had he really meant it? She tried to visualize his face when he'd said it.

Although she'd never doubted Amy's love, Devin had been another matter. Unable at the time to shake the belief that he'd wooed her just to satisfy his need for revenge. How blind she'd been, never taking into account the look of pure, deep adoration he'd had on his face then, combined with the desperate eyes of a man seeing his life sifting through his fingers. No actor could have feigned that sincerity. It had been his heart speaking. The black clouds surrounding her heart parted, allowing the warmth of the sun through to melt the ice. A smile transformed her face.

"Belle," she called, jumping to her feet. "Belle, I need a large box." She plucked the Not for Sale sign from atop one of the castle's turrets. "I'll be right back. I have to buy some very special birthday paper, with happy-colored balloons on it."

Struggling through the curtain with a box she'd been saving for this very occasion, Belle chuckled as Jenny disappeared out the door and dashed toward the gift shop two stores away.

On the long drive to Claymore, Jenny found that making the decision to attend Amy's party had been the easy part. With each mile bringing her closer to the time when she would have to face Devin and Amy, her apprehension grew. By the time she pulled into the driveway, her body was being victimized by a colossal case of nerves.

She'd barely stopped the car when the front door burst open and Amy catapulted through it and down the stairs. Her brace-free legs showed beneath the hem of her mint green dress. Her lustrous black hair bounced around her shoulders in long, exuberant ringlets. She looked like a Madame Alexander doll.

"Mommy! Mommy! You came! You came!"

Amy's words took a second to penetrate. Another second passed before she realized Devin must have told Amy who she was. A deep-down warmth invaded her soul and spread over her like warm honey, smothering her entire world in love. *My baby,* she thought, squatting to gather her daughter's small body close as she sailed into her mother's arms.

Why hadn't she ever guessed Amy was her daughter purely from the chemistry between them? From their very first meeting, she'd felt something special for Amy, some unreasonable attachment, more than that of a friend for a friend or an adult for an adorable child. There had been a linkage there always, that instinctive love of a mother for the child to whom she'd given birth.

"Mommy." Amy squirmed out of Jenny's viselike embrace. "You're squishin' me."

"Oh, I'm sorry." Jenny swiped at the tears blurring her vision. "My goodness, I've squished your lovely dress, too." She smiled and brushed the wrinkles from the crushed fabric.

"It's okay. Hugs are s'pose to be hard. Popie says, if they aren't, people don't know you really mean it." Her forehead furrowed. "Was mine hard enough?"

"Oh, yes, angel, it was real hard."

"Good. 'Cause I want you to know how much I love you."

Tears rolled unchecked over Jenny's cheeks. "I love you, too, Scamp."

Amy grinned. "I know, 'cause you squished me real hard." Again, she paused thoughtfully. "Mommy, will you stay here now, forever and ever?"

Standing on the outer fringes, Devin watched the interaction between the woman he loved and their daughter. He'd imagined this scene a thousand times, imagined he'd realized his lasting love for Jenny the day he stepped into her shop. But he suddenly realized his imagination involving Jenny and Amy had always been superseded by another vision.

From deep in the recesses of his mind, he saw a little boy waiting endlessly for the return of his mother. He knew now that there was only one thing that would clear the air once and for all between him and the woman he loved, something he hadn't told another living human being. But it would have to wait. And this time, he wouldn't put it off with half-baked excuses. This time he had no fears about the outcome.

He shifted slightly for a better view of Jenny. She was noticeably thinner, had a fragile air about her that brought home to him how the tension between them had taken its toll. Suddenly he couldn't wait a minute longer for her to answer Amy's question.

"Will you stay, Jenny?"

Jenny had been so caught up in her daughter, she hadn't noticed Devin's approach. She straightened and looked at him with starving eyes, her gaze imprisoned by the green warmth of his, able at last to see beyond the misunderstandings to the man, the man she'd kept hidden in her heart for so long. Here was a man who wanted nothing more than the home and family he'd never had.

She'd expected him to understand her urgent need to give their child a home without telling him of its existence. Understanding him had been far from her immature mind. Her words of accusation came back to haunt her. It wasn't Devin who had been the selfish one. It was her, demanding he give up his career without reason, solely because she thought it would solve all their problems, demanding he forget his pride as a provider and drag a wife and child from one state to another.

Worst of all, she'd deliberately seduced him, never taking into consideration that protection was unavailable, never taking into consideration the possible consequences of her impetuous actions. And still, he could forgive her self-centeredness, her distrust, her harsh words, and love her, despite betrayal, pain and separation.

After her visit to Dr. Hines, it hadn't taken long for her to understand why Devin had been so angry, why he'd plotted his revenge. Having grown up without his parents, he must have found it a devastating blow to find not only that he had a child, but that she'd been stuck in a place very much like the one in which he'd spent his lonely childhood.

"Well, Sam, do we get an answer?" His voice was hushed, hesitant.

Her insides flipped at the sound of her nickname. He wanted her. The warmth of his love washed over her, chasing the chill of their separation from her bones.

"This is the only place I've ever wanted to be," she whispered as she stepped into his waiting embrace. Wrapping her arms around his neck, she squeezed with all her might, just so there would be no doubt about how much she meant it.

"When was the last time I said I love you, Sam?" His lips were a breath away.

"A lifetime ago," she replied, and cut off any further conversation by pressing her lips against his.

Their mouths melded into a kiss that held the promise of becoming much more. He pulled back slightly and smiled down at her. "You're still a wanton hussy, Sam."

"Don't kids get to be kissed, too?"

Mother and father drew apart slowly. With a burst of laughter, they picked Amy up, sandwiched her between them and smothered her with kisses.

"This is the best birthday ever," she squealed, hugging them both as tightly as she could.

"Let's make it even better," Jenny said, extracting herself from the tangle of arms and setting Amy back on her feet. She went to her car, opened the back door and began tugging on the large box in the back seat.

"Let me," Devin offered, brushing her lips lightly as he bent to grasp the box.

Amy stared at it with wide eyes. "Can I open it now?" she cried, clapping her hands and jumping up and down.

"Soon," Devin admonished her. "But right now, young lady, you're neglecting your duties as hostess of this gala affair. Suppose you go back and make sure Harriet has the cake and ice cream ready. Mommy and I will see to it that this monster is placed with the rest of the loot."

Everything inside Jenny turned to hot mush at the sound of that word on Devin's lips. That one word verified, better than any of the inscriptions in the Clinton family Bible, that Amy was truly hers. She didn't seem able to stop drinking in the two people who were her family.

"Mommy, you'll stay, won't you?"

"Wild horses couldn't drag me away, Scamp." Amy gave her one more hug and dashed off to her guests.

"Do you want help carrying that thing?" she asked, suppressing a giggle as Devin staggered under the weight of the box.

"Witch," he growled, and set the box aside. With a sweep of his arm, he captured her waist and pulled her to him. "That can wait—this can't." The last word was mumbled against her lips. His gentle kiss promised a million tomorrows, and all the love he could possibly put into each day. When he lifted his head, his eyes were misty. "God, I missed you. My heart told me you were always mine, but my head told me I was a fool to think you could forgive me. Please, Sam, don't ever leave me again. It would kill me this time."

"Then you have a long life to look forward to, my love. Leaving you has always torn a piece from my soul. It seems the only way I can remain whole is to stay in your arms."

"Sam, I need you. I need to know this isn't a dream."

Taking a deep, cleansing breath, Jenny stepped back to look into his eyes. "Hold that thought for a while. Right now, we better deliver this gift before the hostess comes looking for us."

Reluctantly Devin released her and picked up the box, straining under the weight. "What in the name of God is in here?"

"You'll see." She giggled at the face he made and guided him up the stairs.

On the patio, Harriet had begun to serve cake and ice cream, under Amy's expert guidance. The trees sparkled with fairy lights, twinkling like millions of lightning bugs. Rainbow-colored streamers and balloons hung from the colonnades and railings of the upper gallery. It was exactly as Amy had described it to her in the gazebo the night of their picnic.

Devin's arm slid around her waist, pulling her close to his side. "I want you to stay right here where I can see you," he growled, his lips caressing her ear.

"I don't plan on going anywhere," she said, looking deep into his eyes, telling him without words that she loved him.

"Jenny, don't look at me like that in front of all these kids. It has to be X-rated."

"Mommy, can I open my present now?" Amy was barreling across the lawn toward them with a flustered Harriet in hot pursuit.

"I'm sorry, Miss Tyson," Harriet gasped.

"It's all right, Harriet," Devin said, stepping in. "We'll take over for a while. You rest. It was inevitable, you know," he told her with a smile as he led her to a lawn chair. "There's not a woman alive who can resist the temptation of an unopened package." He smiled at Jenny, who stepped back within the circle of his protective arm. "Come on, Mommy, let's help our daughter open the offerings of her court."

Amy ran at full speed toward the mountain of gift-wrapped boxes.

"Devin, when did Amy get her brace off?"

"Last week." His gaze followed his daughter. "She hasn't walked anywhere since."

"Is she . . . is she okay?"

"Perfect. Just like her mommy," he said, managing a quick kiss before Amy latched on to his hand and dragged him away, impatient to begin.

"Mommy's first," Amy called, the children backing her decision with hoots of encouragement.

Obediently Devin maneuvered the box to the front of the table, where Amy attacked it without hesitation.

"What's in there, rocks?" he panted, coming back to throw an arm around Jenny's shoulders, not quite convinced she was actually there.

She nodded, but never took her eyes from her daughter. A peal of laughter issued from her as she watched Amy divest the box of the paper she'd so carefully chosen, stand on tiptoe and peer in.

"Oh, Mommy, it's beautiful! Popie, take it out, take it out!" she shrieked, her eyes as large as the multihued balloons floating above her head.

Caught up in his daughter's enthusiasm, Devin looked into the box and grinned. His gaze sought Jenny. "Jenny's castle," he whispered. "I thought it wasn't for sale."

"It's not. It's for giving." She walked to his side and helped him lift it from the box and place it on the patio stones.

An immediate circle of animated children surrounded Amy and her gift. The other presents were forgotten.

Standing in the circle of Devin's arms, her head on his shoulder, Jenny smiled in satisfaction at the delight on Amy's face when she discovered the figure of the little princess.

"It's funny, but I think I knew, deep down, that someday my child would play with it. There's a lot of me in that castle."

"What better gift for a mother to give her child than part of herself," Belle said softly from close by Jenny's side, grinning when she saw Jenny's surprised face. "I got my invitation the same day you did." Seeing Jenny look past her, she explained, "Harry's been up to his ears in kids since he stepped from the car. Whenever he's around, they stick to him like glue." Leaning closer to Jenny, she said in her stage whisper, "Between you and me, I think he loves it."

Over Belle's shoulder, Jenny caught sight of Harry with a child of about two on his knee shouting with glee as he bounced him up and down. "I hope so, because I think Amy may have adopted you and Harry. She was quite adamant about including you on her guest list."

"Belle," Devin said, unable to hold himself in check a minute longer, "do you think, with Harriet's help, you can baby-sit this pack of miniature females for a while? Your boss and I have some talking to do."

"'Bout time you made an honest woman of her," Belle said, her stern tone softened by a broad wink as they hurried away.

"Where's my birthday present?" Devin asked when he'd guided her through the house and into the privacy of his bedroom.

"Your birthday's Halloween." She laughed as he pulled her into his arms.

"Not anymore, Sam," he whispered, all playfulness erased from his tone. "I'll celebrate today as the day of my birth from now on. For six years, I've been dead inside. Having you here has brought my soul to life."

For a moment, she looked into his mesmerizing eyes. The amber halos were expanding, the moss green darkening. She cupped his face in her hands. "Devin Montgomery, I thought I'd lost everything I held dear. Now I have more than any woman could hope for. Our child and your love have made me whole. I love you with every breath I take." She sealed her words by gently kissing his warm lips.

"Marry me, Sam. Marry me and have my babies. I want to be there this time to watch you grow with my child. I want to share with you all the things we missed the first time." He crushed her to him. "I love you, woman."

Tears gathered in her eyes. "Oh, yes. I want to fill this white castle of yours with our babies."

"Jenny's castle, Sam," he corrected. "It was always Jenny's castle, right from the moment I first saw it."

"How did you know?"

"I didn't then. But after you walked out the second time, I prayed more frequently and more ardently than a Buddhist monk. I know now I never stopped looking for you in every face, needing you, loving you, planning to spend my golden years with you at my side." He stepped back, holding her at arm's length.

"There's nothing I want more right at this moment than to throw you on that bed and make love to you for a week, but there's something I need to tell you."

This time, the old wariness Jenny had always experienced when Devin said something like this never showed itself. After all the pain of the past days, she'd come to trust him. He said he loved her and wanted to marry her, and she couldn't think of anything that was left to make her feel afraid. Placidly she allowed him to lead her to the two chairs beside the fireplace.

Devin seated her in one and took the other. When she would have protested the intervening space, he raised his hand to stop her. "I can't say what I have to say when you're close. I find you totally distracting." He smiled gently. "Once I've said what I have to say, I'll never keep you at arm's length again. I promise."

Contented, Jenny leaned back and waited for him to begin.

"The earliest memories I have of myself as a child are standing on the steps of some building, watching my mother drive away in a car. She'd left me there with a promise to come back. The next morning, a man took me to an office building. I fought him all the way. I just knew she'd come back and I wouldn't be there.

"The office building, I realized years later, had been Social Services."

Jenny's relaxed posture stiffened. She wanted to reach out to him, to soothe the pain he must have felt, but she sensed his need to say this all at once, without any interruptions and remained where she was.

"That was the beginning of a long line of moves for me. I was shuttled mercilessly from foster home to foster home. Each time I hoped my mother would come and take me away, but she never came.

"Until I was ten, I was convinced it was because of the constant moves I made that she didn't come. On my eleventh birthday, I ran away. I had the warped idea that if I could just get back to that building, she'd be waiting for me." He made a sound caught somewhere between a chuckle and a sob. "I'd barely gone a block when they caught me and dragged me kicking and screaming back home—or at least what they referred to as my home.

"The next day, a man came. I didn't know who or what he was then, but now I know he was a clergyman of some kind. He sat with me and patiently explained that my mother wouldn't be coming back. She and the man she'd been going off with had had an accident three days after they found me. They both died instantly."

Unable to keep still any longer, Jenny rose and walked to his chair. Kneeling beside him, she wrapped her arms around his waist and held him as if he were still that little boy. "I'm sorry, Devin."

"So am I, Sam, so am I. I really thought I was past the pain, but I know now that I wasn't. When I saw you and Amy on the lawn today, it all came rushing back, like a bad dream. I knew that under all the excuses I'd made for what I did to you, there was that one thing that perpetuated it."

She tried to shush him, tried to tell him that it was all over, that there was no need for him to go on hurting himself with memories that could never be changed, but he kept talking.

"I've been blaming you for everything. I guess when I found Amy in the children's home, I blinded myself to anything that could possibly excuse you. In my mind there could be no excuse for a mother leaving her child."

"Devin, you couldn't have known any more than I did what my grandfather had done." She looked into his face and saw the evidence of his anguish in the moisture running unnoticed down his cheeks. Gently, she brushed it away.

"And when I found out you thought our child had died, I used my pride as the excuse."

He clutched her close, holding her so close she could barely take a breath, but she didn't protest. He needed the security of having her to hang on to at that moment, and she promised herself there would never be a time in their lives when she wouldn't be there to offer that security to him.

Jenny was feeling her own anguish and shame. She knew she'd hurt him when she walked out six years ago, but she hadn't had the foggiest idea how much until now.

"Jenny, you were the best part of my life. You held out to me all the things I ever wanted—love, a family, a home, but I was afraid to take them, afraid I'd lose it all again." He moved her away to look into her face. "I hope I never do anything to chase you away again."

She smiled through the tears in her eyes. "I don't think you could chase me away now. I'd lose too much."

He stared at her for a while. He could not believe she was his, finally, unconditionally and forever his. Covering her lips in a kiss that sealed their love, he promised silently to do everything in his power to erase those years of pain and loneliness from her mind.

"Hey," she said, moving a fraction of an inch away. "I seem to remember a man who said he'd like nothing better than to throw me on that bed."

Devin grinned, showing the first real humor since he'd begun his tale. "You're leaving out the best part."

"Oh?"

"I said I'd like to throw you on the bed and make love to you for a week." As he spoke, he stood her up and began slowly to remove her clothes. Moments later, she stood gloriously naked before him.

"This is grossly unfair," she murmured, and began unbuttoning his shirt.

By the time things were on an equal basis, their bodies were locked in passion on his large bed. They touched and explored each other with the same enthusiasm the children had exhibited with the castle, missing nothing. Whoops of joy, however, were replaced with moans and avowals of love.

Devin's touch painted paths of fire over her skin, caressing and penetrating all her secret places. His lips closed over her breast, enveloping the tip in the warm suction of his mouth.

Glorying in the freedom to explore his masculine beauty again, Jenny extracted tortured groans from his twisting body with her touch. She feathered her fingers through the hair on his chest until she found a flat nipple. With her fingertips, she aroused it to a stiff peak and moved lower. Dragging her nails lightly over his stomach to his swollen manhood was all Devin could take.

"Too much," he whispered, his aroused state cutting his words short. "I need to feel you around me."

He pulled her beneath him and very slowly entered her warmth. A sigh issued from him.

But Jenny wasn't willing to settle for slow and gentle. She wanted proof of a frantic joining to tell her this was not just another dream. Wrapping her arms and legs around him, she pushed him on his back and took charge.

"Jenny," Devin groaned, and settled back, allowing her to have her way. "Sam," he choked out, "it'll end too soon. It's been too long."

She stopped only long enough to kiss him. "We have forever, my love."

"And ever," he added.

The house was finally quiet. An exhausted Amy had bid goodbye to her guests and been carried to bed by her father and mother.

"Are we a family now?" she asked sleepily, just seconds before her eyes closed.

"Yes, sweetheart, we are," Jenny answered, taking Devin's hand across the sleeping body of their daughter.

While Devin checked to see the house was closed up for the night, Jenny went to the master bedroom, where he found her curled up on his big bed, leafing through the Clinton Bible.

She dropped her hands to her lap, still clutching the edges of the book. "I should never have walked out on you that night. I should have let you explain. I was just so hurt that I needed to get away. You deserved to know about the baby," she said, dragging her eyes from the book to look at him. "Those letters I wrote were so pointless and futile. I could have found you, if only I'd tried. He burned them when they came back unopened. He said it was to protect me."

"It probably was," he agreed softly. "Can you forgive him, Jenny?"

"Maybe someday, but not right now. The pain is still too raw. Can you forgive him? You were hurt, too."

"Yes, I can, in a way. I think I'd have done something desperate, faced with the possibility of your death. He really did think he was doing what was best for you."

"But if I'd have known sooner, I would have come back sooner. He had no right to burn my letters. If I'd had them, I would have had some hope that you still cared. I needed you so much. Why didn't I just come back right away?"

Pulling her into his arms, Devin kissed her soundly. "Because you were young and scared. Because you weren't sure that I hadn't deserted you. You were facing a frightening situation. All you could think about was not having to face it alone. Fear has a way of erasing common sense. We act without thinking. It's not until later, when the fear is gone, that we think rationally.

"I have my own sins to atone for in this," he went on. "I should have told you from the beginning that I wanted to marry you, but that I was scared to death I couldn't take care of you without a job. But worst of all, Jenny, I should have told you about Amy that first day in your shop. It was nothing less than cruel to prolong your grief the way I did."

"That's water under the bridge," she said soothingly, caressing the frown lines from his forehead. "Neither of us can undo the past. I'm just thankful you never stopped loving me."

Quietly Devin got up and went to his desk. From one of the drawers, he took a book and returned to the bed, laying it in her lap.

"*The Real People,*" she read, "*A Collection of Old Sayings and Customs of Tennessee,* by Devin Montgomery. This is the book you were writing at the cabin," she murmured. In the corner of the jacket was a sketch of the cabin. She outlined it with love, feeling the memories seep into the tip of her finger.

"Look on the dedication page."

She opened the book and reverently thumbed to the page he indicated and read, "To Sam, my love, my future. Gone, but never from my heart." It was dated four years ago.

"Do those sound like the words of a man who was ready to give up the woman he loved?"

"Oh, Devin," she said in a choked voice, closing the book and cradling it against her heart. "I made so many mistakes."

He removed the book from her hands, laid it on the bedside table, switched off the light and pulled her down next to him. "We've all made our share of mistakes. But we have a whole glorious future ahead of us. Let's squander our energies on it and forget the rest."

Curling into his protective, loving embrace, she nodded. They had years of happiness ahead, here in this great house. Together, as a family, they would live and love and fill these rooms with miniature Montgomerys.

* * * * *

COMING NEXT MONTH

#607 LOVING EVANGELINE—Linda Howard

No one had ever dared to cross American Hero Robert Cannon, until someone began stealing classified information from his company—a situation that Robert intended to remedy himself. But when the trail led to beautiful Evie Shaw, Robert found both his resolve—and his heart—melting fast.

#608 A VERY CONVENIENT MARRIAGE—
Dallas Schulze ***Family Ties***

Sam Walker and Nikki Beauvisage got along like water and oil. So neither was too happy about having to get married! But though their vows were just a charade, they quickly found their roles as husband and wife a little too easy to play....

#609 REGARDING REMY—Marilyn Pappano
Southern Knights

Wounded Special Agent Remy Sinclair needed some down-home TLC, and nurse Susannah Duncan seemed like the perfect candidate. Almost *too* perfect. And before long, Remy had to wonder if his tantalizing angel of mercy had come to help—or harm.

#610 SURROGATE DAD—Marion Smith Collins

Luke Quinlan had noticed sexy next-door neighbor Alexandra Prescott long before her son urged him into action. But she considered him too straitlaced for her tastes—until trouble visited her door. Then Alexandra experienced firsthand Luke's fierce protectiveness—and unquenchable desire.

#611 NOT HIS WIFE—Sally Tyler Hayes

She'd loved him forever, but Shelly Wilkerson knew Brian Sandelle would never be hers. To him, she would always be just a friend. But when someone began threatening Shelly, Brian became a man impassioned, both in his pursuit to save her life—and his desire to claim her heart.

#612 GEORGIA ON MY MIND—Clara Wimberly

He'd sworn he would never return home, but Cord Jamison had to find his sister's killer. Soon, solving the small-town scandal became the least of his worries when Cord came face-to-face with ex-love Georgia Ashley, the woman whose memory still haunted his dreams.

MILLION DOLLAR SWEEPSTAKES (III)

No purchase necessary. To enter, follow the directions published. Method of entry may vary. For eligibility, entries must be received no later than March 31, 1996. No liability is assumed for printing errors, lost, late or misdirected entries. Odds of winning are determined by the number of eligible entries distributed and received. Prizewinners will be determined no later than June 30, 1996.

Sweepstakes open to residents of the U.S. (except Puerto Rico), Canada, Europe and Taiwan who are 18 years of age or older. All applicable laws and regulations apply. Sweepstakes offer void wherever prohibited by law. Values of all prizes are in U.S. currency. This sweepstakes is presented by Torstar Corp., its subsidiaries and affiliates, in conjunction with book, merchandise and/or product offerings. For a copy of the Official Rules send a self-addressed, stamped envelope (WA residents need not affix return postage) to: MILLION DOLLAR SWEEPSTAKES (III) Rules, P.O. Box 4573, Blair, NE 68009, USA.

EXTRA BONUS PRIZE DRAWING

No purchase necessary. The Extra Bonus Prize will be awarded in a random drawing to be conducted no later than 5/30/96 from among all entries received. To qualify, entries must be received by 3/31/96 and comply with published directions. Drawing open to residents of the U.S. (except Puerto Rico), Canada, Europe and Taiwan who are 18 years of age or older. All applicable laws and regulations apply; offer void wherever prohibited by law. Odds of winning are dependent upon number of eligibile entries received. Prize is valued in U.S. currency. The offer is presented by Torstar Corp., its subsidiaries and affiliates in conjunction with book, merchandise and/or product offering. For a copy of the Official Rules governing this sweepstakes, send a self-addressed, stamped envelope (WA residents need not affix return postage) to: Extra Bonus Prize Drawing Rules, P.O. Box 4590, Blair, NE 68009, USA.

SWP-S1194

JINGLE BELLS, WEDDING BELLS:
Silhouette's Christmas Collection for 1994

Christmas Wish List

*To beat the crowds at the malls and get the perfect present for *everyone,* even that snoopy Mrs. Smith next door!

*To get through the holiday parties without running my panty hose.

*To bake cookies, decorate the house and serve the perfect Christmas dinner—just like the women in all those magazines.

*To sit down, curl up and read my Silhouette Christmas stories!

Join *New York Times* bestselling author Nora Roberts, along with popular writers Barbara Boswell, Myrna Temte and Elizabeth August, as we celebrate the joys of Christmas—and the magic of marriage—with

Silhouette's Christmas Collection for 1994.

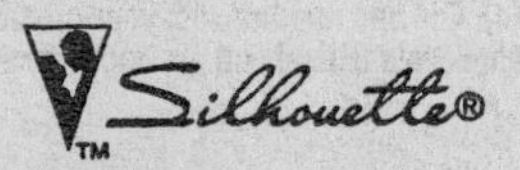

JBWB

by Marilyn Pappano

Award-winning author Marilyn Pappano's **Southern Knights** series continues in December 1994 with REGARDING REMY, IM #609.

Wounded Special Agent Remy Sinclair needed some down-home TLC, and nurse Susannah Duncan seemed like the perfect candidate. Almost *too* perfect. And before long, Remy had to wonder if his tantalizing angel of mercy had come to help—or harm.

And don't miss A MAN LIKE SMITH, featuring Assistant U.S. Attorney Smith Kendricks. His story is coming your way in April 1995.

So immerse yourself once again in the Southern style of living and loving, as three men bound by honor and friendship find the women of their dreams, only in...

INTIMATE MOMENTS®
™ Silhouette®

To order your copy of *Regarding Remy*, or the first Southern Knights title, *Michael's Gift* (IM #583), please send your name, address, zip or postal code, along with a check or money order (please do not send cash) for $3.50 ($3.99 in Canada) for each book ordered, plus 75¢ postage and handling ($1.00 in Canada), payable to Silhouette Books, to:

In the U.S.	**In Canada**
Silhouette Books	Silhouette Books
3010 Walden Ave.	P. O. Box 636
P. O. Box 9077	Fort Erie, Ontario
Buffalo, NY 14269-9077	L2A 5X3

Please specify book title(s), line and number with your order.
Canadian residents add applicable federal and provincial taxes.

KNIGHT2

Another wonderful year of romance concludes with

Christmas Memories

Share in the magic and memories of romance during the holiday season with this collection of two full-length contemporary Christmas stories, by two bestselling authors

Diana Palmer
Marilyn Pappano

Available in December at your favorite retail outlet.

Only from

Silhouette® ™

where passion lives.

XMMEM

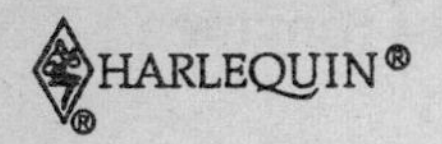

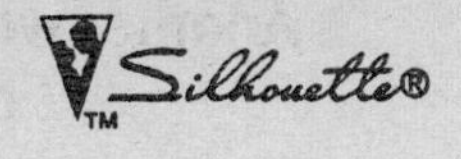

The movie event of the season can be the reading event of the year!

Lights... The lights go on in October when CBS presents Harlequin/Silhouette Sunday Matinee Movies. These four movies are based on bestselling Harlequin and Silhouette novels.

Camera... As the cameras roll, be the first to read the original novels the movies are based on!

Action... Through this offer, you can have these books sent directly to you! Just fill in the order form below and you could be reading the books...before the movie!

48288-4	Treacherous Beauties by Cheryl Emerson $3.99 U.S./$4.50 CAN.	☐
83305-9	Fantasy Man by Sharon Green $3.99 U.S./$4.50 CAN.	☐
48289-2	A Change of Place by Tracy Sinclair $3.99 U.S./$4.50CAN.	☐
83306-7	Another Woman by Margot Dalton $3.99 U.S./$4.50 CAN.	☐

TOTAL AMOUNT $
POSTAGE & HANDLING $
($1.00 for one book, 50¢ for each additional)
APPLICABLE TAXES* $__________
TOTAL PAYABLE $__________
(check or money order—please do not send cash)

To order, complete this form and send it, along with a check or money order for the total above, payable to Harlequin Books, to: **In the U.S.:** 3010 Walden Avenue, P.O. Box 9047, Buffalo, NY 14269-9047; **In Canada:** P.O. Box 613, Fort Erie, Ontario, L2A 5X3.

Name: ____________________
Address: ________________ City: ____________
State/Prov.: ____________ Zip/Postal Code: ____________

*New York residents remit applicable sales taxes.
Canadian residents remit applicable GST and provincial taxes.

CBSPR

"HOORAY FOR HOLLYWOOD" SWEEPSTAKES

HERE'S HOW THE SWEEPSTAKES WORKS

OFFICIAL RULES — NO PURCHASE NECESSARY

To enter, complete an Official Entry Form or hand print on a 3" x 5" card the words "HOORAY FOR HOLLYWOOD", your name and address and mail your entry in the pre-addressed envelope (if provided) or to: "Hooray for Hollywood" Sweepstakes, P.O. Box 9076, Buffalo, NY 14269-9076 or "Hooray for Hollywood" Sweepstakes, P.O. Box 637, Fort Erie, Ontario L2A 5X3. Entries must be sent via First Class Mail and be received no later than 12/31/94. No liability is assumed for lost, late or misdirected mail.

Winners will be selected in random drawings to be conducted no later than January 31, 1995 from all eligible entries received.

Grand Prize: A 7-day/6-night trip for 2 to Los Angeles, CA including round trip air transportation from commercial airport nearest winner's residence, accommodations at the Regent Beverly Wilshire Hotel, free rental car, and $1,000 spending money. (Approximate prize value which will vary dependent upon winner's residence: $5,400.00 U.S.); 500 Second Prizes: A pair of "Hollywood Star" sunglasses (prize value: $9.95 U.S. each). Winner selection is under the supervision of D.L. Blair, Inc., an independent judging organization, whose decisions are final. Grand Prize travelers must sign and return a release of liability prior to traveling. Trip must be taken by 2/1/96 and is subject to airline schedules and accommodations availability.

Sweepstakes offer is open to residents of the U.S. (except Puerto Rico) and Canada who are 18 years of age or older, except employees and immediate family members of Harlequin Enterprises, Ltd., its affiliates, subsidiaries, and all agencies, entities or persons connected with the use, marketing or conduct of this sweepstakes. All federal, state, provincial, municipal and local laws apply. Offer void wherever prohibited by law. Taxes and/or duties are the sole responsibility of the winners. Any litigation within the province of Quebec respecting the conduct and awarding of prizes may be submitted to the Regie des loteries et courses du Quebec. All prizes will be awarded; winners will be notified by mail. No substitution of prizes are permitted. Odds of winning are dependent upon the number of eligible entries received.

Potential grand prize winner must sign and return an Affidavit of Eligibility within 30 days of notification. In the event of non-compliance within this time period, prize may be awarded to an alternate winner. Prize notification returned as undeliverable may result in the awarding of prize to an alternate winner. By acceptance of their prize, winners consent to use of their names, photographs, or likenesses for purpose of advertising, trade and promotion on behalf of Harlequin Enterprises, Ltd., without further compensation unless prohibited by law. A Canadian winner must correctly answer an arithmetical skill-testing question in order to be awarded the prize.

For a list of winners (available after 2/28/95), send a separate stamped, self-addressed envelope to: Hooray for Hollywood Sweepstakes 3252 Winners, P.O. Box 4200, Blair, NE 68009.

CBSRLS

OFFICIAL ENTRY COUPON

"Hooray for Hollywood"

SWEEPSTAKES!

Yes, I'd love to win the Grand Prize — a vacation in Hollywood — or one of 500 pairs of "sunglasses of the stars"! Please enter me in the sweepstakes!

This entry must be received by December 31, 1994.
Winners will be notified by January 31, 1995.

Name ______________________________

Address ______________________ Apt. ______

City ______________________________

State/Prov. ____________ Zip/Postal Code ________

Daytime phone number ____________________
(area code)

Mail all entries to: Hooray for Hollywood Sweepstakes, P.O. Box 9076, Buffalo, NY 14269-9076.
In Canada, mail to: Hooray for Hollywood Sweepstakes, P.O. Box 637, Fort Erie, ON L2A 5X3.

KCH

OFFICIAL ENTRY COUPON

"Hooray for Hollywood"

SWEEPSTAKES!

Yes, I'd love to win the Grand Prize — a vacation in Hollywood — or one of 500 pairs of "sunglasses of the stars"! Please enter me in the sweepstakes!

This entry must be received by December 31, 1994.
Winners will be notified by January 31, 1995.

Name ______________________________

Address ______________________ Apt. ______

City ______________________________

State/Prov. ____________ Zip/Postal Code ________

Daytime phone number ____________________
(area code)

Mail all entries to: Hooray for Hollywood Sweepstakes, P.O. Box 9076, Buffalo, NY 14269-9076.
In Canada, mail to: Hooray for Hollywood Sweepstakes, P.O. Box 637, Fort Erie, ON L2A 5X3.

KCH